Out of the Woods

Also By Lyn Gardner:

Into the Woods

★ "This gothic, wildly adventurous romp through the dream country of fairy tales celebrates the power of sisterhood. . . . The breathless plot, which pulls readers into an escalating series of dangerous situations, hairbreadth escapes, bitter defeats, and surprising triumphs, is grounded in the realistic personalities of the sisters. . . . It should have wide appeal as a family read-aloud or absorbing read-alone."
—*School Library Journal,* Starred

"Gardner has crafted a fast-paced and entertaining adventure filled with cheeky humor and wordplay. . . . It's a blast of a journey."
—*Publishers Weekly*

Out of the Woods

by
LYN GARDNER

pictures
by
MINI GREY

A Yearling Book

For my Mother

 Published in the United States by Yearling, an imprint of Random House Children's Books, a division of Random House, Inc., New York. Originally published in hardcover in Great Britain by David Fickling Books, an imprint of Random House Children's Books, a division of the Random House Group Ltd., London, in 2009, and subsequently published in hardcover in the United States by David Fickling Books, an imprint of Random House Children's Books, a division of Random House, Inc., New York, in 2010.

Yearling and the jumping horse design are registered trademarks of Random House, Inc.

Visit us on the Web! www.randomhouse.com/kids

Educators and librarians, for a variety of teaching tools, visit us at www.randomhouse.com/teachers

The Library of Congress has cataloged the hardcover edition of this work as follows:
Gardner, Lyn.
Out of the woods / by Lyn Gardner ; pictures by Mini Grey.
p. cm.
Summary: The Eden sisters are lured to the fair by Belladonna, a witch who wants Aurora's heart and Storm's powerful musical pipe.
ISBN 978-0-385-75154-4 (trade) — ISBN 978-0-385-75156-8 (lib. bdg.) —
ISBN 978-0-375-89537-1 (ebook)
[1. Sisters—Juvenile fiction. 2. Magic—Juvenile fiction. 3. Sisters—Fiction. 4. Magic—Fiction. 5. Fantasy.] I. Title.
[Fic]—dc22
2010277275

ISBN 978-0-385-75226-8 (pbk.)

Printed in the United States of America
10 9 8 7 6 5 4 3 2 1

First Yearling Edition 2011

Random House Children's Books supports the First Amendment and celebrates the right to read.

Contents

ADMIT ONE
ZEUS THE LION
Mr Prometheus' Famed Funfair

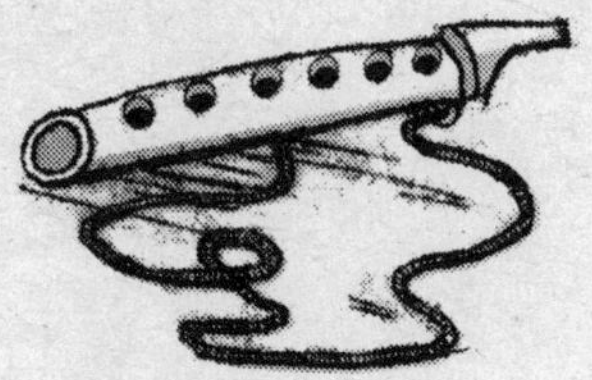

Prologue

The little musical pipe rested almost hidden in the sand at the bottom of the sea. The pipe had been there for nearly a year and gradually, day by day, centimetre by centimetre, it was being swallowed by the seabed. In a day or two it would be completely covered by sand, never to rise again. But the tip could still just be glimpsed, a little glint of magic in the sand, and if there had been anybody there to see it, other than a shoal of tiny iridescent fish, they would have noticed that the tip was glowing and

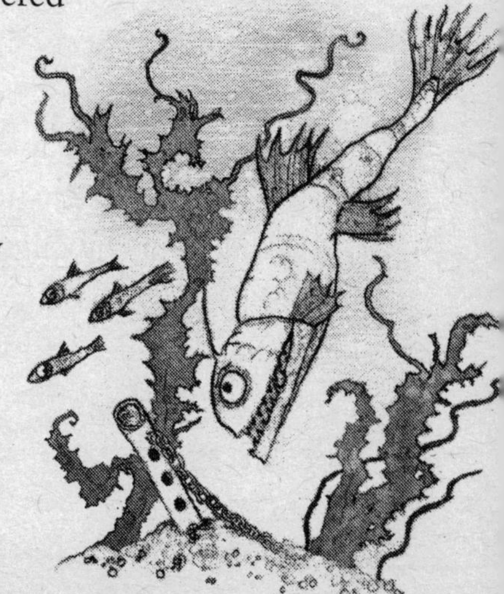

vibrating as if the pipe was trying to speak or sing.

Up above, the little fishing boat bobbed its way across the sparkling sea towards Piper's Port. The waves danced around the small vessel as if they were welcoming it back. The boat had been away from Piper's Port for not quite a year and the fishermen were eager to get home. The skipper, an affable man whose skin was all salt and leather after forty years of seafaring, turned the wheel towards home, and as he did so he heard the most beautiful song inside his head and he was overcome by a sudden, inexplicable urge to make one last catch before they reached dry land. Well, why not, he thought to himself, the fishermen would all be happy to return home with a basket of fish so fresh it tasted of the waves.

Prologue

Down on the seabed, the pipe vibrated and its song grew louder and more insistent.

'Lower the nets,' he ordered. The fishermen looked surprised by this unexpected command so close to home. A thin beautiful boy with freckles and the most astonishing emerald eyes ran to do his bidding.

'You all right, Kit?' asked the skipper as he watched the boy lower the net with a graceful expertise. Kit nodded and grinned so his green eyes sparkled as if the sea was in them.

'Soon be home, and you'll be able to take a fish with you. The biggest fish that we land will be yours, I promise you. You've worked hard, you deserve it. You can take it home,' said the skipper.

Kit pondered the word home as he carefully let out the nets. He didn't have a home of his own. He believed himself to be an orphan. If he had ever known his parents, he couldn't remember them. The rackety little fishing boat on which he'd spent the last year had been the

closest he had ever had to a real home, even though he knew that he would always be welcome at Eden End. Kit smiled as he thought of the impetuous, red-haired Storm Eden and her plump little currant-eyed sister, Any, and his warm heart grew hot as freshly buttered toast as he thought of Aurora, the girls' older sister. Aurora was the most beautiful girl in the world, and even after a year at sea, Kit was more in love with her than ever. He wanted to marry her, but as he owned nothing but the clothes he stood up in, he knew that he could never ask her. But he could take her and her sisters a fish. He knew that they would be delighted as they lived a hand-to-mouth existence. Kit smiled as he rolled out the nets – he would give the Eden sisters a really big surprise when he turned up unexpectedly with the most enormous fish that they had ever seen.

Down in the depths the tiny fish swam this way and that, their minute tails glinting in the gloom. They took no notice of the old musical pipe glowing ever more brightly just beneath them as if it was alive and wanted to be noticed. The luminous fish darted in and out of the deep-sea plants like tiny silver arrows. Suddenly, above them a dark shadow loomed, and the tiny panic-stricken fish scattered as a monstrous fish swam into view, his huge mouth wide open. The giant fish was as ugly as a gargoyle and he was almost all head, and his head was almost all mouth and his mouth was almost all teeth. Lazily, the great greedy fish swam along the seabed guzzling any tiny fish that got in his way like a living vacuum cleaner. He was so busy gobbling that he didn't notice the net coming ever closer towards him across the ocean bottom. He sucked down more little fish and smacked his lips. He saw something shimmer and sensed the vibrating movement on the seabed. He thought it might be an especially tasty fish. He opened his mouth and took a great gulp. The pipe slid down his gullet and as it did so, the net swept him up and he was hoisted to the surface in a tangle of flapping fins and tails.

The fishermen heaved the net onto the little boat. Lying amid the other smaller fish was the huge monster fish.

'There you are, Kit,' laughed the skipper. 'You are a lucky boy! I've seldom seen such a big fish. He's an ugly brute, but he'll taste delicious baked in the oven with some rosemary and lemon juice. He's all yours.'

1

Storm Goes Into the Woods

Storm Eden was talking to her mother, even though Zella had been dead for almost two years. A wild tangle of unbrushed red curls fell across her face as she kneeled in front of her mother's grave, cleared away a small patch of snow to reveal the mossy green below, and laid a posy of snowdrops on the grassy mound.

'I love you,' she whispered, hugging the small silver birch sapling which had sprung up almost overnight by Zella's grave following her burial. Storm's green eyes filled as she thought of Zella, her beautiful, neglectful, lazy mother with her smile like warm sunlight, lying all alone in the cold earth.

'I love you and I miss you,' repeated Storm, clinging to the slender tree as if it were Zella herself. Zella had been the most negligent of mothers when alive and had barely seemed to notice her middle daughter. It was only after her mother's death that Storm had discovered how much her mother had loved her, and it made the loss all the harder to bear. She had taken to coming to the grave every day, lying spread-eagled on the mound and talking to Zella as if she was really there. Sometimes in milder weather Storm would bring a picnic – cheese and watercress sandwiches, a couple of the scrumptious madeleines made by her elder sister, Aurora – and munch them on the grave while chatting away and telling Zella what was happening at Eden End. She told Zella how many times Aurora had tidied the linen cupboard that week and whether her new recipes for quaking pudding and giggle cake had turned out well, and how fast Any was growing up. These one-sided chats made Storm feel less lonely.

It wasn't that her sisters didn't love her to bits, she knew that they did. But Aurora was always so busy, and Any had special privileges as the baby of the family, and sometimes Storm just felt like the one squashed in the middle who nobody really noticed, because she could look after herself. Even Netta, who Storm thought of as her own personal fairy godmother, seemed to have mysteriously given up coming to visit in recent weeks, making Storm feel more bereft than ever.

When there was enough money to buy the ingredients, Storm would take some of the dark chocolate truffles that her mother used to savour so much, and leave them beneath the silver birch tree. The next day the truffles would be gone, and although Storm guessed that they were being eaten by wild animals, it brought a smile to her face to think of her mother sitting up in the night and nibbling on the chocolate with her perfect white teeth.

'Right,' said Storm, pushing back her unruly curls and scrambling to her feet. There were several rips in her skirt caused by climbing trees. 'I've got to go, Mother. I want to check that Aurora's all right. She's been worrying so much about money I think she's making herself ill.' She ran across the park, occasionally reaching into her pockets and throwing a few firecrackers ahead of her that danced and shimmered with red and green sparks.

A few minutes later, Storm ran into the kitchen at Eden End to find Aurora sitting at the table weeping. She was surrounded by a large number of brown envelopes and pieces of paper across which were written the words FINAL DEMAND in angry red writing. Aurora's exquisite oval face was becomingly pink and the tears that ran down it were gathering in a dimple on her chin.

'What's the matter, Aurora?' cried Storm, hugging her sister and depositing a smear of mud on her pale, porcelain cheek.

'She's trying really hard to make ends meet,' explained Storm's little sister Any, 'but the ends keep moving. It's most inconsiderate of them.'

'Have you checked if there's any money down the back of the sofa?' asked Storm.

'Of course,' said Any scornfully. She screwed up her chocolate-button nose. 'All we found was lots of fluff, two hair grips and a half-sucked peppermint drop. It was still very pepperminty.'

'You didn't eat it, Any?' asked Aurora, who stopped crying and looked shocked. 'That's disgusting and extremely unhygienic.'

'Well, I did pick the fluff off first,' said Any. 'It was still a bit furry, but I expect fur counts as extra protein.'

Aurora began sobbing again. 'See! The poor little babe is starving to death. If only Papa could discover the legendary four-tongued, three-footed, two-headed honey dragon and make the family fortune before Any dies of malnutrition!'

Storm considered her delicious plump little sister, who was bursting out of a dress made by Aurora from an old damask table cloth.

'Aurora, I don't think there's any imminent danger of Any starving to death.' She gave her big sister another hug, depositing more mud, this time on Aurora's pristine but much darned apron. 'I'm going to talk to Papa.'

Storm ran to her father's study. On the door was pinned a yellowing notice declaring in large letters:

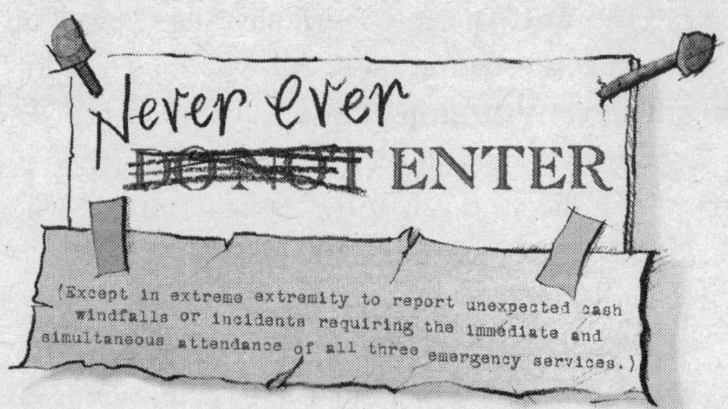

Storm ignored the notice on the study door and marched straight in. As expected, her father was poring over his maps. Captain Reggie Eden was a famed and dashing explorer, but he neglected his family and never earned any money. He was far too busy planning and going on expeditions in search of the legendary four-tongued, three-footed, two-headed honey dragon that was reputed to be at least one hundred metres long and have the sunniest disposition of any member of the lizard family. So far, the honey dragon had remained stubbornly elusive, and the sisters had grown used to their father's long absences and a complete lack of money in the Eden household.

Captain Reggie Eden looked up guiltily at his middle daughter and recognized the determined look in her eye. He gave his wide, easy grin that could charm an angry swarm of bees or a charging herd of white rhinos, but not Storm.

'Don't scold me, Storm. I can't bear it when you give me a ticking off. It makes me feel about eight and three quarters,' he said wearily, and his hair flopped boyishly across his forehead.

'There's no money again.'

'Have you tried down the back of the sofa?'

Storm nodded.

'The cracked ginger jar on the kitchen shelf?' asked Captain Eden a little desperately.

Storm nodded.

'Ah. Well, we'll just have to pawn the Cherished Family Teapot.'

'We already did. Last year. Papa, you have got to earn some money.'

Reggie Eden ran his hand through his hair. 'Give me time, Storm. I really do believe I'm right on the tail of the honey dragon. Of course not literally, because that would make it extremely bad-tempered. But close,

tantalizingly close. One more expedition, and I'm confident I'll find it.'

Storm had heard this all before, and although she didn't care about the lack of money for herself she did very much for Aurora. She sighed. She could see the familiar silver gleam in her father's handsome eye and she knew it was no good suggesting to him that he did something sensible such as becoming a window cleaner or a dentist. Storm felt some sympathy with him, because she thought that being an explorer was a most exciting and romantic way of life.

'Just give me a little more time, Storm. One more expedition, please. If I fail, I promise I'll submit to my doom and train to be an accountant without delay.'

Storm grinned. Like her, Captain Eden had the mathematical skills of a jellyfish.

'All right. It's a deal. But don't go without saying goodbye or leaving any money like you did last time.'

Captain Eden looked fleetingly guilty. 'But I know that you are all so capable and will always look after each other, and I do so hate goodbyes.'

'That isn't an excuse to wriggle off the hook of fatherly responsibility,' said Storm sternly. 'The way you behave you'd think we were full orphans, not half orphans.' But Captain Eden was already buried in his maps again.

The next morning, Storm was crosser than ever to discover that her father and his maps were gone. All he had left his daughters was a note which read:

Am just popping out to find the honey dragon. I may be gone some time. Will try to send some money, but I know you'll all cope if I can't. Fondest love, Papa xxx PS If the bailiffs come, don't let them in. There's nothing worth taking anyway, now that the Cherished Family Teapot has gone. I miss that teapot.

'He misses the teapot, but he doesn't say anything about missing us,' said Storm moodily.

'You can't miss something that you keep forgetting that you've got,' Any said sadly.

'I'm going to search his study,' said Storm. 'Perhaps there's some money squirreled away that he's forgotten about.' She ran out of the kitchen, slid across the polished floor of the hall and came to a halt when she spied something on the doormat. She picked up a bright yellow flyer upon which was written in purple writing:

Her heart beat with excitement. A fair! What fun! They must go at once. Then she remembered: they had no money. Grumpily she marched into her father's study and set about searching the room. It was not easy because Captain Reggie Eden was the second most untidy person in the world after Storm herself.

Nothing. She sat down feeling dejected. An image of the little magical pipe that her dying mother had given to her suddenly popped into her head. The rightful owner was able to harness its enormous power to do whatever they willed. They could control the very stars in the universe. Storm was the pipe's owner, but she had been so alarmed by its corrupting power and the evil Dr DeWilde's persistence in trying to win it for himself, that she had flung it into the ocean. At that moment she wished she hadn't. If she had it now she'd blow it and conjure up a chest of gold coins. But that was impossible, the pipe was beyond anyone's reach somewhere at the bottom of the sea and Storm knew she was well rid of it. The pipe's power had caused the deaths and enslavement of many and brought nothing but trouble.

Accepting defeat, she was just leaving the study when she spied a dusty cracked dragon's egg precariously balanced at the back of a shelf stuffed with old maps. She carefully lifted the egg and gently pulled it apart. Nestling inside were five silver coins, a silky lock of hair and a small picture. The hair Storm recognized immediately as belonging to her dead mother, Zella. The picture was of her father and mother looking blissfully happy. She turned over the picture; scrawled in her father's spidery writing were the words *Reggie and Zella, forever and for always*. Storm's throat felt tight. Blinking hard, she reverently put the picture and hair back inside the egg. Then she ran back to the kitchen and triumphantly threw the coins on the table.

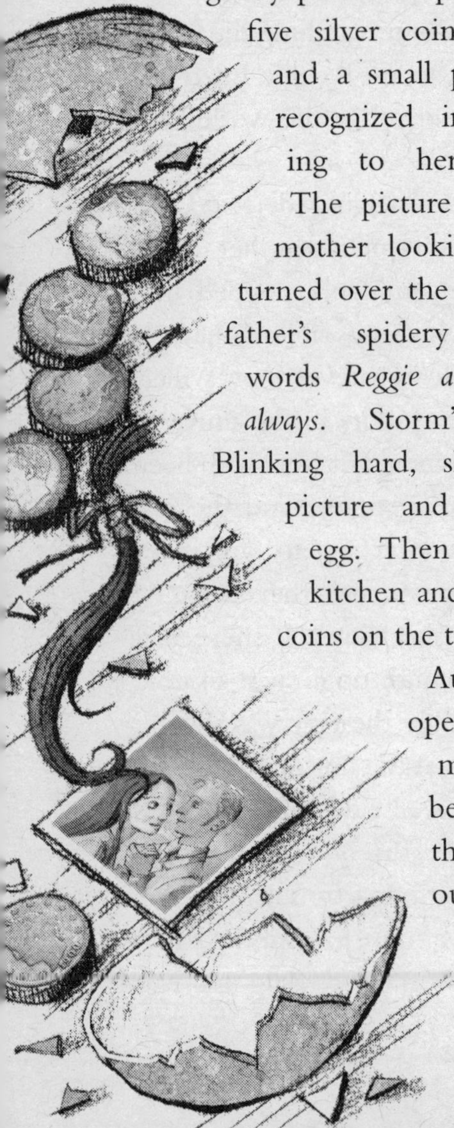

Aurora's mouth dropped open. 'Oh, Storm! You're a marvel. That's magic! I'll be able to settle some of these demands, pay off our bill with Betty at the Post Office and buy more flour and butter.

I'll pop down to the village at once and get some supplies and then we can have a celebratory lunch. Do you want to come with me, girls?'

'I will,' said Any, who hoped that there might be a bag of sherbet lemons in the trip.

'No, thank you,' said Storm politely.

Aurora narrowed her eyes. 'You're not thinking of going into the woods on your own, are you, Storm Eden?'

'I wouldn't dream of it,' smiled Storm innocently. But as soon as her sisters had disappeared down the drive, she headed out of the house, stopping only to pick up her skates on the way. She banged the door behind her so hard that another chimney pot fell off the roof and crashed to the ground, narrowly missing her. As she headed through the park towards the frozen river, she reached into her pocket and pulled out the flyer for the fair.

'Right,' murmured Storm, putting on her skates and peering at the icy river as it slithered into the dark forest. The branches on the trees seemed to be beckoning her. 'Everyone knows that rules are made to be broken. What Aurora doesn't know, will just be one thing less for her to worry about.'

2
Broken hearts and Magic Mirrors

Not long after, Storm stood on the frozen river banks on the edge of Piper's Town, jiggling up and down with excitement. She was wearing her skates around her neck, and her socks were sodden through, but she didn't care. Spread out in front of her was a higgledy-piggledy of caravans, candy-striped tents and booths creating a riot of colour under a pallid winter sun. A silent big wheel towered above her and to her right was a ghost train with a lurid façade of skeletons and grinning ghouls. In the distance, she could see the helter-skelter rising from the ground like a huge twisted sugar-cane. She didn't notice a small silver hare watching her intently as she studied a brightly-painted sign that proclaimed:

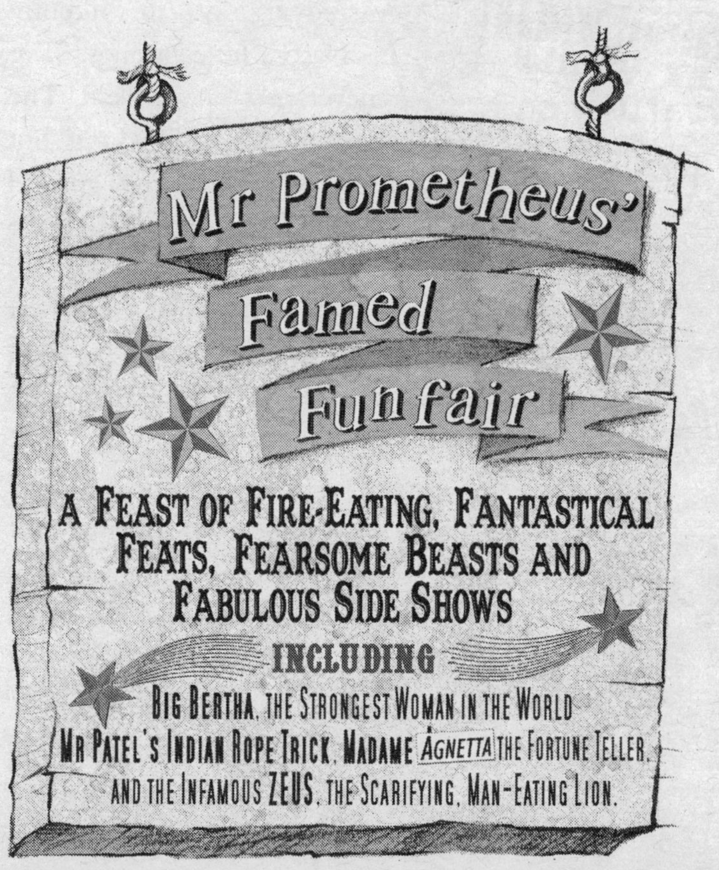

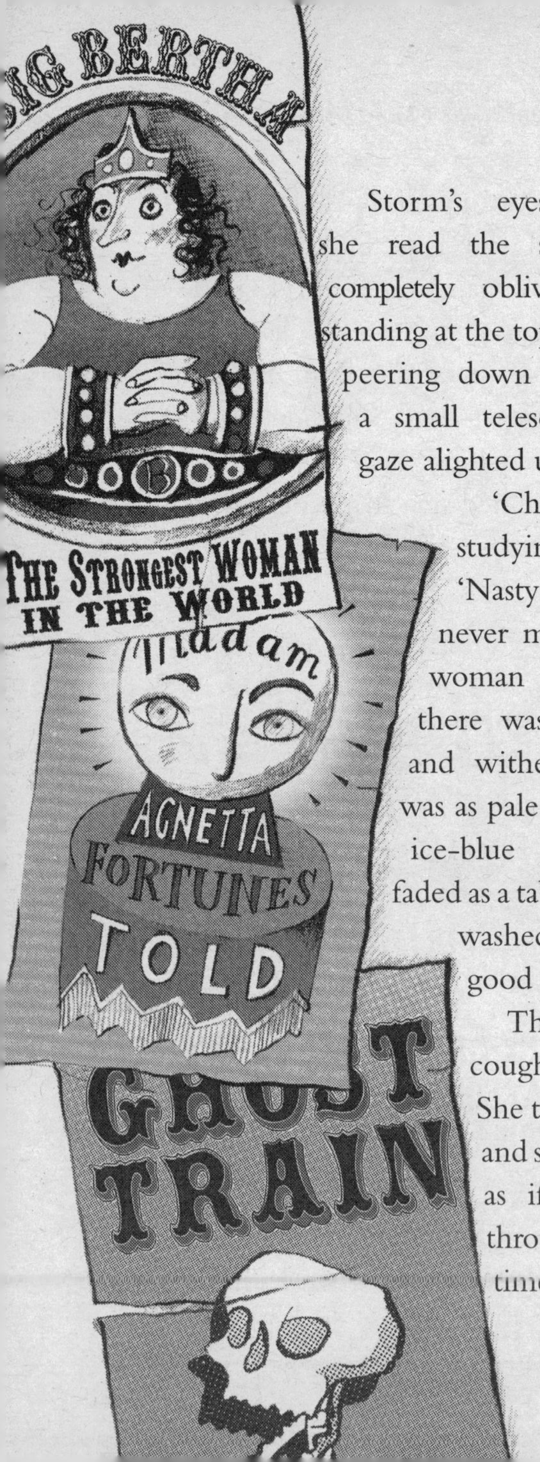

Storm's eyes grew wider as she read the sign, and she was completely oblivous of a woman standing at the top of the helter-skelter peering down at the fair through a small telescope. The woman's gaze alighted upon Storm.

'Children!' she muttered, studying Storm intently. 'Nasty little things. I've never met one I liked.' The woman was still young but there was something gnarled and withered about her; she was as pale as snow and she had ice-blue eyes that were as faded as a tablecloth that has been washed more often than is good for it.

There was a small cough from behind her. She turned. A man so long and spindly that he looked as if he had been put through a mangle three times, bowed so low that

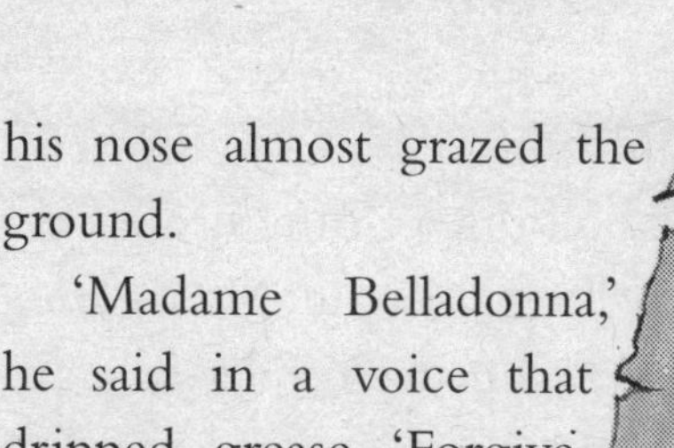

his nose almost grazed the ground.

'Madame Belladonna,' he said in a voice that dripped grease. 'Forgive the intrusion, but your wolves need feeding and that cowardly lion, Zeus, is playing up again. Whenever I go near him he cowers in his cage with both paws over his eyes. He's slightly less terrifying than a newborn lamb. The public will want their money back. Again.'

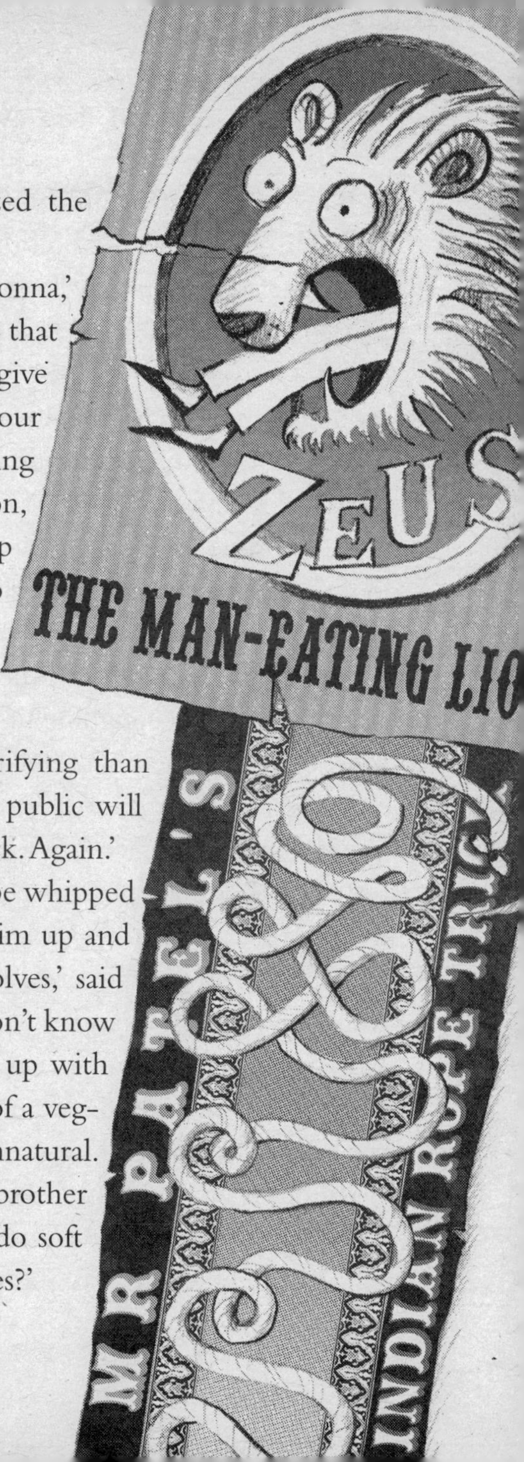

'If that lion won't be whipped into line, I'll mince him up and serve him to the wolves,' said Belladonna softly. 'I don't know why Prometheus put up with him. Whoever heard of a vegetarian lion? It's unnatural. Too soft a heart, that brother of yours. And where do soft hearts get you, Hermes?'

The man shifted uncomfortably and bowed low again. 'Dead with a bolt through the head and hanging as an exhibit in the ghost train, Madame.'

Belladonna gave a wicked grin. 'Yes, let it be a lesson to you. Poor Prometheus, he really shouldn't have objected to my taking over his pathetic little fair or handing over the Dorian mirror. Fortunately for you, Hermes, you are much more sensible than your brother. Still, he does look rather splendid in the ghost train. I've heard several customers comment on how exceptionally real he looks. If only they knew.' She gave a laugh that turned into a coughing fit and she clutched her heart as if it pained her. Her body began to bend and twist like an ancient, deformed tree, and fissures opened up on her face as if a landslip had suddenly occurred there. She put out a hand impatiently. 'Pass me the Dorian mirror, Hermes.'

Carefully, Hermes opened a black velvet box and took out a small looking-glass, its edges wreathed in blue smoke. Belladonna snatched it from him hungrily and muttered an incantation. The surface of the mirror seethed and steamed like an angry, milky sea and the smoky depths turned green and purple then aquamarine. As it cleared, Belladonna's back visibly straightened and the years dropped away from her face. She held the looking-glass aloft and stared into it.

Hermes peered over her shoulder and shuddered. The figure gazing out from the looking-glass and the one gazing into it were clearly one and the same woman. But while the Belladonna holding the mirror was tall and strong and beautiful with clear skin and bright blue eyes, the Belladonna in the mirror was withered, wrinkled and loathsome, with eyes as cruel as a vulture.

'Madame, if I may say so, looks exceptionally beautiful and strong today,' said Hermes in a voice that might have doubled as an oil slick.

'Not beautiful and not strong enough, Hermes,' hissed Belladonna. 'What a curse it is that witch siblings share a single heart. Since my sister Bee was stupid enough to get herself killed, my heart has been shrivelling. Before long it will be nothing but a tiny piece of lead. If I had not known of the existence of the Dorian mirror and its rejuvenating powers I would be long dead by now.'

'We must be grateful for small mercies,' murmured Hermes ingratiatingly.

'I am grateful for nothing,' snapped Belladonna. 'The mirror only keeps death at bay. I must be at the height of my powers when the pipe returns. Have you any news of it?'

Hermes looked frightened. 'I am doing my best, Madame. I have been making extensive enquiries. After Dr DeWilde's death, and that Storm Eden girl threw the magic pipe into the sea, there has been nothing heard of it.'

'The pipe always finds its rightful owner. It will come back to her. Maybe it already has. I must get into Eden End as soon as possible. Did you deliver the flyer for the fair?'

'Yes,' said Hermes. 'That house is an awful wreck of a place. The children are almost orphans. The mother's dead and I spied the father leaving on one of his expeditions – I had to hide in the shadows to avoid being seen.'

Belladonna felt her withered witchy heart twitch

with excitement. 'So the children are alone?'

'Quite alone.'

Belladonna looked thoughtful. 'Poor motherless little things,' she said in a syrupy voice.

Hermes looked surprised. 'I thought Madame had an aversion to children.'

'What a stupid man you are, Hermes. Of course I hate children – unless they are served on toast with a little ground pepper. But I will have to pretend to adore the Eden sisters if I'm going to get into Eden End and find the pipe.'

'How will Madame do that?'

'Simple. I shall be their new stepmama.'

Hermes's mouth dropped open. 'You're going to marry Captain Eden? What if he doesn't want to marry you?'

A flicker of annoyance passed across Belladonna's pale face, which was already starting to age again. 'I won't give him any choice in the matter.'

'But what about the children? How will you get them to trust you?'

Belladonna smiled nastily. 'That's the easy part. The flyer will lure them to us, and when they arrive, you and I are going to make their time here so scary, so hair-raising and so exhausting, that when I appear as their delicious new stepmama, the petrified little babes will be ready to fall into my motherly and comforting arms. What they won't know is that I'm really a witch who only likes children baked in pies or grated over spaghetti Bolognese.'

'Madame is so clever! But are you sure they'll come?'

Belladonna grinned, and momentarily Hermes could see the skull beneath her skin.

'Oh, I know they will, because I know children. A fun-fair! What child could resist such a temptation? Definitely not Storm Eden. It is the perfect snare, and I'll have some fun with her along the way. I have some old scores to settle with Storm Eden. She is a trouble-maker and if it wasn't for her, my sister would still be alive and my heart would still be strong. I want to make her suffer, just as I suffer.' She clutched at her chest as if in terrible pain and her face became more haggard.

'And she will suffer, because not only is she going to lead me to the pipe, but her sister is going to provide me with my new heart.'

'Madame, we must be cautious. We must be absolutely sure that Aurora Eden really is the fairest in the land. The heart cut from the breast of the second fairest in the land would not do at all.

We cannot afford a mistake.'

'No, Hermes, *you* can't afford a mistake. I just hope for your sake that your information about the girl is correct. You wouldn't want to end up in the ghost train, would you, Hermes? I think there's a space that needs filling next to poor Prometheus.'

Hermes turned very pale and his knees knocked together. 'That won't be necessary, Madame,' he assured her, changing the subject quickly. 'Would Madame like to feed her wolves now? Your beauties are waiting for you and they are hungry.'

Belladonna smiled. 'Yes, Hermes, I will enjoy that.'

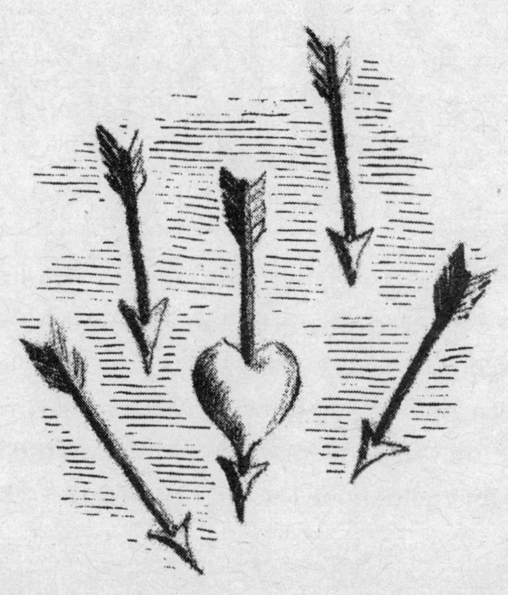

3

An encounter at the Fair

Storm wandered around the silent fair, entranced by everything from the gaily-coloured booths to the smell of candied apples and popcorn. She longed to bring Aurora and Any here to ride on the dodgems and sail high on the swing boats, but she knew it was impossible. Despite the discovery of the five silver coins, the Eden budget wouldn't stretch to a trip to the fair even with reduced rates for almost orphans.

Storm took one last longing look at the big wheel and was about to leave when she heard a whimpering noise coming from a large tent. She ran across and peered inside. A beautiful lion was attached to a large cage by a long chain. A tall, impossibly thin man was cracking a whip and trying to make the lion roar. But every time the whip hit the floor, the animal gave nothing but a terrified whimper. The man took a small pistol out of his pocket and pointed it at the lion.

'Roar, you dratted animal, roar! Or I'll shoot you through the brain – if I can find your brain. Zeus, you are the stupidest, most cowardly lion I've ever encountered. Nobody will pay to see you. I've seen scarier hedgehogs.'

A tear ran down the lion's cheek. The man pointed the pistol at the ground and began firing as close as he could to the lion's

paws. Zeus gave a yelp of fear and began a humiliating hippity-hoppity dance. Storm could bear it no longer. With a loud roar of her own, she ran towards the man and pushed him as hard as she could. Surprise was on her side and he stumbled and fell. Storm picked up the whip and with an expert flick she swept the pistol out of his fingers. She caught the pistol and pointed it at him.

'How dare you! Nobody but a coward would treat an animal like that. I've a good mind to make you dance like poor Zeus, but I haven't got time because I can't be late for lunch. Hand over the key.' The man felt in his pocket and tossed Storm the key. With one hand still pointing the pistol at her enemy, she unlocked the iron cuff around the lion's neck. He was cowering on the ground with his paws over his eyes.

'Run, Zeus, run. Into the woods! You'll be safe there. Don't come back. I'll come and find you later.'

The lion lifted his paws from his eyes and a look of panic crossed his face.

'I'll look after you, I promise,' said Storm gently.

Zeus stopped shaking and advanced towards Storm. He bowed down in front of her with both paws stretched out, and licked her face with his warm rough tongue. Then with a toss of his huge mane and a great purr, he was gone. He bounded through the fairground towards the woods, watched at a distance by a small silver-grey hare which waited until he disappeared and then slipped unseen into the tent.

Storm wondered how she was going to explain Zeus to Aurora when she brought him home. She kept the pistol aimed at the sulky-looking man and waited until she was certain that the lion would be far away. Then she threw it down and marched towards the door.

'Not so fast, my girl. You'll pay for this.' Back on his feet, the man grabbed Storm by the arm. Storm screamed, wriggled and bit his hand. He screeched and biffed Storm hard in the stomach. Storm fell to the floor and he quickly tied her hands behind her back just as Belladonna appeared.

'What's going on here?' she said in a dangerously silky voice, taking in the empty cage, her dishevelled servant and the angry child.

'Madame, forgive me, but this wicked girl set Zeus free.'

Fury disfigured Belladonna's face. 'It was very careless of you to let her, wasn't it, Hermes?'

'Yes, Madame,' he whimpered. 'Please forgive me. It won't happen again.'

'It had better not,' said Belladonna. She raised a finger as if to let loose a hex, but then thought better of it. Her health problems had made her spells tediously unreliable.

'Stand up, girl,' she ordered. Storm rose sulkily to her feet. 'What's your name?'

Storm looked desperately around. She wondered if she could make a run for it, but with her hands tied behind her back she knew she wouldn't get far. She had no choice but to co-operate.

'Storm Eden,' she mumbled.

An amazing transformation crossed Belladonna's face. Where there had been thunderclouds there was now sunshine. 'Storm Eden? Storm Eden of Eden End? The daughter of the famed and dashing explorer Captain Reggie Eden? The sister of Aurora Eden, who it is said is the most beautiful girl in the land, if not the entire world?'

'Yes,' said Storm hesitantly, confused by Belladonna's sudden change of mood. 'Do you know them?'

'Oh, if only I did. I'm such an admirer of your father. If I may say, it is quite obvious that like father like daughter when it comes to courage. I fear that there has been a little misunderstanding here. Untie this delightful and utterly heavenly child.' Belladonna glared at Hermes and muttered, 'You fool! You might have ruined everything,' then she leaned closer to Storm and whispered, 'My manservant, Hermes, is well-meaning but he is not very bright.'

'He was mistreating Zeus,' cried Storm hotly.

'Ah, my darling Zeus. How I love that lion. He's such a big softie. He's my special pet. I adore him and he adores me.'

'Really?' said Storm uncertainly.

'Yes,' said Belladonna firmly. 'It was love at first sight for both of us, and there will be severe punishment for anyone who mistreats my beloved lion.' She glared hard at Hermes, whose knees were knocking together like castanets, and hissed quietly, 'Idiot! Why didn't you recognize her?'

She turned back to Storm. 'Come, let's go to my caravan and have some candy-floss and lemonade.'

'I can't,' said Storm. 'I'll be late for lunch and my sisters, Aurora and Any, will be getting worried.'

'Ah, Aurora! We wouldn't want worry to disfigure her beauty in any way. I think that you and your sisters deserve a treat,' said Belladonna, producing three golden tickets from behind her back. 'Compliments of the management and in the hope that you'll accept our profound apologies for any misunderstanding over the lion. Free passes for all three of you to come to the fair this afternoon. It guarantees you six free rides and a stick of candy-floss

each. And it allows you to go to the front of all the queues.'

Delighted, Storm reached out her hand. Then she hesitated. Although she wanted to show Aurora and Any the fair more than anything, she wasn't at all confident that this Madame was as friendly as she seemed. But the lure of the fair was too great and Storm pocketed the passes, made her thanks and left.

Belladonna and Hermes watched her go. 'Do make sure that you bring Aurora with you. I can't wait to see her,' called Belladonna. A satisfied little smile played across her lips. 'It couldn't have worked out better. What fun we'll have! We'll scare them out of their wits. Aurora's heart will soon be mine, and then I can simply sit back and wait for the pipe to return to Storm. Pass me my mirror, Hermes. I shall need all my strength. The pipe is within my grasp and when I have challenged that girl to a contest and won it from her, I will use its power to bend the whole land to my will. I will enslave thousands, I will start wars just for the fun of it.' She snatched the mirror and swept towards the exit.

'But what if the girl refuses to accept your challenge?' asked Hermes.

Belladonna turned. 'She can't. The owner of the

pipe must accept any challenge, or forfeit ownership. Although the owner does have the right to choose the nature of the contest. Keep a look-out for the Eden girls, Hermes. I'll be back shortly. I'm just going to find their father. He can't have gone far.' She smiled nastily. 'The good Captain may not know it, but he is about to get a new wife.'

Belladonna threaded her way through the fairground, oblivious to the pair of silver-grey eyes that watched her closely.

4
A Family Outing

'There's a fair! In Piper's Town! We must go! Now! This second!' gasped Storm as she burst into the kitchen at Eden End, where Aurora and Any were making pancakes. A stack of freshly-cooked pancakes were being kept warm by the cooker, their frilled edges like charred lace.

'A fair? How do you know?' asked Aurora sharply, simultaneously tossing a pancake and looking askance at the trail of water that Storm was leaving in her wake.

'I saw it,' replied Storm with a little squelchy skip of excitement, causing more water to drip from the sodden hem of her dress.

'How many times do I have to tell you, Storm Eden, that you are not to go into the woods on your own,' said Aurora sternly. 'You know it's not safe. Just twenty minutes ago, Betty from the Post Office knocked to say that her cousin's cousin's little girl got hopelessly lost in the forest, was chased by a lion and would almost certainly have been gobbled alive if some boy who was taking his cow to market hadn't rescued her in the nick of time. They had to give him the last of their beans as a thank-you.'

Storm blanched. That would explain why there had been no sign of Zeus even though she had called and called for him. Storm suspected that it was Betty's cousin's cousin's little girl – a spiteful little no-neck monster – who had been doing all the chasing and not the other way round.

'Lions,' said Storm casually, 'can be rather charming beasts. I've heard they make very rewarding pets.'

'And I've heard that lions think humans make tasty snacks,' said Aurora sternly. 'Don't go looking for it, Storm. Stay away from the woods.'

Aurora had always been scared of the thick woods that surrounded Eden End, and her fear had increased after she and her sisters had been chased through the trees by evil Dr DeWilde's wolves. They had escaped, but it had been a close-run thing. The wolves hadn't been glimpsed for months, but Aurora had still forbidden her sisters to step foot in the woods alone, a command that Storm conveniently managed to forget most days.

'I didn't actually go into the woods,' retorted Storm indignantly, tossing her red curls. 'I skated down the river through the middle of the woods. It's turned so cold, it's completely frozen over.'

'That doesn't make it any safer,' said Aurora firmly.

'Yes, it does,' piped up Any. 'Wolves can't skate. They can never find boots to fit all four feet.' Her eyes were shining. 'I want to skate down the river and go to the fair.' She hugged her teddy tightly. 'Ted-Bear has never seen a fair. And neither have I. We're deprived,' she added indignantly.

'You're not deprived,' laughed Aurora. 'You're spoiled rotten.'

'That's because I am an infant phenomenon,' replied Any, and it was true that she was. She had been able to talk since the day she was born and although she was not yet two and as lazy as a three-toed sloth, resisting all Aurora's attempts to give her a formal education, she could quite often be found reading the dictionary or weighty tomes with titles such as *Brain Surgery for the Barely Educated* and *Conversational and Dinner Party Eskimo in Under a Week*.

'You're just phenomenally big-headed,' Storm said affectionately. 'Oh come on, Aurora, don't be such a killjoy. Please let's go to the fair.'

'You know as well as I do, there's no spare money for the fair,' said Aurora.

With a flourish, Storm produced the three golden tickets.

'Where did you get those from?' asked Aurora.

Seeing Aurora's suspicious face, Storm decided it wasn't the time for truth telling. 'The fair owner was giving them out. She was worried that people might not come. It's an incentive. Six free rides each. And a stick of candy-floss.'

'Please, Aurora, please,' begged Any. 'I've never tasted candy-floss and, like fudge, it is probably an important food group all of its own, which has been lacking from my diet.'

Aurora's face was serious as she consulted one of the many lists she always kept in her pocket. It read:

Aurora Eden's List of
Very Important Things to Do Today

1. Remind Storm she must not go into the woods.
2. Rearrange linen cupboard
3. Wash Ted-Bear when Any isn't looking
4. Test Storm on rotational symmetry
5. Check Storm is not still using remains of garden shed as fireworks factory.
6. ~~Try to match all odd socks in house~~ HOPELESS TASK
7. Check Storm's pockets for firecrackers
8. Persuade Any that Brussels sprouts are just as delicious as chocolate
9. Self-improvement. Find time to read Greek myths
10. Stop worrying so much

'Well,' she said solemnly, 'my list says you are due for a test on rotational symmetry straight after lunch, Storm, while Any and I clean out the linen cupboard.' Storm and Any groaned. Aurora's eyes sparkled. 'But in the circumstances I think rotational symmetry and the linen cupboard can wait. It's not every day that a fair comes to Piper's Town. We'll go after lunch. But we'll have to take the sledge as well. Any's too little. She won't be able to skate all the way there and back, it's much too far. And you'll have to wrap up warm, Any. You must wear your red cloak, the one I made out of the old dining-room curtains.'

Storm and Any grinned at each other and Storm did a little jig of triumph, creating a small puddle at her feet.

'Storm, go and change your clothes,' said Aurora sternly, giving a pancake an expert flip, 'before you catch your death and ruin my nice clean floor completely. Lunch is just about ready. Mushroom-and-broccoli pancakes followed by my special madeleines. Your favourite. Hurry, before I have second thoughts about the fair.'

'Yes, hurry up, Storm, or before we know it Aurora will be having third thoughts and I'll be condemned to spending the afternoon in the linen cupboard,' said Any mournfully.

'I don't think you can have third thoughts, Any,' laughed Storm.

'Of course you can,' said Any. 'Aurora has them all the time.'

A little while later, after a brief detour via Zella's grave, the sisters were standing goggle-eyed just inside the entrance to the fair, listening to the enticing tinkle of the merry-go-round and watching the big wheel turn high above.

'Madame, they are here!' cried Hermes excitedly from their perch atop the helter-skelter.

Belladonna snatched the telescope from him and trained it on the children. 'Just as I had planned.

Everything is falling into place,' she purred with a satisfied smile. 'Let me get a better look at the older sister.' Painfully, her bones creaking, she readjusted the focus of the telescope, but at that moment a wedding party in all their finery weaved their way through the crowd, and Aurora turned to get a better look. The bride and groom were looking lovingly at each other. Storm caught Aurora's eye and knew that she too was thinking of Zella and their father, Reggie, who had loved each other to distraction. Any, who had never known her mother, was entranced by the laughing bride and groom.

'Do you think Papa will get married again one day?' she asked. 'I do so want to be a bridesmaid, and I'd like to have a mother. A pretty mother just like that bride.' She was so busy gazing at the wedding revellers that she didn't notice the look of shock and surprise that passed between Storm and Aurora.

'He wouldn't, would he? He wouldn't get married again. He loved Mama too much,' whispered Storm fiercely.

Aurora shrugged. 'I wouldn't rule it out completely, Storm. He only had eyes for Zella, but they do say that time heals. And as you know, Papa will always do what he wants without any reference to us. I wouldn't put it past him.'

'I don't want a new mother,' said Storm, her eyes filling with tears. 'I want my old mother back.'

Aurora put her hand gently on Storm's shoulder. Storm looked up into her older sister's beautiful face. She saw sadness there, but also the ghost of a dreamy smile. She realized with a jolt that the wedding party had made Aurora think of Kit, the boy who had captured her heart the previous year.

'Will you marry Kit, Aurora, if he asks you?'

Aurora blushed. 'I think it would be me doing the asking,' she said lightly. 'Anyway, Kit probably won't be back for years and by then you and Any will be quite grown up.'

'But if he did come back?' asked Storm insistently.

Aurora studied Storm's intense face. 'I would never leave you and Any, Storm. You know that. The three of us together. Forever and for always,' she said seriously. 'Come on, which rides shall we go on?'

'You choose first, Aurora.' Aurora was of an extremely nervous disposition and Storm expected her to choose something dull, perhaps the tea cups, but to her surprise her sister – who liked to keep her feet firmly on the ground – opted for the big wheel. Soon they were strapped into a swinging seat – Aurora looking a mite pale – and sailing high above Piper's Town. Any, snuggled into her red velvet cloak, hugged Ted-Bear and made him wave at the crowds below. To the North they could see the mountains and the tip of Piper's Peak, where Dr DeWilde had once enslaved thousands with the pipe. Storm's eye was drawn back towards Piper's Town and the spot where she and her sisters had been imprisoned by the witch Bee Bumble. Bee Bumble had died in the fire that razed the Ginger House and many believed that Dr DeWilde had too. Storm certainly hoped he had. She shivered at the thought of his handsome face with its distinctive scar and his cold eyes that bored into her as if trying to see inside her.

The wheel made its slow rotation and Storm's eyes were drawn towards the distant sea, where she had thrown the magic pipe to rid herself of its terrible power. Slowly they returned to earth and the girls disembarked, unaware that they were being watched closely by Belladonna and Hermes.

'This is the best fun I've had since Storm showed me how to abseil off the roof of the East wing of Eden End,' blurted Any, her eyes shining.

'She didn't! Storm, you are so irresponsible,' cried Aurora, turning white.

'Only winding you up, Aurora,' said Any hastily, and she winked at Storm, who broke into gales of laughter.

5
A terrible Loss

The children went on the merry-go-round, the dodgems, the waltzer (which Aurora said made her feel sick) and then they entered the hall of mirrors.

'Look at me, look at me,' cried Any. Storm and Aurora burst into laughter. Their little sister was blown up like a balloon that was about to burst. Any ran to the next mirror and was transformed into a human fish. Storm streaked past a bank of mirrors that made her look like a gambolling giraffe, all skittish legs. The girls ran around the mirrors calling to each other to come and see, and giggling at each other's weirdly elongated or compressed reflections and strange rearrangements of limbs.

While Storm and Any were making themselves almost sick with laughter by Storm's transformation into a six-headed monster, Aurora found herself in front of an ornate, gilt looking-glass. She gazed into it and was puzzled to discover that it reflected back nothing at all. Aurora leaned forward and as she did so her long blonde hair fell like molten gold across her face. She pushed it back with a delicate hand and revealed dark eyelashes framing wide violet eyes set in an oval face. Her skin had the bloom of an early ripe peach and her mouth was the colour of crushed raspberries.

Concealed behind the mirror – which allowed her to observe unseen anyone who looked into it – Belladonna gave a little gasp and licked her lips.

'Yes,' she whispered triumphantly. 'She is undoubtedly the fairest in the land.' She turned to Hermes. 'How I long to pluck out her heart this very instant and gobble it up.' Her tongue flicked like a serpent's across her lips and she shivered with pleasure. 'I have found my heart's desire, Hermes.'

Blissfully unaware of the evil witch's scheming, Storm, Aurora and Any fell out of the hall of mirrors tent laughing helplessly.

'What next?' asked Aurora. Storm and Any pointed at the roller-coaster.

'You two go,' said Aurora. 'I'll watch.'

She didn't see a great deal because she put her hands over her eyes every time her sisters' car headed for a steep drop. Storm and Any came off the ride with pink cheeks and with eyes shining.

'Candy-floss now,' said Any.

'Certainly not,' replied Aurora. 'It's pink, poisonous stuff. It'll make your teeth rot and fall out.'

'Which will save me the inconvenience of having to brush them every day,' said Any.

'No, no, no.'

'Please, Aurora, you're making me feel so flustrated.'

'Any, I don't think you can say flustrated.'

'Yes I can, because it's exactly what I feel: a mixture of flustered and frustrated because I'm not getting my own way.'

Aurora laughed. Storm listened to her sisters

remonstrating with each other. She knew that in the end Aurora would give in to Any. She watched the two of them heading for the candy-floss stall, still arguing. Storm wasn't interested in candy-floss. It stuck to the roof of her mouth and made her gag.

'I'm going to explore. I'll be back,' she called, threading her way through the brightly-coloured stalls and ignoring the cries of the fair folk.

'Everyone's a winner, dearie,' promised the woman from the Catch-a-Frog stall, with its fake amphibians sitting on fake lily pads in a moat of water. 'You've got a lucky face, pet.' Storm smiled, paying no attention to their entreaties. The air was heavy with the buttery aroma of roasting chestnuts. Around the back of the ghost train she could hear the happy screams and shrieks of customers on the ride. She lifted up a flap of the canvas and a skeleton grinned at her. She stuck her tongue out at it. She saw children bouncing up and down on giant trampolines next to the big wheel, screeching with laughter.

She walked on and the stalls began to thin and the noise of the fair became more muffled. A silver hare streaked across the fairground and into a small tent. Unlike the others, it was not candy-striped

but covered with tiny stars that shimmered and twinkled even though it was broad daylight. There was no sign outside indicating what went on within.

Intrigued, Storm walked up to the tent and peered into the gloom. It was like looking at the glimmering night sky. Shooting stars fizzed across an indigo firmament as if chasing each other's tails. She was about to step inside when she heard Aurora's panic-stricken voice. 'Storm! Storm! Where are you? I need you, Storm. Any's disappeared! I can't find her anywhere.'

A gaggle of interested people surrounded a hysterical Aurora. When Aurora saw Storm, she flung herself at her with such force that she almost knocked Storm over.

'Storm, it's Any. She's gone!'

Storm's heart tumbled into her toes. 'What do you mean gone? Gone where?'

Aurora burst into floods of tears.

'Calm down, Aurora, and tell me exactly what happened,' said Storm, hugging her sister tightly.

Between heaving sobs, Aurora told her story. After the candy-floss, Any had demanded a ride on the ghost train. They had just one free ride left, so Aurora happily agreed to watch (life was quite terrifying enough without ghost trains). She showed their golden ticket to the tall thin man who was taking the fares and watched as Any settled into the final carriage, making Ted-Bear give her a wave. She was the only passenger.

The music started and the train trundled through the doors. Aurora thought she heard a shriek and assumed that Any was enjoying scaring herself silly. But when the doors clunked open again and the train clattered through, the last carriage was completely empty. She asked the ticket man where Any could be, and he gave her a funny look and told her he hadn't had any passengers for at least half an hour.

Aurora's sobs grew louder and her breath came in rusty gasps. 'I screamed at him that my sister, a little girl in a red hooded cloak, had been on the ride, but he just made a gesture as if I was mad and repeated that he had never seen her. It's as if she never existed.'

'Did you search the ghost train?' asked Storm urgently.

'When I realized the man wouldn't help me, I went around the back and looked in. But it was really dark and I couldn't see her anywhere.'

'Come on,' said Storm, taking Aurora's hand. 'We're going to look properly. She can't just have vanished. Maybe she's hiding.'

'She's not, Storm. If she was hiding she'd have heard how upset I was and come out.'

Storm knew that was true. 'Well,' she said, 'she must be here somewhere.'

The girls hurried to the ghost train, watched by a small silver hare that was sitting in the entrance to the star-spangled tent, and by Belladonna, whose face was covered by a muffler. As the crowd dispersed, Belladonna and the hare locked eyes.

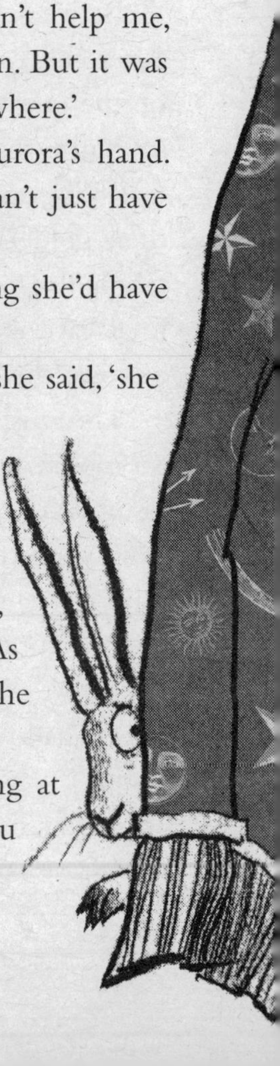

'You!' gasped Belladonna, clutching at her heart in shock. 'I know who you are!' She whipped out a pistol and aimed directly between the hare's eyes. But the little animal was too quick and leaped aside so that the bullet merely grazed its soft forehead. It gave a wounded cry and before Belladonna could fire again it bounded away leaving crimson petals of blood in its wake.

'Drat it,' said Belladonna. 'I won't miss next time.'

Hermes was standing by the ghost train entrance taking the money from the customers who were streaming onto the carriages, laughing and joking. He glared at Storm.

'You! Where's my little sister?' she cried. 'What have you done with her?'

Hermes raised an eyebrow. 'What have you done with my lion? I've never seen your sister,' he smirked. 'I don't know what you're talking about.'

'I don't believe you,' said Storm hotly. 'Where's Madame? She'll help us.'

He shrugged. 'Called away.'

'I don't believe you,' said Storm desperately.

'A medical emergency. A heart problem,' said Hermes with a little grin.

'Madame? Who's Madame,' asked Aurora. 'And what's this about a lion?'

'I'll explain later,' snapped Storm, turning back to Hermes. 'Can I go on the ride and look for Any?'

'Only if you pay the full fare,' he replied. 'If I gave a free ride to everyone who claimed to have lost a friend, a wallet or their wits on the ghost train, the fair would go bankrupt in a week.'

Aurora scrabbled in her purse for some coins. 'Are you sure about this, Storm? I don't want to lose you too,' she said, biting her lip anxiously.

'I'll be back before you know it,' promised Storm, squeezing her sister's hand. She glared at Hermes and slipped into the end carriage.

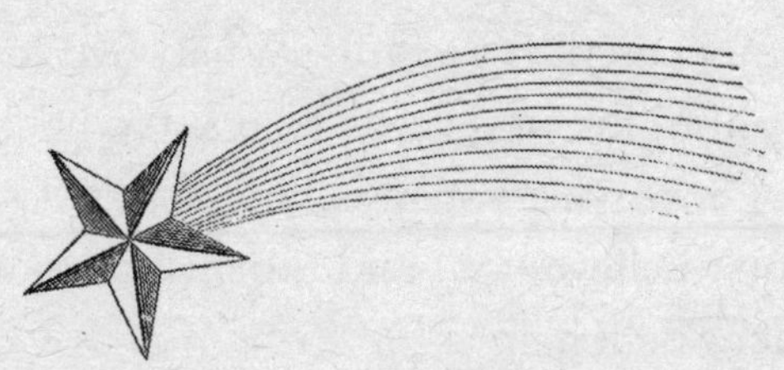

6

Smoke and Mirrors

The train clattered to a start. Storm was suddenly in complete darkness. Something slimy touched her face, then a luminous skeleton leered up at her. The train rattled upwards and then plunged without warning into a dip, and a ghost materialized before her, its mouth open in a silent scream.

The train lurched to the right and several ghouls appeared, cackling with demented laughter. The carriage swung back the other way and she caught a glimpse of a man with a bolt through his head and dark blood dripping from his mouth. He looked disconcertingly real. The carriage oscillated wildly again, allowing Storm to view a tableaux of ghostly wild-eyed women with green-tinged skin being chased by werewolves through endlessly revolving doors.

Around the next corner, she came face to face with a weeping, sad-eyed woman who appeared to be chained in the depths of a smoky freestanding looking-glass. The woman held out her hands to Storm as if silently beseeching her for help. Storm knew it was a visual deception, but the woman seemed so real and in such distress it was all Storm could do to stop herself leaping out of the carriage and going to her aid. The woman opened her mouth in a terrible scream as she was swallowed up by the mirror until all that was left were her entreating, desperate fingers that clawed at the air like boiling crabs.

The train rumbled around another bend and Storm saw a crack of daylight ahead. Her carriage banged through the doors into the light and she caught a glimpse of Aurora's anxious face just before the train entered the tunnel again and began its second circuit.

This time Storm knew what to expect. She passed the leering skeleton, the demented ghouls and the bloody, bolt-head man, all the while peering into the gloom on either side of the track in case she could see any trace of Any. The green-skinned women and the werewolves were still intent on their eternal game of chase. The mirror was next. As Storm's carriage drew level with it, the boiling clouds of smoke that covered its glass suddenly parted, and from deep inside it loomed a desperate, despairing face. The face was Any's and her eyes were wet with tears and hopelessness. She clutched Ted-Bear in one hand and held out the other to Storm in an unmistakable gesture of entreaty.

Storm gave an involuntary cry and leaped from the moving carriage. Any's face had already been swallowed by the mirror, but her small trembling hand was still reaching out to Storm. Storm held out her own hand to grasp Any's, but her fingers passed straight through, as if the child was a ghost. Panic-stricken, Storm called Any's name and reached out again towards the little hand that was being fast consumed by the mirror. Again her fingers passed right through Any's. She thought she heard Any's terrified voice calling 'Storm'. Desperately Storm thrust her hands deep into the cloudy mirror again, but all she felt was something solid and unyielding. She withdrew her hand. The smoke subsided. The surface of the mirror was smooth glass, perfectly ordinary solid glass. She pressed her forehead against its cool surface and then gave a yelp of fury and plunged her fist towards it. The mirror shattered, cutting her knuckles badly.

Gingerly she removed her hand, taking care to avoid the jagged shards of glass. She ran behind the mirror. There was nothing there. She looked wildly around and pushed her way through some thick black curtains. A limp skeleton fell towards her making her jump. She found herself at the back of the tent, which was flapping slightly in the breeze. There was a small gap between grass and canvas, and she kneeled and squeezed her way under the tent and into the open air. There was no sign of anyone. It was quite deserted, apart from an abandoned stick of half-eaten candy-floss lying in the grass.

Weeping with frustration, she ran around to the front of the ghost train and straight into Aurora, who was sobbing loudly that she had now lost not just one sister on the ghost train but two. Hermes stood unsympathetically by and announced to nobody in particular that it wasn't his fault if the customers kept losing their relatives and that Aurora had only herself to blame for such negligence.

'Storm! You're here!' cried Aurora.

'So's Any,' said Storm. 'I've seen her.'

'Where?'

'In a mirror! But it was as if she was just an illusion. I don't like it, I don't like it one bit.'

Aurora put her arms around Storm. 'We'll find her, Storm, I know we will. Remember! The three of us alone, the three of us together. Forever and for always. We're not almost orphans for nothing. We've got through worse than this in the past. We will find her.'

'This doesn't feel right, Aurora. It feels as if someone is playing a game with us.' Storm shivered. It was getting cold and the light would soon be gone. Even if they found Any immediately, the journey home skating down the river in the dark would not be pleasant. 'Come on, let's keep looking.'

For the next half an hour they worked their way around all the stalls asking everyone they met if they had seen a small girl in a red hooded cloak. The replies were always negative and with each one hope ebbed away. The silence between the girls grew heavy with dread.

Having searched every other inch of the fair-ground, they found themselves in the caravan area. There was no sign of Any. Silent tears were pouring down Aurora's cheeks, and a lump that felt like a heavy stone had lodged in Storm's throat. She was overwhelmed with anxiety. They were just about to return to the main fairground, where the fair folk were beginning to close up their stalls, when Storm heard a noise that chilled her to the bone: the long, mournful howl of a wolf. She clutched Aurora's arm as panic flashed across her sister's exhausted face.

Following the sound, Storm took Aur-ora's hand and pulled her around the side of a huge caravan. Just a few feet away was a cage housing five grey wolves. They were mon-strous well-cared-for beasts, sleek and muscled with sharp, bared fangs. And they were intent on pulling apart a small, red velvet hooded cloak.

Aurora gasped and fell to her knees. For a second, Storm felt woozy and then she leaped forward, pushed her arm through the bars, and snatched the cloak from the jaws of the surprised wolves so swiftly that they had no time to bite her. They snapped and snarled and then threw back their heads in a choir of howling.

'Storm, you could have been killed or lost an arm at the very least,' whispered Aurora.

'I don't care,' said Storm fiercely. 'Those wolves may have eaten my baby sister, but I'm not going to let them eat her cloak too.' Then she burst into sobs and her wails mingled with Aurora's wails and the wailing of the wolves in a strange melancholic symphony that was the saddest sound on earth.

'I don't believe it, I won't believe it,' sobbed Aurora, her voice cracked with hopelessness. 'Who on earth would be wicked enough to throw a baby to the wolves?'

'There's only one person in the entire world,' said Storm in a small, dead voice, 'and his name is Dr DeWilde.'

The words were hardly out of her mouth when a small unmistakable voice said indignantly, 'So there you are. I've been looking for you everywhere. Where ever have you been? I know this fair is a brilliant place for hiding from people, but I do think you could have told me that we were playing hide-and-seek. You are both very mean to have left me alone all this time.'

Storm and Aurora stared up in astonishment. Any was standing before them, her face so smeared with candy-floss that she looked as if she had a wispy pink beard.

'I really do think that we should be getting home. It's getting late and Ted-Bear and I are cold, tired and very, very hungry.'

Unseen in the shadows, Belladonna and Hermes watched the children with undisguised glee.

'My moment has come!' whispered Belladonna.

'Yes, but Madame must exert caution,' said Hermes nervously. 'I am sure that Madame knows there are strict rules regarding the taking of human hearts.'

'Rules, what do I care for rules?' said Belladonna scornfully. 'I'm a witch. We don't play by the rules.'

Hermes removed a fat, much-thumbed, battered leather book from his pocket. On the cover was written in faded gold letters: *Taking Heart: The Essential Guide for the Heartless.* He flipped rapidly through it and found a page over which he had scribbled many notes in tiny, spidery writing. He cleared his throat. 'Rule three, subsection 1604: All hearts must be asked for by the recipient or their agents and must be freely given. Instantaneous death is the punishment for anyone who takes a heart that is not theirs to take.'

He flicked further through the book and found a marked page: 'Rule 1,871, subsection 675: Anyone – or their agents – stealing a human heart that has been previously assigned or given away under rule 917, subsection 124, will instantly forfeit their own life . . .' Hermes's thin voice trailed away to a whisper under Belladonna's withering glare.

'Stupid rules,' she said sulkily. 'But it is all the more reason why we must put my plan into action immediately, just in case she's thinking of giving away her heart to somebody else. I won't need to steal her heart because I will make sure that she gives it to me, and only to me. Her brand-new and very loving stepmama.'

'But won't that Storm girl recognize you?' asked Hermes.

'Do you think I'm stupid?' snapped Belladonna. 'I will have to disguise myself.'

Belladonna lifted the Dorian mirror to her face and was unable to conceal a shudder at what she saw there. Then she raised a finger and waved it over the mirror and muttered an incantation. The surface of the mirror seethed, and the outline of Belladonna's body was illuminated as if she radiated a light from within. The light became so strong that Hermes leaned backwards and shielded his eyes.

The edges of Belladonna's body began to dissolve and Hermes watched open-mouthed as Belladonna shrank and disappeared, to be replaced out of a sea of sparks and swirling clouds by a figure so monstrous that Hermes averted his face and whimpered in fear. That figure was swallowed up by more sparks and churning clouds that turned black, then green and vermillion and eventually milky-white. The whirling clouds began to subside, there was a sound like a roaring hurricane, a flash of electric blue light and then out of the clouds stepped a tall woman of icy beauty, with hair the colour of ebony. She extended a hand graciously towards Hermes.

'My name is Belle Eden. So pleased to meet you.'

Hermes's mouth was opening and closing like a fish. 'Belladonna?' he asked hesitantly.

'Of course it's me, you fool.' She snapped her fingers. 'Don't just stand there. We've work to do. To the wolves. It is almost time for the children to meet their new mama.'

Belle Eden stood by the wolf cage as Hermes fumbled with the lock. The wolves sniffed at her suspiciously before howling with pleasure.

'See, they recognize their mistress even though I'm quite transformed.'

Belle threw bits of

raw kidney and liver through the bars at the wolves. 'Sweets for my sweets; titbits for my pretties,' she crooned. The wolves slavered and leaped upwards, snatching the bloody snacks mid-air and gulping them down. Hermes opened the door, and stepped back nervously. The wolves bounded out of the cage and sat at Belle's feet, begging. She threw them each another kidney and let them lick the blood from her hands.

'Enough, my beauties,' she said. 'We must keep you peckish, or you will not obey me.' She tweaked one wolf's nose viciously. It yelped, and the others growled. Belle smiled.

'But you always do exactly what I ask, don't you? Just like Hermes. You are all my faithful servants.' She whispered in one wolf's ear. 'Because you know what I will do to you if you fail me, don't you?' The wolves grumbled and growled. Hermes started shaking, but he noticed that the familiar figure of Belladonna was very faintly visible through the disguised Belle who stood in front of him. She stroked the nearest wolf's head.

'You have your instructions, my pretties. I want those children jibbering. I want you to frighten them so badly that they will welcome me with open arms. Off you go, into the woods.'

She watched them go, then reached for the mirror and considered her reflection. 'Drat it. The spell is unstable. Thank goodness for the mirror.' She started muttering into it again, and the disguise solidified, leaving no trace of Belladonna.

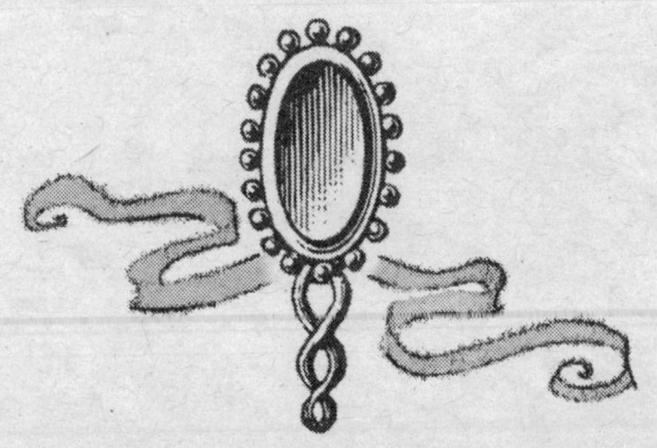

7 Danger! Wolves!

The winter sun smoked low in the sky as Storm and Aurora skated down the frozen river pulling the sledge behind them. Any was now fast asleep clutching Ted-Bear. They had questioned their little sister closely, but Any was quite insistent that it had been Storm and Aurora who were lost and not the other way round.

'I was waiting by the ghost train for you,' she said. 'I didn't budge, although I might have had a nap. It is always good to nap. A nice woman kept giving me free candy-floss.'

'What did she look like?' asked Storm sharply.

'I couldn't see her face properly, she was wearing a muffler. But she was nice. The candy-floss made me sleepy, so I can't remember what she said. I had funny dreams. I dreamed I was locked inside a mirror and I couldn't get out. It was horrid. Maybe it's all that pink colouring in the candy-floss. I think maybe you're right, Aurora, candy-floss is delicious but it probably is exceptionally bad for you.'

The girls skated on in silence through the gloaming. They were so exhausted it was an effort to keep moving. Snowflakes fell from the sky like fluttering white moths; low branches of trees brushed their shoulders as if trying to hold them back.

After a while Aurora said quietly, 'Do you really think this is Dr DeWilde's doing, Storm?'

'Who else could it be?' said Storm grimly.

'But he's dead. He died in the fire. And even if he didn't, what could he want with us? You don't have the pipe any more, Storm. It's safe and entirely out of reach at the bottom of the sea.'

'I hope so, Aurora. I really hope you're right,' said Storm.

Under a darkening sky, the children skated on. The snow was falling so thickly that they didn't see the silver hare moving parallel with them along the frozen river bank. The animal was clearly hurt, a bright wound visible on the side of its head, and although the children were not skating fast it was having trouble keeping up.

They kept to the very middle of the river, where the ice was thickest. Aurora eyed the forest that lined the banks with suspicion, pushing away the branches that hung over the river and pulled at the girls' hair like grasping hands. A sheen of mist clung to the tree trunks as if trying to smother them.

'Why do I feel like we're being watched?' she said.

'It's just the woods making you nervous,' replied Storm briskly. 'We'll be home in a jiffy, and sitting by the fire drinking hot chocolate.'

But they weren't, because a few moments later Aurora tripped over, twisting her ankle. Pain blossomed up her leg.

'Well,' she said, fighting back tears. 'The perfect end to a perfect day. All we need now is for a wolf to come along and gobble us up. I knew we should have stayed at home and turned out the linen cupboard. Nobody ever got injured or eaten while turning out the linen cupboard.'

'No,' said Storm grimly, 'but they do skating through the woods in the dark,' and she pointed back down the river. Aurora gasped. Slinking towards them were five pale-grey, ghostly shapes.

Any woke up and stared. 'Clearly I was completely misinformed about wolves not being able to skate,' she said in a very small voice.

'Yes,' whispered Aurora. 'You were utterly, indisputably wrong.'

The wolves glided over the ice, stopping some distance from the children. They lay down their heads between their paws and watched them. One of the wolves had a distinctive brown stripe running from head to tail. Storm put her arms around Aurora and Any as if shielding them from the gaze of the animals would also protect them from the beasts' sharp teeth, which shone a luminous yellow in the dark. 'Forever and for always,' she whispered.

Aurora squeezed her hand and replied, 'The three of us alone. The three of us together. Forever and for always.'

The wolves stayed where they were, their eyes never leaving the sisters.

'Maybe they're not very hungry,' suggested Any, trying to keep the fear out of her voice.

'I wouldn't bank on it, wolves are always ravenous,' replied Storm tersely. 'Can you walk at all, Aurora?'

'I'll manage,' said Aurora, gritting her teeth.

'All right,' said Storm quietly. 'Very slowly and without any sudden movement, hold on to my arm and manoeuvre yourself onto the sledge.' Aurora did as she was told, wincing as her weight shifted to her damaged ankle. The wolves stayed supine, watching with interest.

'It's as if they're waiting for something,' said Storm. 'I don't like it. Let's try moving and see what happens.'

Very slowly Storm rose to her feet, wrapped her hand around the handle of the sledge and started to haul it after her. It was a mistake. The wolves instantly sprang into life. Sharp teeth snapped by Storm's ear, she smelled the musky scent of fur and heard a warning growl as several of the beasts shot in front of her. The wolves surrounded them. She skidded to a halt and the over-laden sledge turned over, depositing Aurora and Any onto the ice. The wolves growled menacingly, their thin red tongues flicking lazily across sharp teeth. Any whimpered with shock.

From somewhere in the distance came a long mournful howl. The sound hung eerily on the still air and as if on cue the wolves leaped towards the children. Horrified, Storm saw two wolves tear the remains of Any's red cloak off her back. She caught a glimpse of Aurora's frightened face, her arms raised as she tried to defend herself against two snarling wolves. She turned just in time to see a grey shape plummeting towards her. She took a quick side step and the animal plunged nose-first onto the ice, knocking itself out.

Aurora, Any and Ted-Bear were curled together, one tight little ball on the ice under a mass of matted fur. Storm felt desperately in her pocket, pulled out a handful of firecrackers and threw them into the midst of the wolves. The fireworks crackled and hissed and the animals yelped and scattered as hundreds of sparks came into contact with solid ice. Growling and whining, the wolves turned tail and slunk away, but as soon as the sparks and noise had died down, they turned, ready to make a second assault.

As the animals raced towards the children, Storm grabbed the sledge. She swung it round and round and as the line of wolves drew closer she let go. It slid across the ice and careered into the wolves, hitting two of them full on the front legs. The animals reared up, screaming in pain, and limped off into the forest.

The two remaining wolves snarled in rage and advanced threateningly. Storm heard Any shriek with terror. She reached into her pocket again and pulled out a final handful of firecrackers. She threw them and the animals skittered this way and that, yapping angrily as they tried to avoid the tiny explosions of sparks around their feet. One firecracker exploded directly under a wolf. It yelped and bounded away, leaving behind a smell of lightly-singed fur.

The last remaining wolf, the one with the distinctive brown stripe, padded around the children eyeing Storm with a yellow glare. Storm locked eyes with the beast as she felt desperately in her pockets for more firecrackers. All she found was some fluff, a pine cone and a half-eaten cucumber sandwich. Hopelessness washed over her. They were going to be eaten.

Storm pulled herself together. If they were going to be gobbled up by those razor-sharp teeth, she was determined that they would not go down without a fight. She would take the wolf before it took her and at least give her sisters a chance of escape. She bared her teeth and leaped furiously upon the surprised animal, simultaneously shouting 'Run!' to Aurora and Any.

She was aware of her sisters shuffling towards the trees as her head hit the astonished animal's jaw. The animal reared up over Storm and knocked her backwards. There was a sugar and rust taste of blood in her mouth. The animal's bulk loomed over her. She could see its yellow eyes, feel its dank breath, and sense the jagged teeth coming towards her. She braced herself for the pain as those teeth sank into her flesh.

At that moment she heard the tinkling sound of sleigh bells. A shot cut through the air and a bullet whizzed past her right ear and the wolf's left flank. The animal backed away. A second bullet whistled through the air rather too close for comfort. The wolf turned on its heel and bounded into the forest.

Gingerly, Storm raised her head from the ice and looked up into the face of a woman with ice-blue eyes, skin the colour of freshly-fallen snow and lips as red as blood. The woman had a beauty spot on her left cheek and her ebony hair was piled high upon her head in an elaborate arrangement. In her right hand she held a small smoking pistol. The beautiful woman blew on it and smiled at Storm.

'I do so hate it when I miss,' she said.

8
A New Mama

The children stared at their exquisite saviour uncertainly.

Storm suddenly remembered her manners. 'Thank you,' she said quietly as Aurora and Any hugged her. 'You saved our lives. If you hadn't come along when you did, the wolves would have killed us. We'll be eternally grateful.'

'I'm delighted to have been of service,' said the stranger. There was a sudden flash of silver and a small hare streaked towards them across the ice. Casually, the woman raised her pistol and fired. The hare took flight, leaving a trail of fresh crimson blood on the ice.

Storm opened her mouth to protest angrily and then closed it again, remembering that they owed this woman their lives. The stranger glared after the hare, then she extended a white icy hand. 'My name is Belle Eden.'

The children gaped at her.

'Eden?' asked Storm sharply. 'Are you sure?' she blurted.

'Quite sure, thank you,' said the woman. 'Such a lovely name, such a green juicy name, even if I say so myself,' she added with a laugh that was like ice cubes tinkling in a glass.

'But it can't be yours,' Any declared proprietorially, 'because it belongs to us.'

Belle's smooth face didn't betray a flicker of surprise. 'What an amazing coincidence! You must be Aurora, Storm and Any. How lovely to meet you. Reggie told me all about you. As soon as I realized that you would be all by yourselves at Eden End, I flew as fast as I could to be by your side. Clearly I arrived just in the nick of time.' She opened her arms and gathered the three astonished children to her. 'Dearest children, my little babes in the wood, I'm your new mama.'

It was Storm who pulled away first. 'Mother? What on earth do you mean?' she asked. The truth hit her like a blow to the head. She felt dizzy. 'Papa has married again! You are our stepmother! How? When? It's not possible, Papa has been gone for less than twenty-four hours.'

'Indeed I am your stepmama,' trilled Belle. 'It was a whirlwind courtship. We fell head over heels in love with each other. Your Papa was a most decisive man. He swept me off my feet and wouldn't take no for an answer.'

'Was?' said Storm uncertainly.

Belle set her face in sombre mode. 'My dears, I'm afraid I have truly tragic news for you. Your poor father. We had been married less than an hour. A most unfortunate accident. It appears that your father was cruelly mistaken about the four-tongued, three-footed, two-headed honey dragon. It turns out not to have such a sweet disposition, after all. Indeed it is abnormally ferocious and bad-tempered.'

From out of her pocket, Belle produced a

battered hat, which the sisters instantly recognized as belonging to their father. 'This is all that was left of him, I'm afraid.' Belle gave a theatrical sigh and a tear trickled down her cheek.

Aurora fainted, Any screamed 'No!' and Storm stared at Belle white-faced. Dead! Their father was dead! Loss almost knocked her off her feet. She choked despairingly and stooped to help Aurora, who murmured in a daze, 'I suppose that means that we are no longer almost orphans, but proper orphans now.'

'Yes,' whispered Storm, squeezing her sister's icy hand. 'We're entirely on our own.'

'Oh, but you're not!' said Belle triumphantly. 'I'm moving in with you. Your father has left Eden End and you three children entirely in my care.'

The children were so devastated by the news of their father's sudden death that they didn't protest when Belle took over the running of the house. She made herself quite at home and took every opportunity to charm the children into trusting her.

'Look, Aurora, I've found a centuries-old recipe for syllabub that I thought you might find interesting,' said Belle in an exaggeratedly kind voice, placing an ancient recipe book in Aurora's lap. In happier times, Aurora would have been fascinated by the rare old cookery book, but now she barely glanced at it.

'Papa adored syllabub,' she whispered. 'It was one of his favourites. Zella loved it too. She said it tasted like sunshine on a spoon.' Tears boiled over and ran down her cheeks like a stream of lava.

'There, there, you'll make your beautiful eyes all red,' murmured Belle.

At that moment Storm slipped in through the door. She had been out in the woods feeding Zeus on a mixture of left-over vegetarian lasagne and mashed potato. Having seen Belle's trigger-happy attitude to the silver hare, Storm was quite certain that Zeus would not be welcomed as a family pet. Storm entered the room just in time to see Belle patting Aurora's upper arm like a beady-eyed housewife eyeing up a shoulder of lamb on the butcher's slab. There was something about the scene that made Storm feel slightly sick.

Belle caught sight of her and moved away, catching a glimpse of herself in the mirror as she did so. Behind her disguise she could just see the real Belladonna trying to get through. She ostentatiously dabbed her eyes with a black-edged hankie, and hurried to her room to use her mirror. Storm watched her go. She knew that there was something familiar about Belle and felt certain she had seen her somewhere before.

A cloud of mourning had descended upon Eden End. It was as if the old creaky house was wrapped in a cloak of grief. Mist clung to the walls all day and night and the old floorboards and rafters whispered like mourners at a wake. The children were rigid with shock and the agony of loss, and none more so than Storm, who barely spoke, ate or slept, despite the fact that Belle insisted on tucking all three sisters up in bed every night at 7.30 p.m. She claimed that exceptionally early bedtimes were a well-known cure for grief, but in fact it was because she couldn't bear to have the children around her for any longer than necessary.

'Sleepy, sleepy, my little poppet,' said Belle, leaning over Any's bed to tuck her in. Little Any had never had a mother to kiss her goodnight and she clasped Belle to her eagerly. Like all witches, Belle had an allergy to children and an ugly red welt immediately sprung up on her neck where Any's fingers had touched her skin.

'What a darling you are,' soothed Belle through clenched teeth. And how much more darling you'd be dead and buried under the juniper tree, she thought to herself. Planning places to dispose of the children's bones after she had fed them to her wolves was one of her favourite past-times. That moment was drawing ever closer. She had only to get Aurora to promise her heart to her, find the pipe and then win it and she would have no further use for the Eden children.

Her eyes glittered as she went over to Aurora's bed. She looked at the girl ravenously. 'Ah, my beauty!' she said as she tucked Aurora in tightly, imagining that Aurora's heart was already hers and she was tucking Aurora's lifeless body into a coffin.

'Last but not least,' said Belle brightly to Storm, who simply turned her face to the wall. Aurora and Any were passive with grief and patiently bore Belle's endless attempts to win their affection. Indeed Aurora seemed relieved to no longer be weighed down by the full responsibility of caring for her younger sisters. But Storm was far less receptive to her stepmother's attempts to get close to her. She found it hard to accept that her father who had loved Zella so much would have married again so quickly and casually, and she sensed something false about Belle's smiles.

'Oh, my poor damaged little Storm. I know just what you are feeling. My heart is broken too!' cried Belle theatrically to the back of Storm's head, all the while thinking how quickly it would be mended once she had acquired Aurora's heart. She wondered whether Aurora's heart would be best roasted, boiled or fried with a little garlic. Or perhaps she should just eat it raw? She must seek guidance from *Taking Heart: The Essential Guide for the Heartless.* It was too important a matter to get wrong. Belle's icy hand patted Storm's blankets. Storm shivered with a sudden sense of foreboding.

'Goodnight, my little lambs. I hope you all rest in peace,' she said sweetly, and closed the door. 'Yes,' she murmured to herself, 'I sincerely hope it is RIP for all of you, very, very soon.'

Once Belle had gone, all three sisters clambered into a single bed together. As first Any and then Aurora fell asleep, Storm lay awake in the dark, listening to Belle move through the house. There was something so methodical about her stepmother's movements it was as if Belle was searching for something. For what seemed like hours Storm listened to Aurora's little snores and Any's snuffling, then she slipped out of bed and downstairs to the kitchen. She snaffled a handful of madeleines from the cake tin and ran through the pale moonlight into the woods.

'Zeus! Zeus!' she called. There was a sudden crashing through the undergrowth and the beautiful lion emerged from the trees and bowed down before her. Telling him about Aurora's flair for cookery, she hand-fed him the madeleines, which he thought were quite the most delicious things he had ever eaten. Storm buried her face in Zeus's soft fur, and wished she could take him back to Eden End. She gave him another hug and returned to the house.

Hearing a noise, she peeped into the library. Belle was pulling out the books one by one and pressing her long, probing fingers into the spaces behind.

'There's no money, if that's what you're looking for,' said Storm, creeping up behind Belle. 'There's no hidden Eden End treasure.'

Belle gave a little meow of surprise and her face was chalky as if she had seen a ghost. Storm noted that it was almost as if there were two people standing in front of her and not just one. She rubbed her eyes and wondered whether she might need glasses.

Belle smiled smoothly at her. 'Oh, it's only people who pay their bills who need money, and I never do that. Your darling father warned me that he didn't have a penny to his name, and I loved him all the more for it.' She dabbed at her eyes with her handkerchief. 'I was just looking for my pills. A little heart trouble, I'm afraid. It stops me sleeping. Come, would you like some hot chocolate? I can make it with whipped cream and sprinkle it with hundreds and thousands. I know it is very hard for you, Storm, and you have suffered a great loss, but I would so like us to be friends. As your new mama, I want to do my best for you. I do so adore children.'

'I only like Aurora's hot chocolate,' said Storm stiffly, and she marched back to bed.

'Yes, I do adore children,' muttered Belle to herself, 'but only in pies with extra gravy.'

9
An Unexpected Visitor

Belle was suffering badly from her close proximity to the children. It brought her out in an itchy rash and placed extra strain on her already withered heart. She had to make more and more use of the Dorian mirror, which she kept by her constantly, snug in its black velvet box.

'What do you keep in that box?' demanded Storm one lunchtime, noticing the way her stepmother never let it out of her sight.

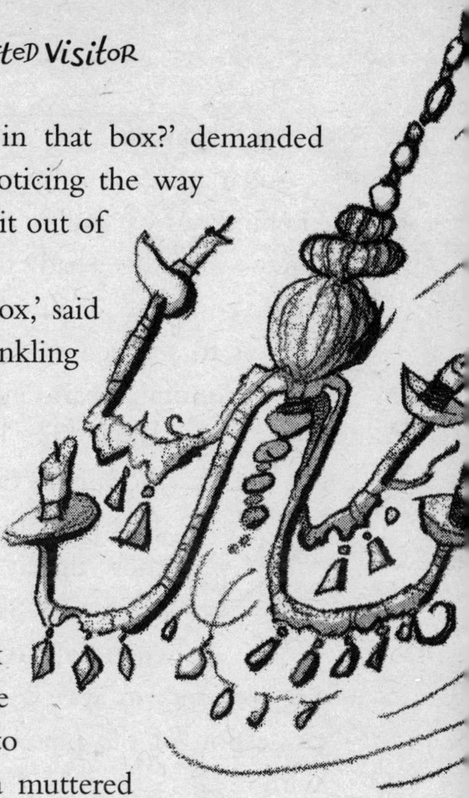

'It's just my beauty box,' said Belle with a little tinkling laugh.

'Can I see what's inside?' asked Storm.

Belle's cheek muscles tightened. 'Of course,' she said with a forced smile. She pushed the box across the table towards the child, but as Storm went to open the lid, Belladonna muttered something and the old chandelier overhead crashed to the floor, narrowly missing Any. In the shock of the moment, the box was forgotten. After that Belle kept the box locked in her room, but Storm had not forgotten about it and was determined to take a look inside at the first available opportunity.

Belle redoubled her efforts to woo the children. She initiated riveting conversations with Aurora about the advantages of duvets over sheets and blankets, and she produced pink sugar mice, as if by magic, from behind Any's right ear. Belle knew that she had to win their complete trust if she was to succeed in gaining Aurora's heart and getting her hands on the pipe. She had searched the house thoroughly and was certain that the pipe was not hidden there, but she knew that it would find its way back to Storm. She intended to be there when it did, and if that meant being patient, it was a small price to pay for possession of the pipe and the power that came with it.

Storm became so irritated by her stepmother's sugary tones that she spent more and more time alone at Zella's grave.

'You left us, and now Papa has left us too. And he didn't even say goodbye. People always leave me. There's no point in loving people if they just leave you,' she railed, the tears making a little snail trail down her cheeks.

'Well, I hope that you are happy together without us. And I hope he's told you about Belle. He can't have loved you all that much if he got married again, and I don't think he loved us at all, or he'd never have left us in the care of that woman.' She burst into furious tears again. The silver birch tree bent over her and its branches rustled as if trying to soothe her.

Returning to the house, she was surprised to find Aurora and Any making cakes with Belle. Both of them had more colour in their cheeks and Belle was smiling solicitously at them.

'What are you doing?' hissed Storm when Belle was in the pantry.

'Making cakes,' said Aurora calmly.

'More like consorting with the enemy,' said Storm fiercely.

Aurora sighed. 'She's not the enemy, Storm. She's poor Papa's widow, and she's trying very hard to be kind. I think we should be nice to her. After all, she's lost her husband, just as we've lost our father.'

'Yes,' said Any, licking the spoon. 'She's grief-stricken, and she's going to let me have a candy-floss-making machine in my room and she said I could have my walls studded with chocolate buttons. Oh, and her lap is very snuggly.'

Storm couldn't believe what she was hearing. 'She's an impostor,' she cried.

Any and Aurora exchanged glances. 'Why would she want to pretend to be our stepmother? What could she possibly gain?' asked Aurora patiently.

'I don't know, do I ?' cried Storm angrily. 'Maybe she wants to get her hands on our inheritance.'

Aurora raised an eyebrow. 'And what inheritance is that, Storm?'

'Eden End. Our home,' said Storm sullenly.

Any looked at Storm pityingly. 'Eden End isn't worth anything, Storm. You know as well as I do it's more of a liability than an asset. It's worthless.'

'Not to me it isn't,' said Storm firmly. 'To me, it's priceless.' She stomped into the larder.

'What's priceless?' asked Belle, emerging from the pantry.

'Storm's imagination,' said Any, and she put her little hand in Belle's, not noticing her stepmother's shudder.

'Are those cakes ready to go in the oven?' asked Belle.

'Yes.'

'Then I'd be honoured if you'd show me how you order the linen cupboard, Aurora, while they're cooking. It would be such a treat to know your system. Your poor dear Papa knew that I liked nothing more than a tidy linen cupboard.'

'Are you sure you're really interested?' asked Aurora eagerly.

'Completely captivated,' said Belle. 'I'm interested in whatever you children are interested in,' she cooed. 'I think a good mama should be. Come, Any, we'll get you a sugar mouse on the way.'

As she ushered the children from the kitchen, a small mouse poked its head out of Belle's elaborate coiffure and ran down her dress and across the floor. Storm bent to pick it up. She stroked it and whispered, 'I bet you couldn't bear her either.'

The mouse looked at Storm with its bright eyes and squeaked loudly as if agreeing with every word.

Storm waited until all three of them were safely ensconced in the linen cupboard. She could hear Aurora earnestly explaining her system through the half-closed door. She knew they would be hours, possibly days in there. It was the perfect opportunity to sneak a look in the black velvet box.

She tiptoed to Belle's door and tried the handle. It wouldn't budge. She produced a hairpin and fiddled with the lock. There was a satisfying click and Storm crept into the bedroom. She glanced around. She couldn't see the box anywhere. She looked in the wardrobe. There was no sign of it. Under the bed. Nothing. The dressing-table drawer held only a brush and comb. Storm crept over to the bedside table and pulled open the drawer. Inside was the black velvet box. With trembling hands she picked it up, but as she did so she glanced out of the window. A familiar figure was walking up the drive. She gave a little cry of delight, dropped the box back into its drawer and ran as fast as she could towards the linen cupboard.

Aurora was enthusing about the best way to arrange the sheets and pillow cases. Belle suppressed a yawn. Any had fallen asleep on the floor, her face sticky with pink sugar. Belle felt as if she had aged five centuries through the sheer tedium of listening to Aurora. She yawned.

'Oh, I'm so sorry, I'm boring you,' apologized Aurora, a look of hurt stealing across her beautiful face.

'But you're not,' simpered Belle. 'I find it all utterly fascinating.' She looked into Aurora's eyes. 'I think that you and I are heart-mates.'

'Don't you mean soul-mates?' said Aurora.

'No, I mean heart-mates. I feel as if our hearts belong to each other.'

'Oh, really?' said Aurora, flustered by this unexpected display of affection. She felt she hardly knew Belle. But then she saw the stricken look on Belle's face and the tears welling in those ice-blue eyes and she felt a pang for her stepmother. Aurora's kind heart swelled. It would cost her nothing, nothing at all, to humour Belle. Aurora took Belle's cold hands.

'I'm sorry, Belle, I know that you are trying to be a loving stepmother to us. I'm growing fond of you.'

'So I can count on your heart, dearest Aurora?' asked Belle greedily.

Aurora gulped. If she said 'yes' she wouldn't be entirely sincere, but it would be rude to say no. Aurora knew the value of good manners. She opened her mouth. 'If it matters so much to you, Belle, then—'

Before she could say the word 'yes', Storm burst

into the linen cupboard.

'Aurora, come quickly, we've got a visitor,' she said, her cheeks pink with excitement. She dragged her sister downstairs, with Any following close behind, sleepily rubbing her eyes.

Belladonna was left quite alone with the linen, which was just as well, as she was so furious that smoke was coming out of both her nostrils.

Storm and Aurora skidded into the kitchen. Their visitor was already knocking on the door. Aurora pulled it open.

Standing on the doorstep was Kit. And in his arms, wrapped in brown paper, its monstrous head and tail poking out from either end, was the biggest, ugliest fish the children had ever seen.

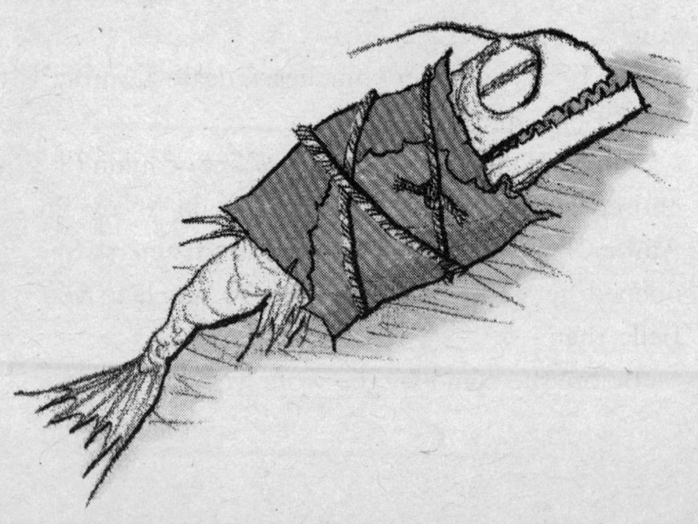

10
The Pipe Returns

Storm drew back behind her mother's headstone and watched Aurora and Kit as they picked their way through the gravestones. She felt badly neglected by them both. She had tried to catch Kit alone and give a full account of Belle's strange arrival in their lives and her suspicions about her stepmother's motives, but he was always with Aurora. They had eyes only for each other. Aurora tilted her head back and laughed, and for a split second she looked so much like Zella that it made Storm catch her breath. She felt the loss of her mother like a sharp pain as if someone was jabbing pins into her side. Aurora and Kit wandered towards Zella's grave and Storm drew back guiltily, ashamed that she might be caught spying. The couple stopped just a few feet away and sat down on the grass. Shyly, Kit took Aurora's hand.

'I love you very much, Aurora, but I'm poor and I can't think of asking you to marry me until I've made my fortune. My mind is made up. With the little money I've earned from fishing, I'm going to set myself up as a dragon-hunter. I've heard that there are towns and villages beyond the great forests that are terrorized by dragons, and will pay well to be rid of them.'

'That's very brave of you, Kit,' gulped Aurora, 'but it is an excessively dangerous choice of career. Couldn't you be a weights-and-measures inspector or a bank manager? It would be so much safer.'

'And duller,' smiled Kit, who knew that Aurora's idea of an adventure was trying out a new recipe for upside-down pineapple pudding. 'Nothing's worth doing unless it makes you a little bit nervous.'

'The trouble is that almost everything makes me nervous,' said Aurora anxiously.

'If you always expect the unexpected, then you won't get any nasty shocks,' said Kit. And he got down on one knee and declared: 'Aurora Rose Grace Eden, I cannot ask you to marry me yet, and I know that you may not want to wait for me, but I will come back for you. In the meantime, I pledge you my undying love and I hope that one day your heart will truly be mine.'

Aurora smiled and took his face gently in her hands. They were so absorbed in each other that neither noticed Storm behind the gravestone – or Belle lurking behind a tree . . .

'If you ever have need of my heart, come and take it. I give it to you gladly, Kit.'

From behind the tree came a cry like that of a wounded bird of prey.

'What was that?' asked Aurora anxiously.

'Just a bird,' said Kit, drawing her closer.

Behind Zella's headstone, Storm clenched her fists. Her mind was racing. If Aurora married Kit, what would happen to Storm and Any? 'The three of us alone, the three of us together. Forever and for always.' Aurora was always saying that, but obviously it meant nothing to her. They were just empty words, because Aurora was clearly preparing to leave with Kit and abandon her sisters to the horrible Belle. How could Aurora even think of such a thing! Storm's world suddenly felt very fragile, as if it might crumble away to nothing. Tears plopped down her face as she ran towards the house, oblivious to the trees that sang to her as she passed and to the tinkle of a roundabout and the low rumble of caravans as the fair moved closer to Eden End.

The cooked fish lay steaming on a huge platter in the middle of the kitchen table, looking ugly and smelling delicious. A mouth-watering aroma arose from its crisp skin, which had been rubbed with olive oil and salt and pierced with sprigs of rosemary. Aurora had baked it in the oven along with some roast potatoes and winter vegetables. There was a most satisfactorily wobbly quaking pudding for afters.

'Let's eat,' said Belle, forcing herself to smile warmly around the table at the three sisters and their guest.

'Yes,' said Any, 'or I'll die of starvation.'

Storm's face was dark and she kept on scowling in Kit's direction.

'What's wrong, Storm? Your face is so crumpled it looks as if it could do with a good press,' laughed Aurora, trying to jolly her sister along. It was the first time she had felt happy since the trip to the fair, and she wanted Storm to be happy too. She couldn't understand why her sister was glowering so.

In between rearranging the larder and preparing the fish, Aurora had been searching for Storm, eager to tell her what had passed between her and Kit. She had looked in all Storm's usual secret haunts, but hadn't been able to find her anywhere. How she longed to make plans with her for a distant future where all four of them would live happily together at Eden End. Obviously Kit would be away dragon-hunting a good deal of the time and Aurora couldn't really envisage Belle as part of it, but she was certain that it would all work out for the best, because Aurora knew that love conquered everything, except perhaps chickenpox and really stubborn stains.

Aurora picked up the fish slice and carefully

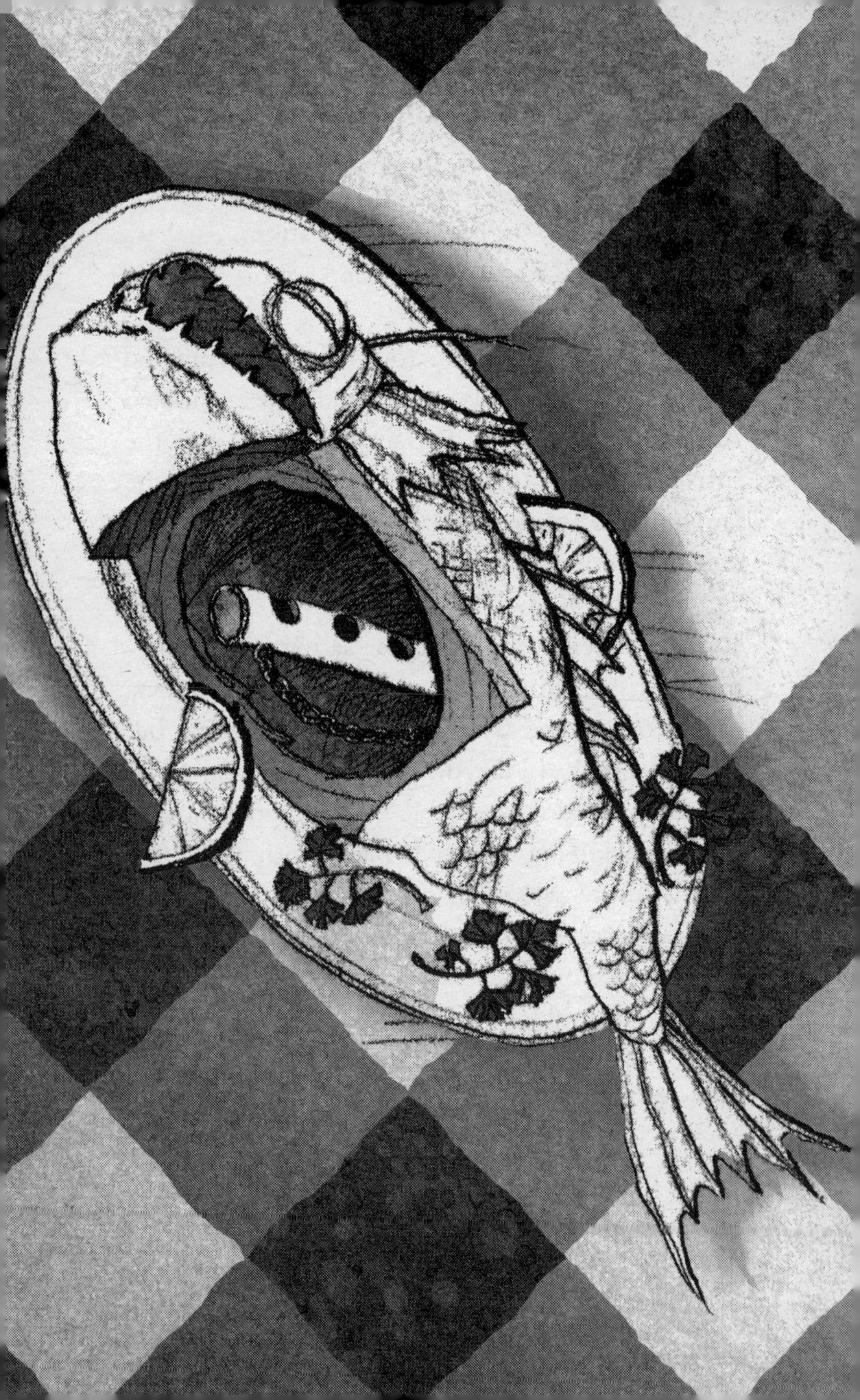

carved down the belly of the fish, a look of intense concentration on her face as she filleted the moist, creamy flesh. She eased the fish slice under a plump chunk of fish, lifted it and gave a loud cry. The fish slice clattered to the ground, raining flakes of fish all over the carpet. Aurora stared, horrified, into the excavated hole in the belly of the fish. Everyone rose to their feet to get a better look. Storm peered into the hole and saw a dull glint. She reached forward and lifted the object into the air.

It tingled and danced in her hand as if saying hello. Any squealed, Kit looked shocked and Aurora burst into tears.

'The pipe has come back to you, Storm. It has found you again!'

'Actually, I think you'll find that the pipe belongs to me,' said Belle in a hard, excited voice. She leaned over, swiped the pipe out of Storm's hand and into a small black velvet bag and swept out of the room.

11 Catastrophe

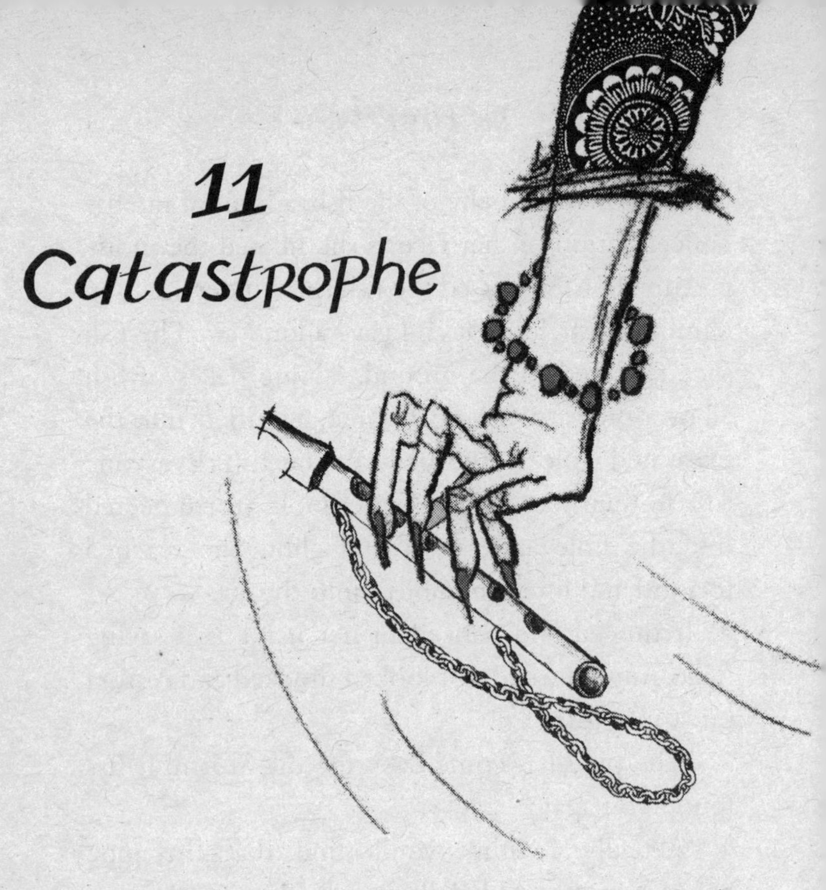

For a split second the shocked children didn't move. Then Storm cried, 'That's it! That's why she's here. It wasn't Eden End she wanted, it was the pipe!' She raced out of the room after Belle.

'Where are you going, Storm?' called Aurora.

'To get the pipe back, of course,' shouted Storm.

'Wait! It's no use to her. It belongs to you!' But Storm was gone, racing up the stairs towards Belle's room. She reached the door just as Belle tried to close it, and leaned against it hard. The door flew open and Storm fell into the room. Belle tried to hex her, but Storm rolled out of the way just in time. The spell hit the carpet, leaving a small singe mark.

'You're a witch!' gasped Storm. Leaping to her feet, she lunged at Belle, who sprang away with surprising agility and slammed the door shut, locking them both inside and unleashing another hex. But her powers were waning and her aim was unsure. The spell merely brushed Storm's shoulder, causing her to stumble into the bedside table. The small black velvet box sitting on top fell to the ground and the Dorian mirror tumbled out, its edges wreathed in blue smoke. Storm grabbed the mirror and held it high. Belle, who was now very pale and growing weaker as every minute passed, gave a shriek of fury and tried another spell but it simply plopped onto the carpet like a tennis ball that has lost its bounce.

Storm risked a quick glance in the mirror. She saw her own face reflected back. What was so special about that? Instinctively, she held the mirror up towards Belle's face. She shuddered at what she saw reflected back: the face in the mirror was undoubtedly Belle's, but the lips were withered to nothing, the nose had collapsed and the lidless, dead eyes were frozen pools. It was like looking into the face of a decaying corpse.

'That's you,' whispered Storm. 'That's what you really look like on the inside, you wicked old witch. It's the mirror that keeps you alive!'

Belle gave a shriek and grabbed for the mirror, but Storm was too quick for her. Belle glared at her and Storm glared back. The two of them were lost in their own bubble, oblivious to the calls of Aurora, Any and Kit, who were trying to batter their way into the room.

'Now,' said Storm, 'I think it's time for a little negotiation. I've got something that belongs to you, and you've got something that belongs to me. We should swap. The pipe is no good to you. You can't use it.'

The sound of axe against wood could be heard outside the door.

'Do you take me for a fool?' croaked Belle, whose skin had taken on a blue hue. 'If I give you the pipe you'll use it against me.'

The wood of the door began to splinter.

'I think you'll have to take that risk,' said Storm sweetly. 'You're not in a very strong position. Remember, I tried to rid myself of the pipe by throwing it into the sea. You have something that is useless to you that I don't particularly want, and I have something that is priceless to you that you want very much.'

With that she raised the mirror above her head. 'I'll break it into a million pieces and grind each one to dust so you can never put it together again.'

'Don't!' screeched Belle.

'When I give you the mirror, you are to leave immediately and never return.'

'How do I know I can trust you?'

'You'll just have to take that chance,' said Storm, and she felt her heart give a little dance of excitement as she thought of the pipe and its tremendous power. She might enjoy having the pipe back again. She could hear it calling to her from inside the black velvet bag in Belle's hand.

A large hole appeared in the door and a hand reached through and turned the lock.

'All right, we'll swap,' said Belle desperately, and she held out the bag towards Storm, who simultaneously stretched out the mirror towards Belle. The witch seized the mirror, but as Storm grabbed the bag, Kit burst through the door and barged into Storm, sending the bag skittering to the floor just out of her reach. Seizing her chance, Belle furiously muttered an incantation into the mirror as Storm got down on her hands and knees and scrabbled for the bag. Storm had it in her grasp and was struggling to open it, when a spell hit her in the back and she and Kit were thrown against the wall in a heap.

Belle had clearly recovered some of her power. She picked up the bag and pocketed it, a nasty smile on her face. 'Well,' she said in a venomous voice, 'who is in the superior position now?'

Storm and Kit struggled to their feet. 'You realize this is entirely your fault,' snarled Storm to Kit. 'If you hadn't intervened, I'd have the pipe now.'

'But you don't and I do,' laughed Belle.

'You are a horrid witch, and I don't believe our father ever married you. Storm's right, you are an impostor,' screamed Any from the doorway, and she raced towards Belle, both hands flailing.

She never reached her. With a wicked smile, Belle pointed one of her long, thin fingers at Any. There was a great deal of green smoke, and when it cleared, sitting on the floor was a very surprised-looking frog.

'Where's Any gone?' asked Aurora in a tiny voice. The frog gave a small croak and hopped towards her. Belle smirked.

'Any? Is that you?' whispered Aurora, although she already knew the answer. She put her open hand on the floor and the frog hopped onto it. Aurora tried not to wince as she felt its clammy flesh against her skin. Aurora drew the frog up to her face. 'Is that really you, Any?'

The frog croaked, and a tiny tear ran down its face. Aurora's eyes filled to the brim.

'Turn her back!' yelled Storm furiously.

'Won't,' said Belle happily. 'Actually, I can't. Don't know how.

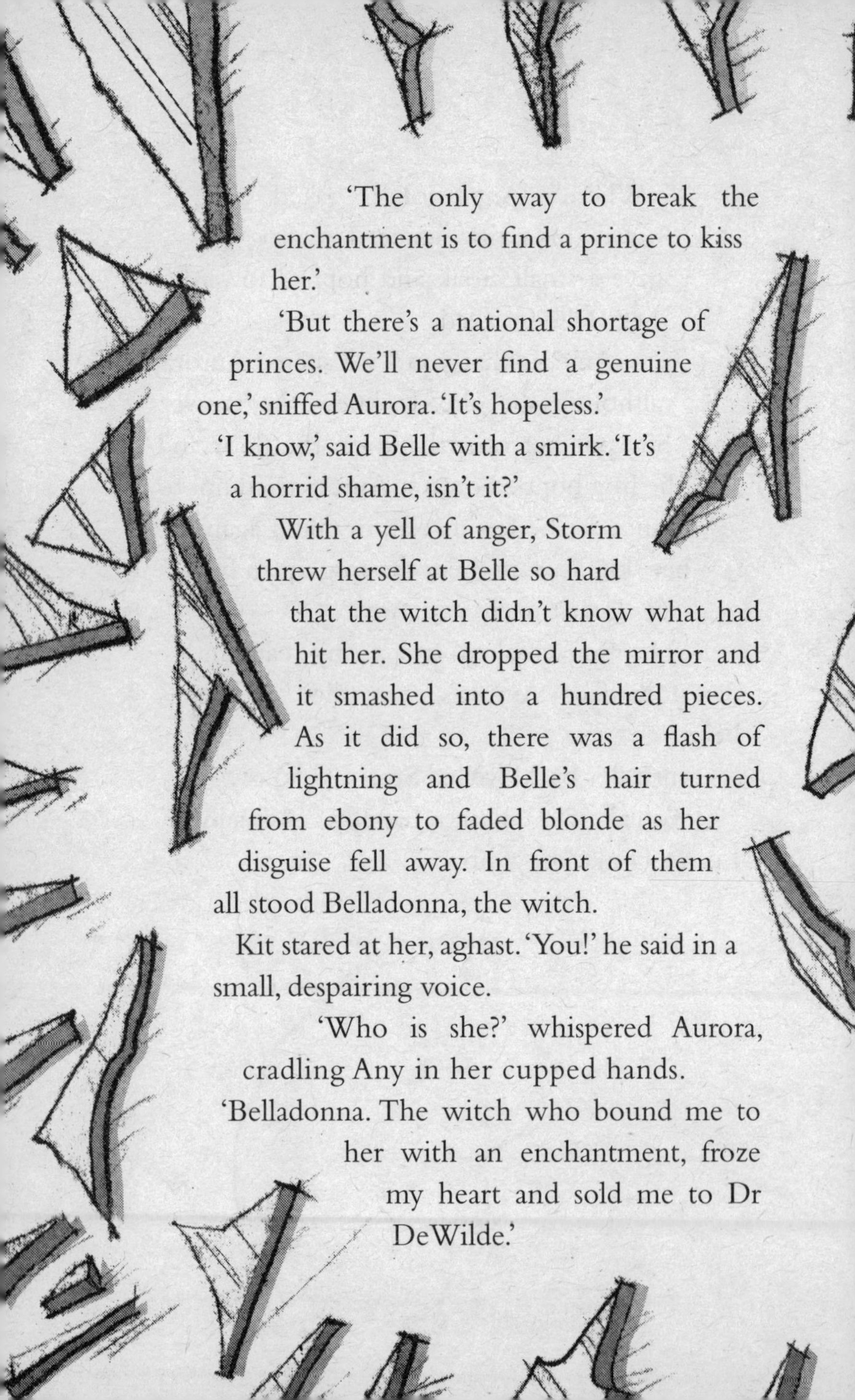

'The only way to break the enchantment is to find a prince to kiss her.'

'But there's a national shortage of princes. We'll never find a genuine one,' sniffed Aurora. 'It's hopeless.'

'I know,' said Belle with a smirk. 'It's a horrid shame, isn't it?'

With a yell of anger, Storm threw herself at Belle so hard that the witch didn't know what had hit her. She dropped the mirror and it smashed into a hundred pieces. As it did so, there was a flash of lightning and Belle's hair turned from ebony to faded blonde as her disguise fell away. In front of them all stood Belladonna, the witch.

Kit stared at her, aghast. 'You!' he said in a small, despairing voice.

'Who is she?' whispered Aurora, cradling Any in her cupped hands.

'Belladonna. The witch who bound me to her with an enchantment, froze my heart and sold me to Dr DeWilde.'

'That's right, you little fool. I'm back and soon the pipe will be truly mine and I will rule you all.'

'Not while I'm here,' yelled Storm, and she rushed at Belladonna again. But this time the witch was ready. Summoning all her power, she hexed Storm, who collapsed in an unconscious heap, causing the shards of broken glass to scatter further.

'Ouch,' said Kit. 'I've got something in my eye.' But only Any heard him, because Aurora was bent double crying over Storm's apparently lifeless body.

'You've killed her!' wept Aurora.

'If only I had, but that's beyond my powers for the present. Still, it will do until I come up with a more permanent solution,' said Belladonna with a satisfied smirk. 'Now, boy, down on your hands and knees and pick up every shard of glass. We must stick the mirror together again. It won't work so effectively, but it will be better than nothing until I can get my new heart.' Belladonna threw a long appreciative glance at Aurora, who was sobbing inconsolably over Storm's limp body.

'I am entirely at your

service,' said Kit in a low voice to Belladonna. Momentarily, surprise flashed across Belladonna's face, then she looked at him through narrowed eyes and broke into a peal of laughter that sounded like moving icebergs.

She beckoned him towards the window, away from the others, and gazed into his eyes. 'My, my,' she said quietly, 'perhaps the smashing of the mirror will turn out to be lucky for me, after all. Have you something in your eye, boy?' she asked in concerned, motherly tones.

Kit nodded. Belladonna gave a delighted smile. 'I rather suspect that when we paste the bits of the looking-glass together again we will discover that the tiniest sliver is missing. We must hope that it sticks in your eye and doesn't dislodge. In a few days it will migrate to your heart. Then the enchantment can never be broken and you will be my creature again, this time forever.'

As Kit began to gather up the shards of glass, Aurora finally dried her eyes and pleaded, 'Please don't be so cruel. Please turn Any back and let us go; we'll all leave and you can have Eden End.'

Belladonna laughed. 'You think I want this mouldy old house?'

'I'll give you anything, anything you want if

you'll leave us alone.'

Belladonna raised an eyebrow.

'Anything?'

'Anything.'

'You promise to give me the thing I most want?'

'What is it?'

'You'll find out soon enough, my dearest Aurora,' said Belladonna.

Aurora bit her lip. She knew it was foolish to make a promise when she didn't know what it was she was promising. But then she looked at poor little Any transformed into a frog and Storm's limp body, and knew she would promise anything to save them.

'All right,' said Aurora. 'Whatever it is, you can have it. I promise.'

Belladonna gave a gasp of joy and Aurora felt a shiver of fear whisper down her spine.

12
A Walk in the Woods

Belladonna surveyed the room smugly. Aurora was weeping, Storm was unconscious, Any was a frog and the boy . . . well, the boy was all hers. At that moment, Hermes arrived, whistling casually and accompanied by several wolves.

'You took your time. You've missed all the fun,' snapped Belladonna.

Hermes bowed low. 'My deepest apologies,' he grovelled, 'but I see that Madame has been exceptionally busy.'

'Yes,' said Belladonna happily. 'It has been a most productive day, no thanks to you.' She showed him the pipe and Hermes's eyes glittered with excitement. Aurora's keening was becoming louder and Any joined her in a cacophony of croaking.

'Now you're here, you can make yourself useful,' snarled Belladonna, whose head was aching from all the noise. 'Take Aurora and that dratted frog outside and get the wolves to keep a close eye on them. Then meet me in the library in half an hour.'

Hermes bundled the protesting Aurora and Any down the stairs and out into the garden where the wolves stood sentry. Every time either girl tried to move too far, the animals snarled and ran their red tongues over their teeth as if speculating on what tasty morsels the girls would make.

'I hope you're good at jigsaws!' said Belladonna to Kit as soon as the others had left the room. 'Down on your knees, boy. You must find every piece of the mirror and glue it together again.'

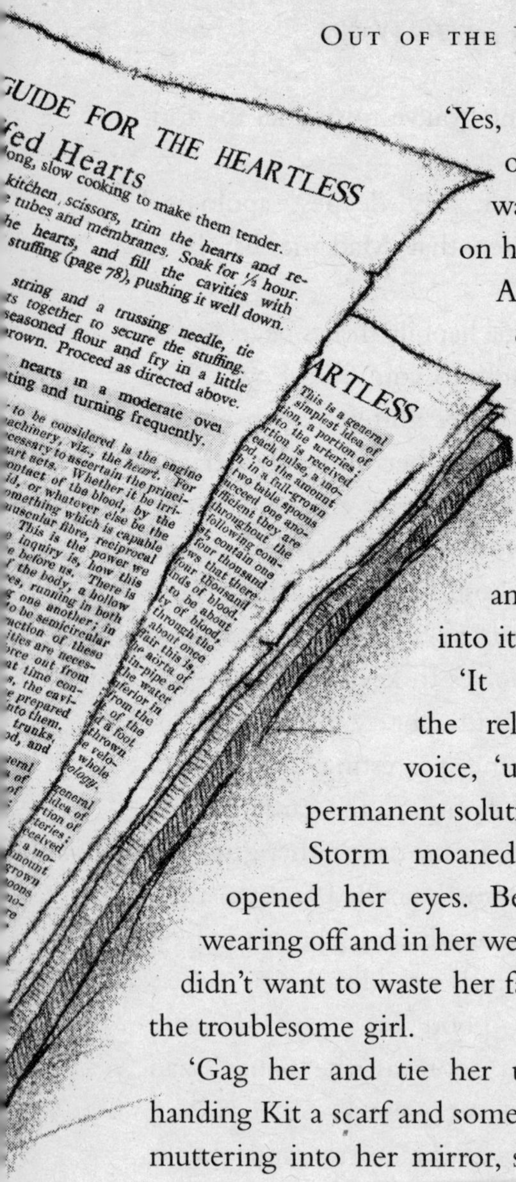

'Yes, Madame,' said Kit obediently, but there was deep sorrow etched on his face.

At last the mirror was complete, but for the one tiny fragment that was lodged in Kit's eye. Belladonna grabbed the mirror and began muttering into its smoky depths.

'It will do,' she said, the relief evident in her voice, 'until I have a more permanent solution.'

Storm moaned and muttered and opened her eyes. Belladonna's spell was wearing off and in her weakened state the witch didn't want to waste her fast-waning powers on the troublesome girl.

'Gag her and tie her up,' she commanded, handing Kit a scarf and some thin rope. Frequently muttering into her mirror, she watched contentedly as Kit bound Storm's arms and legs so that she resembled a squirming parcel.

'There, all done,' said Kit as he tied the last knot. Behind her gag, Storm cursed him, but no sound came out. Her eyes were two black coals of fury. She hoped that Kit could feel her hatred. She had been quite right not to trust him, she thought, quite forgetting that it was her jealousy of his relationship with Aurora – rather than any question of his integrity – that had turned her against him in the first place.

'Well done, Kit,' said Belladonna. Her skin had the waxy sheen of a corpse. Her eyes had faded and her lips were snow-blue. The cracked mirror was greatly diminished in power and would barely keep her alive. She needed Aurora's heart, and she needed it now. She moved closer to the window to watch Aurora down in the garden leaning over the pond with Any in her hand. There was a rapacious look in the witch's eyes.

Reluctantly she turned back to Kit. 'It's so delightful to have you in my service once again. Keep an eye on her. I won't be long.'

Several minutes later, Belladonna eased herself painfully into a battered leather armchair in the middle of Eden End's charming but rather dilapidated library. The table before her was covered with sheets of paper filled with Hermes's spidery writing. *Taking Heart: The Essential Guide for the Heartless* was open at page 11, 595. Just looking at the book made Belladonna feel irritated.

'I'm afraid, Madame, that the Guide is quite clear on the matter,' said Hermes nervously. 'A heart cannot be assigned to two people at the same time.'

Belladonna gave a furious cry and smoke poured out of her nostrils. 'But she promised me anything I wanted. Anything.'

'You are quite certain that before Aurora made that promise to you, you heard her promise her heart to the boy?'

Belladonna nodded angrily.

'The Guide is unequivocal,' sighed Hermes, flipping back to page seven. 'Anyone – or their agents – stealing a human heart that has been previously assigned or given away under rule 917, subsection 124, will instantly forfeit their own life . . .'

'It's ridiculous,' said Belladonna sulkily. 'People must be able to change their minds about who they want to give their heart to. Humans are famous for changing their minds, Aurora in particular.'

'Indeed they can, Madame,' said Hermes, looking very worried. 'Chapter 999 is quite specific:

a heart's owner can reassign their heart at any time. But footnote 21 also makes it clear that the heart's owner must have a full understanding of their actions before any reassigning can be done. I do not believe that Aurora's promise to you constitutes full understanding. Of course the situation would be different if the boy died before he could take the heart . . .'

'We can kill him. What a delightful idea,' said Belladonna. She pouted, 'But it does seem a waste now he is my creature forever.' A sly gleam suddenly flickered in Belladonna's eyes. 'He's as good as dead. He is a puppet entirely under my control.' She laughed nastily. 'So if he is entitled to take her heart, I've no need to kill the boy! I can simply order him to get it for me!'

'Aurora,' whispered Kit, taking her hand firmly.

'Kit! Where have you been? I've been so worried about you and Storm. I thought Belladonna had killed you both.'

'Storm's fine. I've been looking after her. Belladonna said that she would sleep the spell off.'

'I don't believe anything that witch says,' said Aurora. 'I must go to Storm.'

'You can't,' said Kit quickly. 'Belladonna has

locked her in her bedroom. Besides,' he whispered, 'you and I must escape into the woods together.'

'I would never leave Storm and Any. The three of us together. Forever and for always,' said Aurora fiercely.

'We must go, Aurora. It's our only chance. I've come up with a plan to get us all out of here safely, but I need your help, and that means a little walk in the woods for just you and me.'

'Why can't we all go now?' asked Aurora.

'Because the spell has left Storm woozy. It will be a few hours before she's ready to travel.'

'But where will we go?' asked Aurora.

'That's what I want to show you. I know a secret place deep in the woods. You'll be the one to take your sisters there. I need to show you the way.' He squeezed her hand gently. 'You know I'd never suggest anything that I thought might put you and your sisters in danger.'

'I know you wouldn't, Kit,' said Aurora, squeezing his hand back. 'Let's go. But we must be quick.'

As she spoke, Hermes appeared and the wolves ran over to him and set up a loud howling. He started throwing them pieces of raw meat from the bloody bowl he was carrying.

'This is our chance,' said Kit, taking Aurora's

hand and pulling her towards the woods. The wolves snarled and fought with each other and Hermes encouraged their viciousness.

'I must tell Any where we're going.'

'No time for that,' said Kit firmly. 'Come on, while they're distracted.' He pulled her harder.

Any was so engrossed in watching the horror show that was the wolves' feeding time that at first she didn't notice Aurora and Kit slip away. She was only just in time to see them disappearing into the trees. She put her little head on one side and wondered why it was that while Kit held Aurora's hand with his right hand, he held his left arm behind his back and glinting in that hand was a small silver dagger. She hopped after them as fast as she could.

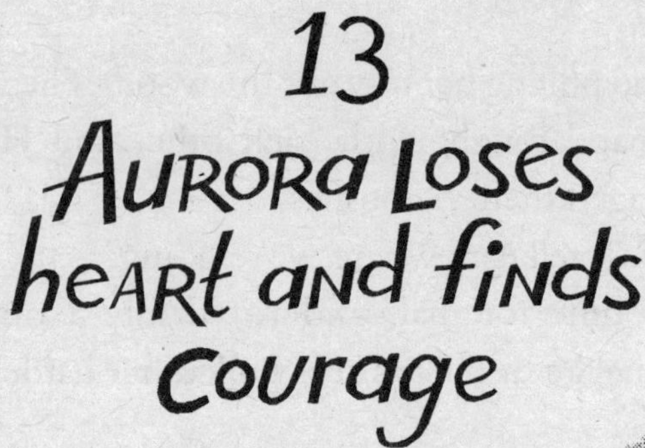

13 Aurora Loses heart and finds courage

Out in the woods, Aurora was surprised by Kit's brusque manner. He was pulling her along almost faster than she could run. She kept glancing at him from under her lashes. There was something odd about him, but she couldn't quite put her finger on it. He was still as beautiful as the day, but something about him had changed.

Aurora Loses heart and finds Courage

'Are we almost there?' asked Aurora as Kit took her into the deepest part of the forest. The trees were so thick here that the branches created a canopy that kept the light out. No birds sang. Kit pulled Aurora roughly onwards through the dense trees. They came upon a small dead deer tangled in some brambles. The poor creature was covered in deep scratches where it had desperately struggled to escape the hunter's trap that had ensnared it. Its blood was still ruby bright, as if it had only very recently given up its exhausted fight for life.

'Oh, poor, poor thing! How frightened it must have been,' cried Aurora, and was shocked when Kit – who was normally as tender-hearted as she – didn't even break his stride. A few minutes later he dragged her into a dank cave.

'Is this the secret hiding place?' asked Aurora, shivering. Kit took her further into the depths of the cave. There was a low boulder, a natural stone altar.

'Lie down and shut your eyes,' ordered Kit.

Aurora looked puzzled. 'Why?'

'Trust me, Aurora,' said Kit curtly.

'I do, Kit, I trust you with my life,' said Aurora, and she slid onto the boulder and stretched out.

'Then prove it by lying quite still and keeping your eyes shut,' said Kit. Aurora put her hands over her eyes and lay as still as a stone effigy in a churchyard.

'Aurora,' whispered Kit softly, raising the silver knife above her breast. 'I've come for your heart.'

'So soon,' smiled Aurora, her eyes shut tight. 'I thought you wanted to wait, but if you need it now, my dearest Kit, then you must take it at once.'

'I will,' cried Kit, but at that moment there came a croak so loud that it was like a small explosion.

Aurora leaped to her feet. 'Any! What are you . . .' she cried. She stopped and saw Kit with the knife in his hand. Confused, she took a step backwards and stared at him.

'That's what's different about you, Kit,' she said in a small voice. 'I should have realized. It's your eye! One of your eyes is blue. That wicked witch, she's enchanted you. Oh, poor, poor Kit, you're as ensnared as that unfortunate deer in the trap.'

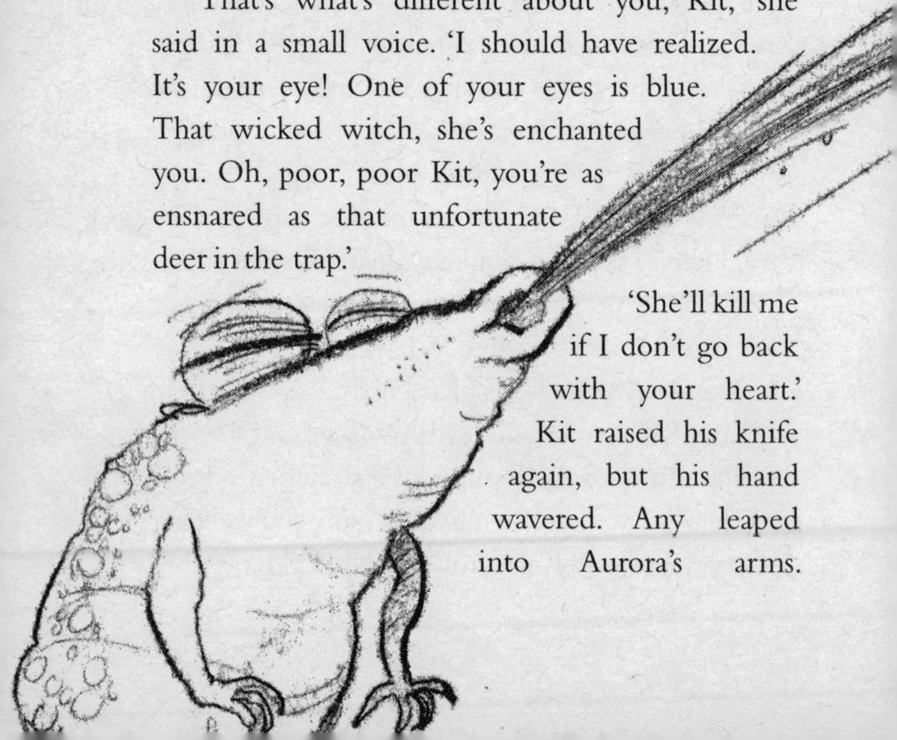

'She'll kill me if I don't go back with your heart.' Kit raised his knife again, but his hand wavered. Any leaped into Aurora's arms.

Kit lunged at Aurora with the knife and as he did so, Any puffed herself up until she was three times her normal frog size and, with perfect aim, squirted poison into his blue eye. Kit dropped the knife and doubled over in pain.

Any croaked again and it sounded very much like 'Run!'

The two sisters fled, but after a short distance, Any stopped and croaked loudly. Aurora could have sworn that Any was saying 'Storm'. 'Are you going back to help Storm?'

The little frog nodded.

'I must come with you,' insisted Aurora.

Any shook her head very firmly. Aurora knew that Any was right. She had to get as far away from Belladonna as possible. She planted a kiss on Any's wet head and whispered, 'Tell Storm, if you can find a way, that we will all be together again one day. We belong together. The three of us alone, the three of us together. Forever and for always.'

Then she turned and plunged into a thicket of trees.

Any sat in a puddle and watched her disappear and then she hopped purposefully back to the small cave.

Kit was still bent double with pain. Any hopped onto his knee. Kit lashed out blindly, trying to swipe the little frog away, but Any ducked his blows and jumped onto his shoulder. His blue eye had turned red with the poison, and glistening clearly in the corner, a tiny sliver of glass from the Dorian mirror could be seen. In a blink, her long thin tongue flicked his eyeball and brushed the piece of glass away. Tears poured out of Kit's eye, washing the poison away.

Gradually his sobbing subsided. Gingerly he put his hand to his eye. 'It's gone! The glass has gone. Oh thank you, Any, you've saved me.'

Any was already hopping resolutely down the path in the direction of Eden End. The little frog moved with surprising swiftness and Kit had to run to catch up.

'Any, wait! I must go after Aurora and beg her forgiveness or I'll have lost her forever.'

Any croaked angrily and shook her head. When Kit tried to turn back, she bounced up and down

on the path in front of him so he couldn't get past without squashing her. At last, reluctantly, he turned back towards Eden End.

'This is ridiculous, Any,' said Kit bitterly. 'I could still catch Aurora up and help her, but if I return to Eden End without Aurora's heart, Belladonna will strike me dead.'

Any just croaked to urge him on. They came to the place where the dead deer had been snared. Any stopped and looked at Kit expectantly.

'What do you want me to do?' asked Kit. 'Bury it?'

Any shook her head. Kit sat down heavily. Any hopped onto his knee and rubbed her nose against the knife. Kit looked at Any and then at the knife.

'Oh, Any, you are clever. I'd give you a big kiss if you weren't quite so slimy.'

Kit pulled out the knife and walked towards the dead deer.

Aurora ran and ran through the dark woods, half blinded by tears and fear. Her breath came in ragged gasps and the branches of the trees reached down to her like hands trying to snare her. She stumbled on and it began to snow, great flakes like white moths fluttering. She was exhausted. She tripped over brambles and tree roots and got lost in tangled thickets. She stopped for a moment to catch her breath, and from far away she heard the freezing cry of a wolf carried on the wind. She staggered on and at last she reached a small clearing in the woods where the earth lay silent and dark under a muffled sky. She fell to the ground, gasping for breath.

When she raised her head she saw a small cottage at the edge of the clearing. Wearily, she scrambled to her feet and walked towards it. Seven pairs of very dirty boots were lined up on the porch. Despite her current predicament, Aurora immediately wished that she had brought some shoe polish with her.

As quietly as a mouse, she got down on her hands and knees and edged warily towards the window. She could hear singing and sounds of jollity. When she reached the window she eased herself upright and peeped through.

Inside the cosy cottage, a bright fire burned in the grate and seven small men with kind, happy faces were dancing and singing with great merriment. Mountains of dirty crockery sat in the sink. Aurora pressed her nose against the window like a child outside a sweet shop. How her fingers itched to get her hands on all that washing up, and the dust that clung to every surface.

She suddenly caught sight of two small notices in the grubby window. The first was very faded and curled sadly at the edges as if it had been there for many years.

Prince Christopher Alfred
Herringbone Alasdair, Gregory.

Aged 7. Very handsome. Charming. Green eyes.
Small distinctive dragon birthmark on nape of neck.
Believed eaten by dragon, but may have survived
and wandered into the woods.

REWARD FOR ANY INFORMATION.
Apply in strictest confidence:
The palace, 1, Palace plaza, Somewhere.

REQUIRED IMMEDIATELY
HOUSEKEEPER

Able to count up to seven,
polish boots, make exceptional
apple pies and tell bedtime stories.

Solid gold remuneration to
the right candidate.

Previous candidates need not reply.

(That means YOU, Goldilocks!
Don't come back again,
we've got a guard dog.)

Aurora gasped with delight. It couldn't be more perfect. She would make herself useful, cooking and cleaning, and stay safe from the clutches of Belladonna in the little cottage until . . . until . . . until what? Kit wasn't going to turn up on a white charger to rescue her. He was in the grip of an enchantment. So was Any, and she didn't know what had happened to Storm after she had been knocked unconscious by Belladonna's spell. Perhaps Kit had been lying and Storm was already dead. It was all she could do to stifle the sob that rose in her throat.

She crept round to the front door. Her fingers had already clasped the knocker and she was about to let it drop when a picture flashed into her mind of herself and Kit together at Eden End when he had first declared his love. Her heart was broken and the mere thought of him was like a rusty ache. Every word that he had said that day was imprinted like a scar upon her mind. With sudden clarity she remembered one particular thing he had said. That nothing is worth doing unless it makes you feel nervous.

Her hand hovered, ready to let the knocker drop. Staying here in the cottage in the woods would be the comfortable choice. What if she spent the rest of her life hiding away from Belladonna and waiting for someone who never came? What kind of life would that be – even if it did allow ample opportunity for her to indulge her passion for housework? For a split second she hesitated. She was scared of the woods, but perhaps somewhere out there in the world beyond she would discover a way to break the enchantments on Kit and Any and rescue Storm. With a tiny wistful sigh, Aurora replaced the knocker so gently that it made no noise at all and without a backward glance, she ran towards the trees and into the deepest, darkest part of the forest.

14
Belladonna gets her heart's desire

Back at Eden End, Storm watched impatiently as the little mouse that had escaped from Belladonna's hair gnawed through the final threads of rope that bound her feet. Just when she had given up all hope of escape, the mouse had scurried under the door and begun nibbling at her bindings.

'Thank you. Thank you so much, little mouse,' whispered Storm as she struggled to her feet. The mouse ran up the wall and onto the window-sill, squeaking loudly. Storm walked over to the window and looked out, wondering whether she might be able to squeeze through the narrow opening and climb down the drainpipe. Beyond the gates of Eden End she could see the fair. It seemed a very strange place to set up a fair, since Eden End was as far from anywhere as it was from everywhere. There would be very few customers.

She saw Kit walking towards the house with Any hopping behind him and wondered where they had been. Did Any and Aurora realize that Kit was not to be trusted? And where was Aurora? Storm's stomach suddenly felt as if someone had sewn a stone inside it. She felt certain that Aurora was in danger. She hauled an old box towards the window and climbed onto the sill. She was fumbling with the catch when she heard the key in the lock.

It was too late. Belladonna and Hermes entered the room. The mouse ran up Storm's leg and into her pocket, where it was delighted to find half a stick of liquorice and a piece of cheese. Storm made a bolt for the door but Hermes stood in front of it, smiling nastily.

'Come, Hermes, bind her hands,' Belladonna said irritably. 'I'm in need of a little rejuvenation. I think a snack is what I require.'

Down in the kitchen, the smell of frying meat was strong. Kit stood at the stove pushing a piece of meat around in a frying pan. He was desperately worried that Belladonna would discover his deception before he could hatch a plan. He knew that the longer Belladonna believed that he had done her bidding, the further away Aurora could get. Any was splashing in the sink amidst the dirty washing up, watched with intense interest by the wolves.

'Is it ready?' demanded Belladonna as she entered the room.

'Almost,' said Kit meekly, careful not to turn around in case she noticed that his enchanted eye was now green again.

'It smells delicious,' said Belladonna greedily. She turned to Storm. 'I'm sure you must be peckish? You look as if you could do with feeding up.'

Storm was puzzled. Why was Belladonna being nice to her?

'I have an idea!' said Belladonna. 'We'll have an eating competition to decide ownership of the pipe. Whichever one of us can eat most of that delicious-smelling meat in sixty seconds can claim the pipe as their own.'

Belladonna gets her heart's desire

An exclamation of horror escaped from Kit's lips. Belladonna looked at him suspiciously, but was too excited by her devious plan to waste time on the boy. Soon she would have a new heart and the pipe.

'Do you agree to the wager, Storm? Or would you prefer another spelling contest – I hear you did so well last time when you were pitted against Dr DeWilde. You would have won if you hadn't made that silly slip. Or perhaps you'd prefer a maths competition?'

'Where is she? Where is Aurora?' demanded Storm.

'Oh, she's close by. We'll bring her to you in a minute,' said Belladonna, waving her arm around airily. 'Now, come along, make up your mind. Which is it to be? Spelling, maths or eating?'

Storm knew that she was rubbish at spelling and maths. She was certain that there must be some trick involved, but at least with an eating competition she would have some chance of winning. Aurora was always calling her a gannet because she bolted her food. She looked over at Any, who was hopping up and down on the edge of the sink in a most agitated manner. Hermes nudged her back into the sink with the back of his hand.

'All right,' Storm said. 'Eating.'

Belladonna pulled the velvet bag out of her pocket and tipped the pipe out into the middle of the table. It sat there looking strangely alive. Storm sensed that the pipe was silently calling her. She had to stop Belladonna becoming its owner, whatever it took. Belladonna had made the challenge and Storm had no choice: she must concede the pipe or take part in the contest and try to keep the pipe in her possession. Those were the rules of the pipe. With a little sigh, Storm sat down opposite Belladonna. She had never felt less hungry in her life.

'An eating contest it is, then,' said the witch. 'If I may say so, an excellent choice. Rotational symmetry is so confusing.' She indicated for Hermes to release Storm from her bindings and called out for plates and knives and forks.

'When can I see Aurora?' asked Storm sharply.

'Any second now,' said Belladonna with a wicked grin. 'Serve the meat, Kit.'

Kit brought the frying pan over and placed it next to the pipe in the middle of the table. Storm stared at him scornfully, but he avoided her gaze. He picked up a carving knife and with a shaking hand carved the meat straight down the middle into two equal halves. He put one half on Belladonna's plate and the other on Storm's. The meat was still a little bloody. Storm screwed up her nose; just the smell made her feel sick. Belladonna was looking increasingly decrepit despite her constant muttering into the mirror. Hermes took out a whistle.

'Ready, steady . . .' The piercing whistle filled the kitchen and Storm cut a large slice of meat, stuffed it into her mouth and began chewing. The meat was extremely tough, and it had been a mistake to put such a huge slice in her mouth. It was impossible to swallow. She chewed frantically and started cutting the next slice before she had swallowed the first piece. She suddenly realized that Belladonna hadn't even picked up her knife and fork. She was just sitting there watching her, a curious smile playing around her bluish lips.

Then Belladonna leaned forward and whispered softly, 'Oh, I quite forgot to say. That's Aurora's heart you're eating.'

Storm's mouth fell open. With a terrible cry she spat the unswallowed piece of meat onto her plate. She swayed in her chair as if about to faint. Her eyes

were great pools of darkness in the white mask of her face.

Belladonna gave another venomous smile, cut a tiny sliver of meat, put it in her mouth, chewed for a second and swallowed. 'Mmm. A real delicacy, I feel better already,' she murmured. 'Thank you so much, Kit, for supplying me with it. You are such a dependable boy.'

Storm's scream of fury competed with Hermes's whistle and Kit's howl of despair. He couldn't bear it that Storm believed he had slaughtered Aurora, but he had to hide the truth from Belladonna for as long as possible.

'Time's up,' Hermes said triumphantly. 'I declare Madame the winner. The pipe and all its power is rightfully hers.'

With one hand, Belladonna picked up the pipe, which danced and tinkled in her palm as if welcoming its new owner, and with the other, she started stuffing the bloody meat into her mouth in a frenzy of excitement. Blood dribbled down her chin and neck.

But Storm didn't notice. She was buried deep in her own avalanche of loss and despair. Aurora was dead, and part of Storm had died with her. She was roused from her stupor by her rage at Kit, which flared and blazed in her heart like a forest fire. Kit had killed Aurora and plucked out her heart. She threw herself at him like a leaping flame and hit him with her full force, felling him like a tree. He toppled over, knocking into Belladonna, who let go of the pipe, which skittered over the floor. Suddenly the room was full of shouts, growls, snarls and confusion. Any leaped into the mêlée, grabbed the pipe in her mouth, and with one giant leap, hopped straight out of the kitchen window with it.

'After her!' yelled Hermes to the wolves, and they streaked out of the door, knocking him over in their eagerness. They gained on Any fast as she hopped down the drive. She could feel their breath and hear their snapping jaws. She only avoided being caught in the wolves' savage teeth by making a huge sideways hop. Her little legs were hurting dreadfully and the pipe was blistering her mouth. She knew that the burning sensation was the pipe's way of telling her that it disapproved of being parted from its rightful owner, but she took no notice.

At the end of the drive she plunged through the fairground, always just one jump ahead of the wolves, and hopped into the hall of mirrors. The wolves followed, yapping with excitement, convinced that they had their quarry cornered. Then they stopped suddenly. They were nose to nose with a dozen huge snarling wolves the size of houses with two heads each. The wolves bared their teeth and the strange giant double-headed wolves bared their teeth too. Terrified, the wolves turned on their tails and, whimpering loudly, they ran as fast as they could into the forest.

Any watched them go with quiet satisfaction. Then very gingerly, because it burned her mouth so, she picked up the pipe and hopped away.

Back in the kitchen, mayhem ruled all around as Belladonna sat quite unconcernedly stuffing more heart into her already full mouth. The witch was puzzled. She had expected to feel and see the signs of rejuvenation of her witchy heart at the first mouthful. But she felt nothing. Her skin was still crêpey and bluish and she was as tired as if she hadn't slept for a century. Perhaps she had to eat the entire thing to feel the benefit? She took another bite as Hermes tried to scramble to his feet. But he was immediately felled again as Kit barged into him, pursued by a furiously pummelling Storm.

Let them fight, thought Belladonna to herself. Soon she would have her full powers again and then she would deal with them. She was confident that the nasty little frog would be no match for her wolves, her beauties. She took another bite of the heart. At last! The magic was working. She had a pain in her chest near her heart. Yes, she was sure something was happening. Her full power and beauty would be restored to her any minute now.

Kit made a dash for the kitchen door with Storm in hot pursuit.

'You killed my sister and I'm going to kill you,' screeched Storm.

'I didn't kill her,' cried Kit in desperation as he pulled the door open. 'Come on, Storm, we've got to get out of here and get to Any before the wolves do.' He aimed a mighty kick at Hermes, who was struggling to his feet again. The manservant toppled back to the floor, badly winded.

Belladonna swallowed the very last piece of heart. She felt exceedingly strange.

'They're getting away! Hex them,' shouted Hermes.

Belladonna rose to her feet. She felt most curious, but this was as good a time as any to try out her new powers. She pointed her fingers at Storm and Kit. There was a tiny little pop and her spell slithered to the floor, where it made a small sticky puddle. She tried again. This time nothing came out of her fingers at all. Her legs gave way and she slumped back into the chair.

Kit was trying to drag Storm out of the door.

'You cut out my sister's heart!' cried Storm accusingly. 'You're as evil as Belladonna.'

'I'm not, Storm,' yelled Kit desperately. He knew he had to tell Storm the truth. 'I didn't kill Aurora. It was a deer's heart. Aurora is alive,' he shouted. There was a tiny electric silence as their eyes locked and the world held its breath. Storm knew that Kit was telling the truth. She grabbed him by the arm and started to pull him outside.

'Come on, Kit, hurry up, stop hanging about,' she grinned. The two of them raced across the lawn towards the woods.

Back in the kitchen Hermes got slowly to his feet, wincing with pain. He hardly dared glance at Belladonna, who had an incredulous look on her face. She kept muttering two words over and over as if she couldn't believe them: 'deer' and 'heart'. She had been duped!

Belladonna gave an enormous burp and felt a sharp stab below her breast bone. She had the most terrible indigestion. Painfully, she fumbled in her pocket for the mirror and started muttering into it. She needed all the strength she could muster. She had failed to get Aurora's heart this time, but she would not fail again.

She watched as Storm and Kit ran into the woods, and shrugged. 'They won't get far. The pipe is no good to those Eden sisters. It is rightfully mine, and it will do everything it can to come back to me. If I didn't feel quite so old and ill, I'd very much enjoy the thrill of the chase.'

15
From Bad to Worse

Storm and Kit lay gasping for breath on the forest floor.

'I've got to find Any,' said Storm.

'I've got to find Aurora,' said Kit. Storm saw the desperation in his eyes.

'We've got to find them both,' they said in total agreement.

'I'm sorry, Kit,' said Storm stiffly, 'I misjudged you. I really thought that you had killed Aurora.'

'Don't be sorry, Storm,' said Kit sadly. 'You were right to despise me. I didn't kill Aurora but I might just as well have done so. I've killed her love.' He explained about the enchantment and what had happened in the forest. Storm listened, her eyes getting wider and her mouth narrower. In her heart she knew that it was not Kit's fault, but all her feelings of jealousy and resentment came bubbling to the surface and stopped her seeing straight. She knew she was being mean and unreasonable, but the burning coal in her stomach meant that she couldn't stop the words coming out of her mouth.

'So you did try to kill Aurora, and when you failed, you left her all alone in the forest?'

Kit nodded miserably.

Storm stood up, her eyes blazing once more. 'Then you have as good as killed her,' she hissed. 'I was right about you, Kit. You're no good for Aurora and Aurora is too good for you. You don't deserve her love. Keep away from her and keep away from my family. You're like a bad penny that keeps turning up. You just bring us rotten luck and trouble. It was you who brought the pipe back and it is because of you that both of my sisters have probably been eaten by wolves. So, please, just go away and never come back. I don't ever want to see you again, and if Aurora is still alive, neither will she.'

Storm marched away, leaving Kit all alone. He slumped to the ground and put his head in his hands. He knew that he had lost Aurora forever and without Aurora his life wasn't worth living. And it wasn't just Aurora. It was all the Eden sisters, who felt like the family he couldn't remember ever having. He felt so utterly alone. All he wanted to do was curl up in the roots of a tree, go to sleep and never wake up.

Fat snowflakes had begun to fall and Kit's eyelids were drooping when he felt something tugging at his trouser leg. It was a small white mouse, squeaking loudly and trying to pull him towards the denser part of the forest.

Kit bent down. 'Are you trying to tell me something?' he asked.

The mouse nodded and squeaked, then jumped off his hand and ran along a path into the forest. Kit followed. Even if he had to search to the very ends of the earth he would find Aurora and prove himself to her.

Storm stopped beneath a large tree. Should she

go in search of Aurora or try to find Any? It was hard to tell who was in more danger: Aurora – who would find being in the forest on her own terrifying – or Any, who in her frog-like state could be so easily squashed and who had the added danger of being in possession of the pipe. All their problems arose from the pipe. They would not be safe until it was destroyed. Storm sighed and turned back towards Eden End, trying – and failing miserably – not to imagine Aurora coming face to face with a wolf in the forest.

She was almost at the edge of the wood when she heard a familiar crashing sound. Zeus joyfully bounded into her like an over-grown puppy, licking her face all over. Storm stroked his mane.

'I'm sorry, Zeus, I haven't got any food for you.'

Zeus shrugged to show he didn't care and redoubled his licking of Storm's face. His beautiful, soulful eyes reminded Storm of Aurora.

Suddenly Storm had an idea. If she couldn't immediately find Aurora and protect her from the worst that the woods had to offer, she could send somebody who could.

'Zeus,' she said to the lion. 'I need you to do

something important for me.'

Zeus put his head on one side and nodded vigorously to show that he understood.

'I want you to find my sister Aurora – the one who makes the madeleines you like so much. She is lost somewhere in the woods. I need you to watch over her for me. It's probably best if you don't actually show yourself to her because she will be scared of a lion that she hasn't been properly introduced to, but if you keep your distance you could still offer her some protection. Will you do this for me?'

Zeus nodded again. He would do anything for Storm and even more for her sister who made those delicious madeleines. He gave a little roar to prove he was no scaredy-cat – although in truth he was, and found the forest almost as terrifying as Aurora – and held out his paw for Storm to shake, as if sealing an important business deal. Storm solemnly shook it and then watched him disappear back into the woods.

She walked on, ignoring the nagging feeling that had settled in her stomach the moment that she'd stormed away from Kit. In the far distance, through the rapidly-falling snow, she could see the chimneys of Eden End. She was certain her life there had ended. Her mother and father were dead; her sisters scattered. Closer by, she could see and hear the fair. The tinkle of the merry-go-round sounded sinister and, even more eerily, the rides were all turning despite the complete lack of customers. She shivered and was about to head towards the house when she suddenly remembered a comment that Any had made on that first, inauspicious trip to the fair. She'd said that the fair would be a good place to hide. Any was a clever little thing, and what cleverer place to hide than right under your enemy's nose? Storm headed towards the fair.

16 Jeopardy on the Big Wheel

Storm walked warily through the fair, keeping a sharp eye out for Belladonna. The big wheel was turning slowly, cackles and shrieks emerged from the ghost train every time the doors clattered open, and the galloping horses on the merry-go-round rose and fell to an endlessly repeating tinny tune. Hot dogs and onions scented the air. But the entire fair was deserted. There was nobody to take the money and no customers. In other circumstances, Storm might have been delighted by the opportunity to ride for free, but she was frightened by the mysterious ever-turning rides. It was as if the entire place was enchanted and just waiting for her arrival. She wondered if she was walking into a trap, but it was a risk she would have to take.

She hurried towards the ghost train and slipped into a carriage. It began to move immediately. With her heart in her mouth, she passed through the double doors and into the darkness. Her eyes adjusted to the gloom and she looked hard for any sign of Any. She held her breath as she neared the point in the ride where she knew the mirror would appear, wondering whether she would see a distressed frog in its smoky depths, but she saw only the desperately entreating woman chained for eternity inside it.

She jumped off the still-moving carriage when it had completed a single circuit, and hurried into the hall of mirrors. She ran up and down the banks of mirrors fruitlessly searching for Any. Every mirror threw back an image of herself, but it was a Storm that she didn't recognize, a strange girl cackling in derision at her attempts to find Any. Almost weeping, Storm ran out of the tent.

Then she saw it: the Catch-a-Frog stall. She rushed towards it and saw Belladonna heading towards it too from the opposite direction. They met on opposite sides of the circular stall and glared at each other. Without a word, they each seized a fishing net and began reaching out for the little frogs sitting on their lily pads.

Belladonna took a frog out of her net, examined it, tossed the plastic creature aside and plunged her net into the water again. Storm scanned the unblinking frogs closely. She was quite certain that Any was hidden here somewhere. She just had to make sure that she got to her before Belladonna. She thought she saw one of the floating frogs twitch. She scooped it up in her net. It wasn't Any. Disappointedly, she scooped again and again. She had one eye on the remaining frogs and one on Belladonna, who was fishing in a frenzy.

There were only five frogs left bobbing around on the moat of water. Belladonna scooped one; Storm caught another. Neither was Any. That left just three frogs. Belladonna and Storm watched each other's closest move. Belladonna scooped up the nearest frog with a little yelp of triumph.

But it was just plastic. There were only two frogs left. They looked absolutely identical as they bobbed around on their fake lily pads. Storm and Belladonna stood poised, like two duellists who know that there can only be one winner.

Storm stared at the frogs, willing Any to make some kind of secret sign. Both frogs sat entirely unblinking. Out of the corner of her eye, she caught a tiny flash of green movement in the candy-floss stall next door. She desperately wanted to turn her head and take a closer look but didn't want to alert Belladonna. The more she stared at the

two remaining frogs, the more certain she was that neither was real and that Any was hiding elsewhere. A candy-floss stall would be exactly the kind of place that greedy little Any would choose.

Belladonna watched Storm through narrowed eyes, waiting for her to make a move. Storm bit her lip. Suddenly she plunged her net into the water and scooped up a frog in a movement so smooth and seamless that she caught Belladonna off guard. She plucked the fake frog out of the net, yelled 'Any' in joyful tones, cupped her hands around it as if it was the most precious thing on earth, and ran.

Despite her decrepitude, Belladonna was after her in an instant, just as Storm had hoped. She led her away from the Catch-a-Frog and candy-floss stalls towards the helter-skelter. Then she yelled 'Sorry, Any' and threw the plastic frog as far as she could.

Just as she had intended, Belladonna veered off after the frog and Storm doubled back to the candy-floss stall. To Storm's relief, Any was there, peeking out cautiously from behind a swirl of freshly-spun candy-floss. She leaped onto her sister's shoulder, and dropped the pipe into Storm's pocket. Storm felt it tingling and burning, and immediately an insistent whisper took up residence in her head, telling her to give the pipe back to Belladonna.

Storm closed her mind to the wheedling voice and concentrated on their escape. By now Belladonna had realized that the plastic frog was a decoy and had sent two wolves after the sisters.

Storm streaked past the ghost train and the helter-skelter with the wolves not far behind. They were gaining on her fast. Storm could hear their snap-happy jaws opening and closing. She put on an extra spurt of speed, but the wolves were speedier still and it seemed inevitable that soon she would be felled by one of their powerful bodies and feel sharp teeth sinking into her flesh.

Weaving between the stalls, she headed towards the ever-turning big wheel. One wolf, nimbler than the rest, surged forward and took a bite out of Storm's skirt; the other wolves bayed and yelped with excitement. Storm ran towards the big wheel and, gathering her very last reserves of energy, she made an almighty leap into one of the double seats as it soared upwards. The wolves, surprised by this unexpected turn of events, sat on the ground howling at the injustice of losing their supper. After a few minutes they bounded away.

Storm sat breathing heavily. The wheel turned, stuttering and stopping every now and again before continuing on its journey. She stared out over the twinkling lights of Piper's Town, then scanned the dark woods that stretched all the way to the distant mountains and thought of Aurora lost and all alone somewhere in their depths.

Suddenly she was aware of Any hopping along the safety rail, croaking in agitation. Storm looked down. Their carriage was beginning to make its descent, and waiting for them at the bottom, as if she hadn't a care in the world, was Belladonna, with Hermes by her side. Storm cast around desperately. She had leaped onto the wheel to save

them from the immediate danger of being gobbled up by wolves, but now it seemed she had simply jumped from one pickle into another. Storm sighed, and the pipe in her head needled and whined.

'Look, Any,' she said, the exhaustion apparent in her voice, 'let's just give Belladonna the pipe. It's rightfully hers. The contest may not have been fair, but she won it. Maybe once she's got the pipe, she'll leave us alone, and let us get on quietly with our lives at Eden End.'

Storm didn't believe a word of what she was saying. She knew that if Belladonna got her hands on the pipe there'd be no peace and quiet for anyone. But she also knew that they couldn't go on running for the rest of their lives. Belladonna would always track them down.

Any bounced up and down on Storm's lap, croaking angrily. She clearly wasn't ready to give up.

As their carriage grew ever closer to the ground, the smile of odious joy on Belladonna's face was enough to rouse Storm. Despite her aching limbs, she clambered precariously over the rail and onto the inside frame of the wheel. Then she climbed upwards on the frets against the direction in which the wheel was turning. Any obviously didn't like the vertiginous view from Storm's shoulder because she hopped into her sister's pocket. Storm looked down. Belladonna was prodding a reluctant Hermes with one of her long bony fingers. A look of intense annoyance on his face, Hermes came after them, clambering up over the frets with surprising agility. Storm climbed faster, but she was exhausted by her earlier exertions and Hermes was gaining on her fast.

Storm's legs felt as if they were made from sponge but Any's croaks of encouragement spurred her on. If she could just reach the summit of the wheel, climbing down the other side would be easier.

She hauled herself upwards. Hermes grabbed hold of her leg. She kicked out, almost hitting him in the face. It was enough to gain the tiniest advantage. She scrambled to the top of the wheel. Hermes reached out for her again. Storm kicked again. She was precariously balanced and feeling a little dizzy. Hermes scrambled onto the top of the wheel. The two kneeled there trying to keep their balance as the wheel turned. Their eyes locked for a second, and then Hermes gave Storm a hard shove. She tumbled off the wheel, arms and legs semaphoring distress as she plunged downwards. In a moment she knew that it would all be over. She and Any would be squashed quite flat, and Belladonna would simply remove the pipe from her lifeless body.

An image of her mother and Aurora together – both of them so beautiful and so alike – floated before her eyes. She felt strangely peaceful in the downward rush of wind. She braced her body for impact, hit something solid and found herself rising up into the air again and falling back towards the earth. As she rebounded upwards once more, Storm opened her mouth in astonishment. She was not dead! Instead she was bouncing up and down on an enormous trampoline.

After several more bounces she came to rest,

gasping for breath. Lying flat on her back on the trampoline, she looked up at the Ferris wheel and saw Hermes slowly climbing back down. Belladonna was hobbling painfully towards them, her legs creaking with every tiny step. She didn't have enough energy to even think about casting a spell. Storm sat up, felt in her pocket for Any, whose delight at being alive was only slightly tempered by the fact that she was half squashed, and jumped to the ground. This was no time to hang around, they needed somewhere to hide. Spying the tent covered with tiny, shimmering stars, Storm ran pell-mell towards it.

Hermes joined Belladonna.

'You let them get away, Hermes. That was very careless of you.'

'Yes, Madame. I'll make it up to you, Madame.'

Belladonna glared at him. 'Yes, Hermes, you will, or it will be most unfortunate for you. Stay here and catch them. I'm going into the woods to find the boy and the sister. I can wait no longer for her heart. Without it I have only a short time to live. Once I have it, I can deal with the others in my own time.'

'Madame must be cautious about taking what does not belong to her,' said Hermes, reaching into his pocket for *Taking Heart: The Essential Guide for the Heartless.* 'Under rule 21,877, paragraph five, it says—'

'I don't care what it says,' interrupted Belladonna. 'The girl promised me whatever I wanted, and what I want is her heart. And nothing will stop me getting it. I'll kill the wretched boy and the entire family if I have to.'

Hermes watched her go and then turned back towards the fair, just in time to see Storm apparently disappearing into thin air.

17
The Quest

Storm ran through the entrance of the tent with Any hopping close behind. Inside, the canvas roof was a peepshow of stars that gave off a beautiful soft glow. A woman stood up from behind a large crystal ball.

'Ah, Storm and Any,' she murmured, 'I've been expecting you.' She let the magenta scarves that covered her face fall, and standing in front of them was Netta, the woman who Storm had come to think of as her fairy godmother. It had only been with Netta's help and that of Netta's brave pony, Pepper, that she had saved her sisters and escaped the clutches of Dr DeWilde.

'Netta,' cried Storm, running into the young woman's outstretched arms. Netta hugged Storm, who caught a whiff of caramelized pineapple, a smell which reminded her of Zella. For a moment, Storm's heart ached with longing for her dead mother. Netta picked Any up and planted a kiss on her froggy head. Any snuggled happily into Netta's hand.

'Belladonna! She's a witch and she's after us. Hide us, quick!' cried Storm.

'Calm down,' said Netta soothingly. 'I just saw Belladonna leaving the fair. In any case, the tent is enchanted – only we can see it. You are quite safe here.'

Any did a little froggy jiggle and croaked something that sounded suspiciously like, 'In that case we won't be leaving. Ever.'

'What are you doing here?' Storm demanded.

'Waiting to help you,' said Netta simply. 'Belladonna will stop at nothing to gain your sister's heart and get the pipe.'

Storm felt in her pocket and brought it out. The tin object glinted dully.

'So it came back to you, Storm,' said Netta sadly. 'I had hoped that it would never rise again from the seabed. As time went by, I was beginning to feel confident that we had seen the last of it. But the pipe always has a way of finding its rightful owner.'

'Belladonna is its rightful owner now,' said Storm. She explained about Belladonna and Kit's arrival at Eden End, the eating contest and how they had lost Aurora.

'That's all the more reason why you must get rid of it once and for all,' said Netta.

'How?' asked Storm.

'There is only one way. You must return it to the person who let it out into the world in the first place.'

'But he must be centuries dead,' said Storm, looking puzzled.

'She is,' replied Netta.

'Then how can I give it back to her?' asked Storm impatiently, struggling to silence the pipe's siren song in her head telling her to ignore Netta. 'It's not possible.'

'It is.'

'How?' snapped Storm.

Netta looked at her with sad grey eyes. 'You must travel into the land of the dead and then on to the Neverafters. The pipe's original owner is called Pandora. She will put it back in her box, where it belongs. She has never forgiven herself for her foolishness in allowing it to escape from her box. It has caused war and suffering all over the world. Once it has been returned to its box in the Underworld, it must remain there for all eternity.'

'And what about me,' whispered Storm. 'Will I have to stay there for eternity too?'

Netta had tears in her eyes. 'Few ever return, but I have heard that it can be done.'

'So if I do this, I could die in the process?'

'It is a real possibility,' agreed Netta gently.

'And if I refuse to go?'

'It's up to you, Storm. You don't have to go. Nobody will make you. But as long as the pipe remains here, your family is in peril and so are we all. If the pipe falls into Belladonna's hands, nobody will be safe. She will be able to control the very stars in the universe and use its power to make slaves of us all.'

'So actually I don't have a choice,' said Storm bitterly.

'It's your decision, Storm. Nobody will think the worse of you if you refuse to undertake the quest.'

'Yes, but I'll think the worse of myself, won't I?' said Storm angrily. 'If I don't try, and Belladonna gets the pipe, I'll be sorry for all eternity. Like that poor woman Pandora, there will be no end to my regret.'

Suddenly a little white mouse ran across the tent, up Storm's leg and onto her shoulder, where it sat gently nibbling at her neck.

'That mouse,' asked Netta curiously. 'Have you known it long?'

'It came with Belladonna,' said Storm. 'It was living in her hair. But it didn't like her one bit. It tried to help me escape when she had Kit tie me up.'

'How interesting,' said Netta, and she leaned forward and squeaked at the mouse. The mouse's little eyes brightened and it squeaked loudly back. Netta replied with a series of squeaks.

'Netta, I'd no idea that you spoke mouse-ish,' said Storm admiringly.

'Oh, I'm pretty fluent, but it doesn't come naturally. I find owlish and goldfish much easier.'

'It's a pity you don't speak froggish,' said Storm.

'Oh, that's a fiendishly difficult language. I tried to learn but it defeated me. I couldn't get to grips with dragonish either,' said Netta, and she went back to squeaking with the mouse. After a while the squeaking ceased. Netta turned to Storm.

'Your mouse tells me that he has seen Aurora out in the forest. So we know that she is still alive. But he has also seen Belladonna and she's not far behind.'

'We must get to Aurora first,' said Storm, turning to leave.

'You must,' said Netta. 'I think you'll find that the entrance to the Underworld is in the direction you'll be travelling,' she added casually. 'Who knows, along the way you might find a prince to kiss Any and break the enchantment.'

'Where exactly is the entrance to the Underworld?' asked Storm.

'It tends to move around,' replied Netta. 'But your best bet is to head for a place called Somewhere. It's quite close to Nowhere, and I have every confidence that you will find Aurora there.'

'Aren't you coming with us?' demanded Storm.

'I'm afraid not,' said Netta. 'I have other work to do, and besides I'm not entirely well.'

Storm gazed into Netta's face and realized that indeed she looked grey and drawn. She suddenly noticed that Netta's fringe disguised a large graze on her forehead.

'Netta, you're hurt. What happened?' cried Storm, giving her a hug.

'It's nothing,' said Netta lightly, 'just an unfortunate collision with a bullet. But it is enough to prevent me accompanying you. I will see you soon, I hope, and I can help you escape from here, although it won't be easy. As soon as you step outside the tent you'll be visible to Hermes. You will have to evade him. Make for the merry-go-round, you'll find help there.' Netta hugged Storm and Any again, making sure not to squash Any, and once again, being enfolded in Netta's arms made Storm feel quite sticky with need for her dead mother.

Netta looked out of the tent and peered anxiously around. There was no sign of Hermes. 'Now go,' she urged, and then added quietly to Storm, 'I know that you will make the right decision, Storm, I have every faith in you, as if you were my own daughter. Keep your eyes on the road ahead, and don't look back. You'll only trip over your own feet.'

With Any perched on her shoulder, Storm ran out of the tent, zig-zagging across the fairground in the direction of the woods. She had only got as far as the Catch-a-Frog stall when she heard the thunder of paws close behind. She had been spotted! She wondered whether she should try and double back towards Netta's tent. But when she turned to look, the tent had disappeared entirely.

She ran towards the merry-go-round, leaped onto the platform and threaded her way through the brightly-painted horses that rose and fell as they galloped in an eternal circle. What did Netta mean? What was here on the merry-go-round that could help her? She could see that the wolves and Hermes

had almost reached it, and in the same second she heard a whinny and realized that the horse she was standing by was not wooden like the others, but made of warm dun-coloured flesh with a beautiful dark mane and tail and the most intelligent, brown eyes.

'Pepper!' she cried, greeting the handsome Connemara pony like the old friend that he was, and leaping into his saddle. Pepper – who was Netta's horse, and had proved himself a brave warrior in their battle against Dr DeWilde the previous year – gave a happy neigh of welcome, jumped off the merry-go-round, and headed for the woods, with the first wolves hot on his heels. They gave chase, but Pepper galloped faster than any wolf, snorting with excitement and pride, and very soon the wolves were left far behind.

A short while later, Pepper came to a halt in the graveyard on the edge of the woods. He stood by Zella's grave and neighed and pawed the ground as if waiting for something. Storm slid off his back and kneeled by her mother's headstone. Any hopped a little distance away and started catching flies with her long tongue.

'What shall I do?' whispered Storm, hugging the slender silver birch tree. 'I want to take the pipe to the Underworld so it can do no more harm, but I'm so afraid.'

Tears fell down Storm's cheeks. The wind rustled through the trees and somewhere on the breeze Storm thought that she heard her mother's voice saying, 'Come to me, Storm. Come to me. I would like to see you one last time.'

The wind dropped and the graveyard was still. Storm stood up and she was smiling softly. 'Right, Any,' she said. 'No dilly-dallying. We've got a job to do. We need to find Aurora before Belladonna does, and deliver the pipe to the Underworld.'

18 Out of the Forest Into the Frying Pan

Aurora opened her eyes and blinked. The last thing she could remember was a feeling of being followed and then she'd turned around and seen a lion. Betty from the Post Office had been right! After that, everything had gone black and she had expected to find herself on the forest floor staring into the jaws of a hungry lion, but instead she was tucked up in bed. Her eyes wandered around the room taking in the large highly-polished range, the red-and-white checked curtains, and the mirror so sparkling that even Aurora's eagle eyes couldn't detect a single smear. Framed on the wall was a signed photo of a pretty teenager wearing a crown and a handwritten note which read:

Dear Granny Ridinghood,

I wish you no happiness at all in your retirement, after your distinguished service as the palace cook. It is very mean of you to leave to spend more time with your granddaughter when you could have spent more time with me. Only you know how to make my nightly hot milk exactly how I like it.
I shall miss you and I shall miss your double chocolate brownies with hot fudge sauce even more, particularly as every bite reminded me of my poor lost brother who used to love them so much.

You will be welcome to return as palace cook any time because although I have interviewed 1,927 applicants for the post, none of their brownies are a patch on yours.

I shall probably starve to death.

Yours most regally and grumblingly,
her Right Royal Highness,
The Princess,
The Palace, 1 Palace Plaza, Somewhere.

Aurora smiled. The princess sounded like a little madam. Granny Ridinghood, she decided, must be an exceptionally nice person to put up with her. She let her gaze wander further around the room and admired the large array of hand-painted stones of differing sizes that sat on the mantelpiece. Granny Ridinghood was clearly artistic as well as house-proud, a combination that Aurora couldn't fault. She would like to meet her.

Aurora sat up and found herself looking into the face of an elderly woman. Her cap was slightly askew and her grey hair had a distinctive brown stripe down the middle. The old lady pulled her cap forward and smiled sweetly. 'My name is Granny Ridinghood,' she said. 'You fainted in the forest. So lucky that I came along when I did, or you would have been eaten by wild beasts, which would have been a waste. Would you like a drink?'

'I'd love some hot milk,' said Aurora.

'I'm afraid I don't know how to make that,' said Granny.

'Oh,' said Aurora, surprised. 'But didn't you make it all the time for the princess?'

'The princess?' Granny looked puzzled.

'The princess you used to work for as palace cook.'

'Oh yes. The princess. How silly of me.' Granny gave a growly little laugh. 'I'm getting so forgetful.'

Feeling sorry for her, Aurora slipped out of the bed and into the kitchen and made her own hot milk. She wondered whether Granny's duties as palace cook had got too much for her.

'Would you like a bath?' asked Granny.

'Oh, yes please,' said Aurora enthusiastically. She strongly believed that a long soak in a hot bath was a cure for most ills except perhaps in-growing toenails and blocked gutters.

'I prepared you one while you were asleep, with my own special infusion of herbs,' said Granny, beaming.

'You're too kind,' said Aurora, and she went into the bathroom. She slipped wearily into the warm water. The smell of lemon and rosemary wafted around her.

'This smells delightful. It's just like a marinade I use for barbecuing,' she called to Granny through the door.

'Yes,' called back Granny, 'it will make you as soft and tender as a newborn lamb. I do so hope you will be staying for lunch.'

'I'll help you with the lunch,' said Aurora kindly, drying herself off on a soft, freshly-laundered towel. 'I'm quite a good cook, although I'm sure you could teach me a thing or two. I'm ravenous.'

'So am I,' said Granny.

In the kitchen, Aurora admired the gleaming stove and sparkling saucepans. 'I know,' she said. 'Let's make your special double chocolate brownies with hot fudge sauce.'

'Ah,' said Granny. 'I can't remember the recipe.'

'It'll be in here,' said Aurora, taking down a handwritten book from the shelf which was neatly labelled: *Granny's Very Special Recipes.* Granny smiled and Aurora caught a flash of the biggest, sharpest teeth she had ever seen. The teeth were rather worrying but Aurora tried to put them out of her mind.

'Here we go,' she said, finding the recipe. 'Oh, they look delicious.'

'Yes, you do,' said Granny.

Aurora stared at Granny, and noticed the hairy chin and hands like paws. 'You're not Granny Ridinghood, you're a wolf!' she gulped. 'Where is the poor old lady? What have you done with her?' She ran for the door. 'I really must be going. Thank you for having me.'

'But I haven't had you yet,' said the wolf, licking her lips and barring the way. She smiled at Aurora.

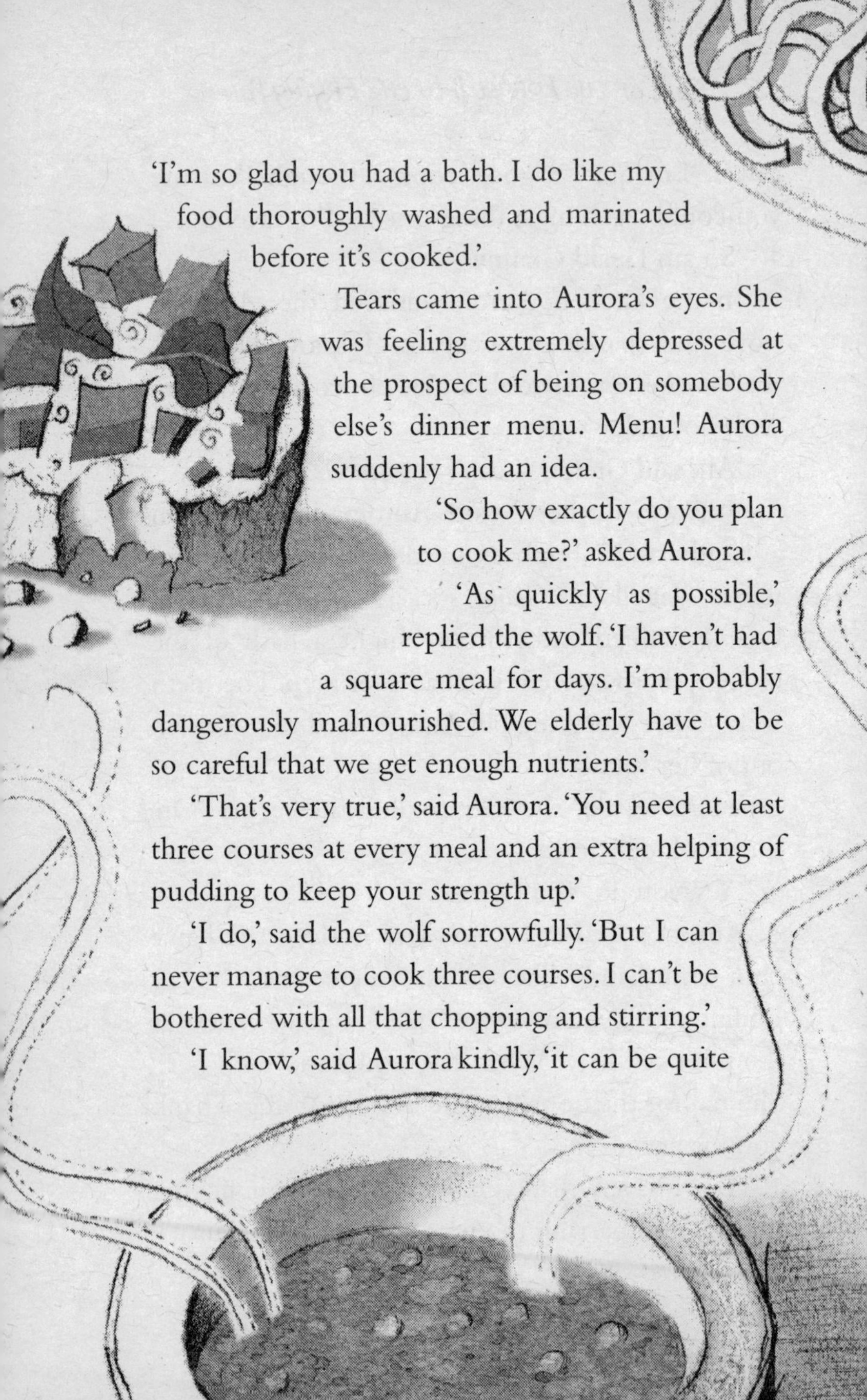

'I'm so glad you had a bath. I do like my food thoroughly washed and marinated before it's cooked.'

Tears came into Aurora's eyes. She was feeling extremely depressed at the prospect of being on somebody else's dinner menu. Menu! Aurora suddenly had an idea.

'So how exactly do you plan to cook me?' asked Aurora.

'As quickly as possible,' replied the wolf. 'I haven't had a square meal for days. I'm probably dangerously malnourished. We elderly have to be so careful that we get enough nutrients.'

'That's very true,' said Aurora. 'You need at least three courses at every meal and an extra helping of pudding to keep your strength up.'

'I do,' said the wolf sorrowfully. 'But I can never manage to cook three courses. I can't be bothered with all that chopping and stirring.'

'I know,' said Aurora kindly, 'it can be quite

exhausting, but of course I could cook lunch for you.'

'Could you? How very good-natured of you to offer. But won't there be insurmountable difficulties in cooking yourself?'

'It might be rather tricky,' conceded Aurora, who had started chopping a tomato and a little basil and onion together while simultaneously making toast. 'But we could talk about it over lunch.'

She rubbed some garlic all over the toast, piled a little of the tomato mixture on top and popped a piece into the wolf's mouth.

'That's scrumptious,' she said. 'Can I have some more?'

'Help yourself. Eat it all up,' said Aurora,

peering into the well-stocked larder, 'and then I can make you wild mushroom soup, followed by spaghetti Bolognese and lemon meringue pie.'

'Could I have two helpings of lemon meringue pie?'

'You can have three if you like,' said Aurora.

'In that case,' said the wolf, 'I'll save you for my dinner. It's always good to have food in hand. I can't bear the thought of running out.'

Aurora cooked as fast as she could and soon the wolf was sitting down to a slap-up feast. She gulped down every scrap including four and a half helpings of lemon meringue pie. She gave three very loud burps and then she settled down in the rocking chair for her afternoon nap. In a very few minutes she was fast asleep and snoring.

Aurora waited until she was quite certain that the wolf was asleep and then she crept over to the door. But the hinges had not been oiled for a very long time and they screeched as Aurora tried to ease the door open. The wolf leaped up from her chair, grabbed Aurora and pulled her back.

'You weren't trying to leave, my pretty one?' said the wolf sorrowfully. 'Whatever would I have eaten for my dinner?' She smiled wickedly, and Aurora got a rather closer look than she would have liked at two rows of razor-sharp teeth.

'My,' murmured Aurora faintly, 'what sharp teeth you have.'

'All the better to eat you with, my dear,' chuckled the wolf. 'I am looking forward to my tea.' With that she settled back to sleep.

Aurora waited until she heard the wolf's snores and then she tried the little window in the kitchen, but it was far too small to squeeze through. The only way out was through the front door. Aurora realized that she would have to be patient. She stoked the fire and then she busied herself in the kitchen. After her nap, the wolf was famished again. Aurora served up tomato soup, mushroom omelette with chunky chips and toffee cheesecake and the wolf couldn't resist, resolving to eat Aurora tomorrow instead.

After every meal the wolf announced that she would eat Aurora at the next, and when that meal arrived Aurora always came up with another mouth-watering menu that the greedy wolf found impossible to refuse. Aurora was cooking as if her life depended on it – and it did. But provisions were beginning to dwindle. Aurora knew that she must escape before the contents of the larder ran out and she herself rose to the top of the menu. But how to get out of the cottage and away? The screeching hinges always foiled her attempts, and even if she did get through the door she knew that the wolf – although elderly – would easily be able to outrun her. She was worrying about this as she chopped butter into small pieces to make the pastry for an apple and apricot strudel. Butter! Why hadn't she thought of it before? She could put butter to another use besides cooking.

Through the kitchen window, Aurora could see the wolf prowling around the garden. While she let the pastry rest, Aurora began the dusting. It had

become a matter of honour to Aurora to keep the cottage at the same exacting standards as its owner, Granny Ridinghood, who Aurora was certain had been gobbled alive by the wolf who had assumed her identity. She picked up one of the decorated stones to dust underneath it. It was small but heavy. She turned the stone over in her hand and suddenly she had an idea. She rushed to the kitchen, took out the strudel pastry and flattened a piece. Then she put a little of the apple and apricot mixture in the middle and pushed the stone into the centre, and then she wrapped the whole thing up into a wolf-bite-sized parcel. She quickly made several more. Then she made four individual steak and kidney puddings, secreting one of the stones inside each of the puddings. After that she made her favourite chocolate madeleines – each one with a hidden stone at its sweet centre.

'Am I having you for my supper?' asked the wolf, entering the cottage.

'I've got something far more delicious,' said Aurora, sliding a warmed plate in front of the wolf. Sitting in the middle in a puddle of gravy was one of the steak and kidney puddings. The wolf speared the pudding with her fork and despite its size she swallowed it in a single gulp.

'Would you like some more?' asked Aurora. The wolf nodded. She ate all the steak and kidney puddings as well as the accompanying mashed potato, and she ate all the individual strudels with the heavy stones hidden inside.

'I'm full up,' said the wolf with a satisfied sigh.

'Oh, what a pity,' said Aurora sweetly. 'I've made some of my special madeleines that you like so much.'

The wolf's greedy eyes brightened. 'Maybe I'm not quite as full as I thought,' she said. 'I am sure I could manage one.' In the end the wolf managed twelve of the madeleines, guzzling them down so quickly that she didn't notice the stone hidden in the centre of each one. When she had licked the last crumbs from her hairy chin, she gave an enormous burp and waddled towards the bed, her stomach so hugely distended that all the poppers on the back of her dress flew off. She heaved herself under the lace counterpane.

'You know, my dear, that meal was on the heavy side. I need a lighter diet. In fact I need you. I expect you to serve yourself up for breakfast, and if you don't I'll just have to swallow you whole. Don't forget. Goodnight.' With that the wolf started snoring.

Aurora waited until the wolf's breathing became more regular, and then she put some extra madeleines – minus stones in their centre – in her pocket, scooped up a piece of butter and crept to the door. She rubbed the butter carefully over the hinges. The wolf gave a louder snore and turned over. Aurora froze. The wolf's breathing became more rhythmical again. Aurora got back to work with the butter and when she was satisfied that the hinges were well covered, she pulled the door carefully towards her. It opened without a sound, and Aurora fled out into the dark forest.

She had not gone far when a gust of wind blew the door shut. Awoken from her dream in which she had been feasting on little boys (rather tough and chewy), the wolf sat up and gave another loud burp. She realized at once that Aurora was gone. With a growl of fury she leaped out of bed and gave chase. But the stones in her vastly swollen belly weighed her down and the wolf could do nothing but snarl in rage as she watched her breakfast escape through the trees. She followed Aurora's scent and arrived at a fast-flowing river just in time to see Aurora scrambling up the bank on the other side. The wolf plunged into the water but weighed down by the stones, she immediately sank without trace.

19
A Rosy Red Apple

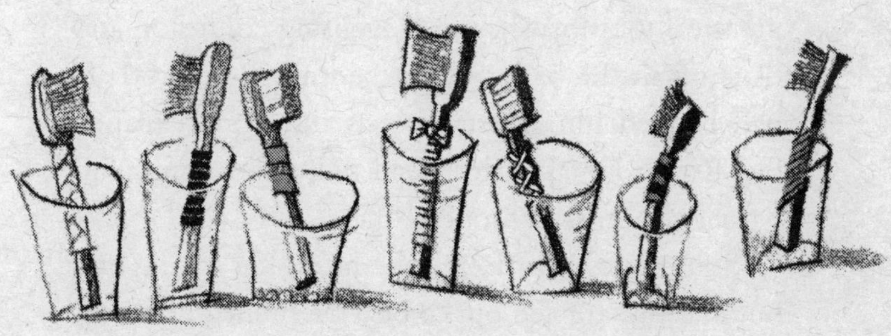

Kit sat on a fallen log in the middle of the forest with his head in his hands. He had found no trace of Aurora. On one occasion he thought that he had glimpsed a lion disappearing through the trees. During the night he had seen an even stranger sight: a drowning wolf wearing a bonnet. He had met no humans since he had stopped at a cottage in the woods where he had been welcomed in by seven brothers who had the small, stocky stature of men who worked underground hewing gold and precious metal from the rock. They had not seen Aurora, but they welcomed him in and fed him on sausages and mash and treacle tart with cream. In return he had polished their boots and came up with an ingenious method of colour-coding the brothers' seven identical toothbrushes so preventing confusion and fisticuffs in the bathroom at bedtime. The brothers had begged him to stay on as their housekeeper, but Kit had shaken his head sadly and continued wearily on in search of Aurora.

Sometimes Kit thought he heard her crying out, but it always turned out to be a frightened deer that would turn on its heel and flee away from him with the same wounded look in its eyes as Aurora had given him when she had seen the knife in his hand. Even if he found her safe and well, how would she ever forgive him? How could he ever forgive himself? Falling prey to an enchantment once could be dismissed as bad luck, but for it to happen twice could be considered a fatal flaw of character. Perhaps Storm was right, and he should just stay away from Aurora. He wondered whether perhaps his own family had abandoned him because he was ill-starred. Wearily he stood up and continued on, his legs aching and his stomach rumbling as if it had been badly plumbed.

Not far away, Aurora sat on another fallen tree trunk and nibbled a madeleine. She heard a twig break and looked around nervously. Once again she was certain that she was being followed. Twigs snapped and popped nearby, and she could hear the swish of branches as if something large was coming her way. Aurora had had enough experience of almost being eaten by now to know it is not wise to wait around to see if you are on the menu. She dropped the madeleine and ran, her arms flapping nervously like a bird winging wildly across the ferny forest floor.

Zeus the lion emerged from the thickest part of the woods, just in time to see Aurora disappearing through the trees. He hadn't slept since Aurora had vanished, convinced that he had failed her and she had been eaten by a wolf or suffered a terrible accident. He vowed never to let her out of his sight again! With a little skitter of joy, the lion bounded after her, only stopping to snaffle the rest of the discarded madeleine.

Aurora pushed her way through brambles that

scratched jealously at her beautiful face and past branches that tried to claw at her skin. The trees around her seethed and whispered as if they were gossiping viciously about her. It was beginning to snow again. Aurora shivered, and at that moment she heard a forlorn cry.

'Help! Will somebody please help me?'

Aurora didn't hesitate. She turned in the direction of the cry and fought her way through the thicket. An old woman, her back to Aurora, was bent over in the brambles, apparently ensnared.

'Help, please help, or I'll die here,' came the feeble cry again. Aurora thought of the poor deer she had seen tangled in another bramble bush and she ran to help. On reaching her, she realized that the old lady was a peddler: her tray with its pretty combs and a single beautiful red apple lay discarded on the forest floor. Assessing the situation, Aurora saw at once that the old lady was not badly trapped, but she guessed that panic and feebleness had prevented the old lady from helping herself. Quickly she removed the offending brambles.

'There, all done,' she said soothingly, gently helping the bent woman up. The old peddler straightened a little, although her back was still as crooked as an ancient apple tree. The hood of the woman's cloak fell back, and Aurora found herself staring into the face of Belladonna. Aurora's mouth formed a little O of surprise and she stepped back, appalled, not just by the proximity of the woman who had tried to kill her and claim her heart, but also by Belladonna's face, which was so withered that she looked like a corpse that had already been a month in the grave. Despite everything, Aurora felt a pang of sympathy for this broken figure.

Belladonna looked at Aurora through hooded eyes. 'You look shocked, my dear,' she rasped in a voice like a key in a broken lock. 'I assure you that I shock myself every time I look in the mirror. I who once was so proud and strong and beautiful. Now I am nothing but a rotting husk. The Dorian mirror keeps me alive, but it is only a half life. Since the mirror was smashed and lost a fragment, its power has waned.'

Aurora took several steps back. 'You want my heart!' she whispered.

Belladonna gave a long sigh that sounded like a death rattle in her throat. 'I did,' she agreed, looking at Aurora slyly, 'but not any more, my dear. It is too late for me. Your heart is no use to me now. I am merely using what strength I have left to make my way home to the mountains, where I will die unmourned, uncoffined and unremembered. The birds will peck out my eyes and the wolves will gnaw on my bones.'

'Oh, that's so sad,' said Aurora, and her gentle heart softened further like butter on a window-sill on a warm spring day.

'It is,' said Belladonna with a quick sideways look at Aurora, 'but I've led such a wicked life, it's hardly surprising. Before I die, I would feel so much better if I thought you had forgiven me for the very terrible wrong that I did you.'

'Of course I forgive you,' said Aurora warmly.

'Ah, you are as beautiful inside as you are outside,' said Belladonna, and as she cast a longing eye over Aurora's slender frame she involuntarily licked her lips. 'I wonder whether you would do me a great favour. Please take this apple and eat it as a gift from me to you. It would mean a great deal to me, a symbol of your forgiveness and our new friendship.'

Aurora looked at the apple. It was the most beautiful apple she had ever seen: green on one side and rosy red on the other. It was very tempting. She reached out her hand towards it, but something in Belladonna's eye – a hungry gleam – made her hesitate.

Belladonna gave another rattling sigh. 'Oh, my dear,' she said, 'I don't blame you for a minute for not trusting me. Why should you after everything I've done to your little family? I am a very, very wicked witch. The worst witch in the entire world. Even if you forgive me, I cannot forgive myself.' A tear ran down her ravaged cheek.

'There, there,' said Aurora, patting Belladonna comfortingly. 'I'm sure you're not half as wicked as you're making out.'

'You are such a kind girl, but even you don't trust me enough to share an apple with me.'

'Well,' said Aurora, 'if we are going to share the apple, how can I refuse? No harm can come of sharing.'

Quick as a flash, Belladonna whipped out a silver-bladed knife and cut the apple in two. She took the green side for herself and gave the rosy half to Aurora. Belladonna raised her half of the apple to her lips and took a large bite. One of her few remaining teeth fell out. The old witch chewed with difficulty and swallowed. Aurora raised her half of the apple to her lips. It had the sweetest perfume. She was just about to take a bite when there was a piercing shout, and Kit crashed out of the forest and knocked the apple out of Aurora's hand.

'It's a trick, Aurora!' he cried. 'The apple is poisoned. She will stop at nothing to get your heart!'

Belladonna screeched with disappointment. 'I want your heart, and I will have it,' she screamed. 'You silly, silly girl. "Oh, I do forgive you. I'm sure you're not half as wicked as you think",' she said, imitating Aurora's voice in simpering tones. 'I'm *twice* as wicked. You deserve to die for being so gullible. Stupidity appears to be your only redeeming vice,' and her knife slashed through the air, just missing Aurora's shoulder as she stood paralyzed with shock.

'Run, Aurora! Run! I'll catch you up,' cried Kit as he dodged Belladonna's knife, narrowly avoiding having his right ear sliced off.

Aurora looked wildly around. She had been such a fool, and would now be dead if Kit had not arrived in the nick of time. Her heart swelled with love and gratitude, and would quite possibly have burst if she hadn't had to make a swift leap to the left to avoid Belladonna's knife. The witch was clearly not quite as decrepit as she had made out. She must help Kit. She shoved Belladonna hard in the back, but although the witch stumbled she regained her footing and swiped the air with the knife. It would have gone straight through Aurora's heart if Kit had not grabbed at Belladonna's arm.

'Run, Aurora,' pleaded Kit, struggling desperately.

'She won't get away,' cackled Belladonna. 'You, boy, may have managed to escape the Dorian mirror enchantment, but she will not escape my knife.'

'Just run, Aurora,' yelled Kit.

'Yes,' shouted Belladonna nastily as she dodged Kit. 'Why don't you run away like a good little girl. Just like your sisters ran. Not that it did them any good.'

Aurora froze. 'What do you mean?' she whispered.

'They're dead,' spat Belladonna. 'My wolves, my beauties, dealt with both of them. It wasn't pretty.'

Aurora swayed, she turned the apple-white of an early snowdrop and fell to the ground in a dead faint.

20 A Death and a New Life

Belladonna laughed, a sound reminiscent of a badly-blocked drain. She picked up the rosy half of the apple that had fallen on the ground and turned to Kit.

'She's not going anywhere, so now I can give you my full attention. You've been nothing but trouble, boy. I wish I'd never stolen you away from your wretched parents in the first instance. You have only brought me bad luck.'

'My parents? You know who my parents are?' gasped Kit, desperate to know more about the family he could not remember, despite the danger he was in.

Belladonna laughed nastily. 'I expect they were pleased to see the back of you.' She advanced towards him with the knife. Kit dodged out of the way and circled back behind Belladonna, but she saw him coming and whipped round. Kit stumbled over a bramble and fell to the ground, twisting his ankle badly. He tried to stand but Belladonna was already on him, holding the point of the knife teasingly at his throat. She smiled viciously.

'Well, well! How very convenient! I'll kill you, so voiding Aurora's promise to give you her heart. Then I'll be able to pluck my heart's desire still beating from her breast.'

Kit opened his mouth to protest, and Belladonna shoved the apple between his lips. Surprised, Kit bit down and, in a reflex action, swallowed. For a moment he looked puzzled and then his eyes closed and he fell back, hitting the ground with a thud that sounded very final. Belladonna checked his pulse, gave a sigh of satisfaction and walked over to Aurora's prone body. Just as she had raised the knife directly over Aurora's heart, Zeus blundered out of the forest and leaped towards Belladonna with an almighty roar. Zeus was not brave, but the sight of the witch poised to dispatch his beloved Aurora filled him with courage.

Belladonna took one look at the lion and laughed her tinkling ice cube snigger. 'Zeus! The world's biggest scaredy-cat and only known vegetarian lion,' she sneered.

Remembering Storm's instructions and seeing both Aurora's and Kit's lifeless bodies, Zeus gave another furious roar and advanced on Belladonna. For a moment she hesitated and then she saw a wild gleam she had never seen before in Zeus's eyes, realized that he meant business and ran as fast as her bandy legs would take her into the forest. Zeus bounded after her.

When Zeus was quite sure Belladonna had gone, he retraced his steps. He padded over to Aurora's prone body, lay down beside her and very gently began licking her face. Aurora stirred a little. She smiled sleepily.

'Don't do that, Kit, it tickles,' she murmured. Zeus licked her face again. Aurora opened her eyes. She saw the lion and tried to scream but nothing came out. Aurora scrambled up. She felt a little woozy and her mind was hazy. She could hear her heart beating very hard, so she knew that Belladonna had not claimed it. But where was Kit?

The lion sobbed. He didn't want to frighten Aurora, he just wanted her to love him.

'You poor thing,' said Aurora kindly, dabbing at the lion's eyes with her handkerchief. 'Are you hurt?'

Zeus shook his head.

'Are you hungry?'

Zeus nodded his head vigorously.

Aurora reached into her pocket and pulled out two rather squashed madeleines. Zeus's heart did a little back flip of joy. He was in love. Suddenly he felt rather brave. In fact he felt exactly as he felt sure

that a lion should feel. Love had given him courage. From now on he would always be the bravest lion in the world.

Aurora's dazed brain was clearing and as it did, her heart began sinking as if attached to a very large stone. She cast her mind back like a fishing rod to the events that had led up to the moment when she had fainted. Storm and Any were dead! A sob escaped from her throat. She looked around. There was no sign of Belladonna but she couldn't see Kit either. Then she spied one of Kit's feet sticking out from behind a bramble bush. She ran over, her heart thumping as if it was trying to escape from her body. Kit lay on his back with his eyes closed. He looked just as if he was sleeping.

Aurora smiled and gently shook him. 'Wake up, sleepyhead,' she whispered. He didn't stir. She kissed him gently on the forehead, his unmarked pearly skin warm to her touch, a bloom on his cheeks. He didn't move. She shook him harder. Nothing. Somewhere from deep inside Aurora a sound welled, a cry of absolute despair so desolate that it frightened the birds and deer as it echoed around the woods. She gathered Kit in her arms and held his warm, dead body and as she cried, the sky wept with her and snow fell on her cheeks and eyelashes and mingled with her tears.

Zeus padded quietly over and leaned his big soft body against hers. They stayed like that for some time until Aurora rose shakily to her feet.

'We must bury him,' said Aurora, 'or the wild animals will eat him.' But the ground was iron-hard and unforgiving and they could make no dent in it. In the end they gathered dry dead leaves from the forest floor and covered Kit's body, creating a gossamer blanket. Aurora gathered a pillow of leaves on which to rest Kit's head. As she gently raised his head to lay it upon the foliage she noticed a faint, unusually-shaped birthmark on the nape of his neck.

When they were done, Aurora hugged Zeus and he licked away the tears that sat like dull pearls on her cheeks. A little white mouse and a silver hare watched them, unseen. Aurora remained immobile by the grave as if she had been turned to stone by grief. After a while Zeus nudged her.

'Leave me alone, I'm going to stay here until I die. I can't bear to be parted from him,' wept Aurora. It began to snow heavily. Zeus nudged her again.

'Go away, my life is ended,' whispered Aurora sorrowfully. 'Without Kit, Storm and Any there is no life.' Zeus nuzzled her face.

'You must go,' said Aurora kindly. 'You can't stay here with me. There's nothing to eat. You'll die or get eaten by wolves.'

But despite all Aurora's pleading, Zeus refused to budge. After some hours, his nose began to turn blue and he shivered uncontrollably. Aurora knew that if they didn't move, he would die with her.

'All right, for your sake I'll go on,' she told the lion, and they set off into the forest together. The path unwound in front of them and as they trudged on in the deepening gloom through a brittle arctic wind, it seemed to Aurora as if she could see her entire chilly life stretching before her – a life without Storm, Any and Kit, a life in which she would grow old unembraced, unkissed, unloved and entirely without hope.

After a while they came to a small roughly-hewn signpost. It had only two arms: one pointed back in the direction from which they had come and read NOWHERE. The other pointed forward and read SOMEWHERE. Tacked to the signpost was a small notice.

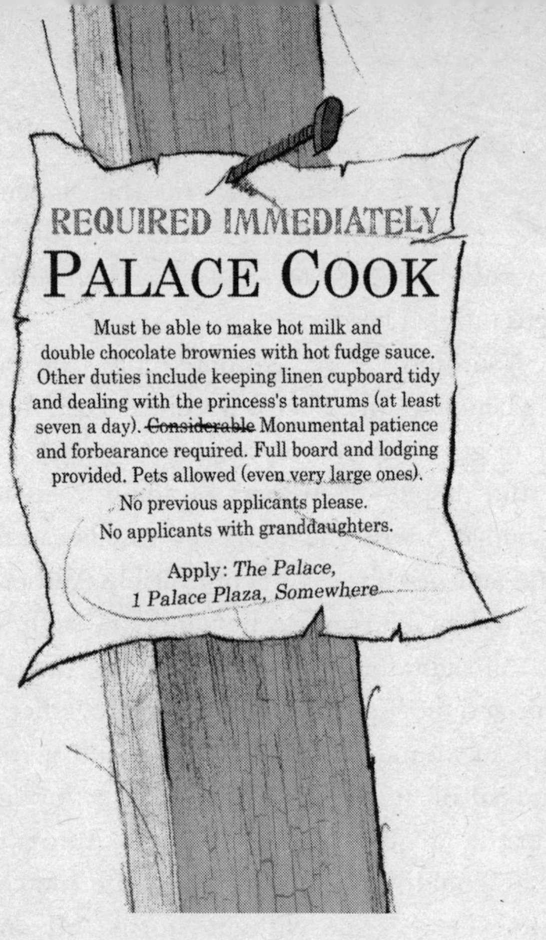

Aurora looked at the notice for a long time. Then she turned back to Zeus and said in a small, broken voice, 'Come on, we're going to Somewhere. Maybe that's where our future lies.'

They set off walking, and Aurora's eyes were so blurred with tears that she would have stumbled on every step if Zeus had not guided her gently along the road.

21
The Legless Frog

Pepper, Storm and Any were exhausted. They had travelled so far. Pepper yearned to lie in a stable and eat sweet hay, but he trotted stoically on. Storm was longing to lie down too. She anxiously scanned the forest looking for Aurora, but the woods rustled with secrets that they refused to divulge. Early in their journey they had passed a pretty cottage. Storm had knocked but got no answer. Through the window, she saw seven unmade beds and piles of dirty washing up and knew that Aurora had not been there.

Much later they came to another cottage and received a warm welcome from the granny who lived there and her granddaughter. They found oats for Pepper, put Any on a lily pad in the pond so she could catch flies and offered Storm what food they had, apologizing that the larder was so bare. When the granny told them that she had just returned home from holiday to find her cottage mysteriously spic and span and dust-free, Storm was quite certain that Aurora had passed this way. She knew that they must waste no more time and continue onwards even though it was getting dark and the stars hung like scabs in the sky.

It was almost midnight when the path they were on opened out into a rutted track. They turned a bend and saw an inn. Any bounced up and down on Storm's shoulder in an agitated manner.

'What's wrong?' asked Storm crossly. Any's jiggling was giving her a headache. The pipe in her pocket was well wrapped up, but she could still feel its heat, and she had to endure its insidious whispering in her brain, telling her to stop and go back. Any pointed at the sign over the door. The inn was called the Legless Frog.

'Well, I can see that from your point of view it's not the most encouraging name,' said Storm, 'but there's not likely to be another inn for miles.' The song of the pipe grew louder in Storm's head, urging her to stay the night at the inn. Storm felt too exhausted to resist even though she knew that anything the pipe advised was likely to prove dangerous.

'We should stop. Pepper's exhausted and so am I. If we stay the night, we'll make better time in the morning.' Any shook her head violently but Storm took no notice. She felt the pipe stir as if deeply satisfied. She led Pepper to the stables behind the inn. A tall thin man lurked unseen in the shadows. Any kept jiggling on Storm's shoulder, chattering away and urging her sister onwards.

'Oh, do be quiet, Any,' snapped Storm. 'If you don't shut up at once I'll turn back and not even try to find Aurora or take the pipe to the Neverafters.'

Any burst into tears and Storm immediately felt terrible. 'I didn't mean it, Any. Of course I'd never stop trying to find Aurora. I'm just completely exhausted. I need to sleep.'

Any sighed and crept into Storm's pocket,

avoiding the one with the pipe in it, because it always made her feel uncomfortable.

As Storm walked in, the entire inn fell silent and everyone's eyes swivelled towards her. It was most disconcerting.

'Do you have any food?' Storm asked the barman. The customers went back to their conversations as he handed her a menu. Storm read:

'Do you have anything other than frogs' legs?' asked Storm, who had rather lost her appetite and was acutely aware of Any in her pocket.

'Cook might be able to do you toad in the hole, but only if he's got some holes left in the larder. We won't get a new delivery until the end of the week.'

'I'm not really that hungry,' said Storm apologetically. The pipe was insistently chanting *stay the night, stay the night.* Storm was so tired, it felt as if someone had drawn the curtains in her head.

'Do you have a room available?'

'Straight up the stairs, last on the left. It's the only one left.'

'Actually,' said Storm shyly, 'I've no money.'

The barman looked her up and down and saw how exhausted she was. 'You've got two arms?' Storm nodded'. 'Cook can always do with some extra help with the washing up in the morning.'

Thanking the kind barman, Storm made her way up the stairs. The impossibly thin man who had been sitting half hidden in the corner of the inn followed her. Once in the room, Any began croaking Froggish words that Storm felt quite sure were not used in politer amphibian circles. She guessed that Any was

OG. A small tailless, amphibious ptile of which there are about hundred varieties, spread almost throughout the world.

True Frog

aradoxical Frog

Long-fingered frog

Slender-toed Frog

Narrow-mouthed Frog

Noisy frog

SPOTTED FROG

Glass Frog

commenting on the menu. Storm pulled the covers over her head and tried to block out Any's angry chattering. She could hear the pipe again, and it was as if it was singing the most exquisite lullaby to her. Her eyelids flickered and she whispered into sleep.

Any croaked loudly but Storm could not be roused. She hopped onto the window-sill. Beyond the roof of the stable in a far field she could just see the top of the big wheel. She knew that if the fair was here then so was Hermes and maybe Belladonna. Feeling sure that they were in terrible danger, Any hopped over to the door and squeezed herself underneath. If Belladonna or Hermes were lurking, she wanted to know exactly where, so she could warn Storm.

She hopped down the stairs and threaded her way under the tables, a perilous journey for one so prone to being squashed, particularly as in this particular location she was likely to end up on the menu. She had one or two near misses, and a very close shave when seven small, stocky brothers who had drunk too much beer, started doing the conga to much stamping of feet from the other customers. A boot suddenly appeared over Any's head and would have crushed her, but just in time she was carried through the air in the palm of a hand. She found herself at eye-level with an elderly man who was staring at her with interest.

'Look at this, Jacob,' said the professor to his companion. 'If I'm not mistaken, this is a short-legged, long-tongued frog. It's not a native of these parts. I think I will add it to my collection of amphibians.'

'I wouldn't bother, Wilhelm,' said the other professor. 'That species of frog is very short-lived. They never survive past two years, and that one looks as if it's at least that. You can tell its age by the spots on its back.'

Any's little heart beat very fast, but she made an enormous leap off the professor's hand and as luck had it, a tall thin man, his face hidden, was just leaving and Any hopped out of the door after him before it slammed shut.

Outside, she felt rather faint. Her species of frog seldom lived past two years old! Any had been almost two when she had been transformed by Belladonna's spell. She couldn't have very long left to live! Her tiny heart thumped in her body as she hopped around to the stable, where Pepper was fast asleep. The pub started to empty and the stable yard filled up as customers collected their horses and yelled 'Goodnight' to each other. Any stayed out of sight in the straw – she wasn't going to risk being squashed by somebody's hobnail boot again. She saw the seven small brothers weaving their way unsteadily into the forest, singing as they went.

She was about to creep out of her hiding place when she heard a familiar voice say, 'She's here.' Any peeped through a crack in the stable door. It was Hermes! He was talking to Belladonna, whose face was caught in the glow from the stable yard lamp. Any gasped. The witch looked as if she was a thousand centuries old; her entire face was crumbling like a cliff face suffering from terrible erosion.

'Has she got the pipe?'

'I haven't seen it,' said Hermes, 'but I'm quite certain that she has. Apparently she's taking it to the Neverafters in the Underworld.'

'We must stop her. Once it is in the Neverafters it must stay there for ever. There can be no delay, I want the pipe tonight.'

'I'll go and get it for Madame immediately,' said Hermes.

There was something about his tone – just a little too eager – and the feverish look in his eye, that made Belladonna hesitate. Where the pipe was concerned it was better to trust nobody.

'I'll get it myself,' she snapped. 'Which bedroom is she in? I don't want to go waking up the entire inn.'

'I'll mark the door frame at the bottom on my way to my room,' said Hermes, producing several pieces of chalk from his pocket and jiggling them in his open palm. One piece fell to the ground unnoticed. 'Wait a while before you come up, then everyone will be asleep and no one will hear you.'

'Have you seen the little sister?'

'No, but she's probably in the girl's pocket. There's no sign of the boy.'

'He won't trouble us again,' said Belladonna happily. 'He's dead. A most unfortunate fruit allergy. Next time I meet Aurora Eden, her heart will be mine. I'll be taking her up on her promise.' She gave a little chuckle of pleasure.

Hermes opened his mouth to urge caution but was silenced by Any's involuntary croak of horror. Kit was dead!

'What was that?' said Belladonna sharply.

'Probably just one of the frogs in the kitchen. This inn is famed for its frog cuisine.'

A tear ran down Any's face. Kit was dead. Aurora would be devastated. She knew that her sister would still love Kit, even though he had tried to kill her. Aurora had the most forgiving nature, and would have understood that he had been under an enchantment. But now there could be no happy ever after.

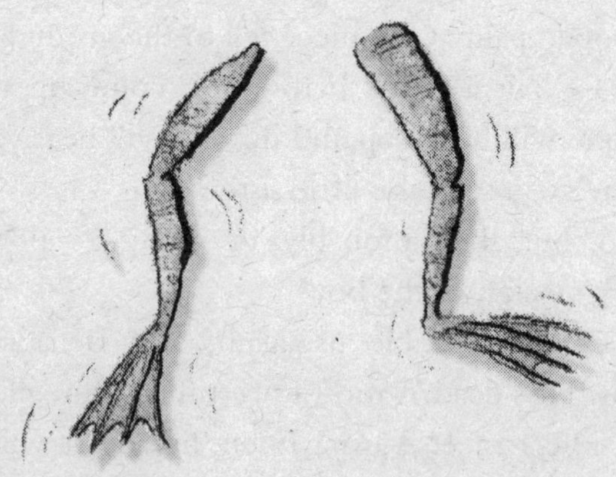

22
Squashed!

Miserably, Any watched Hermes make his way back to the inn. Unseen by Belladonna, who was muttering into the Dorian mirror, Any crept after him, only stopping to snaffle the piece of chalk that he had dropped.

In the corridor the bedroom doors were all shut. Loud snores were coming from several of them.

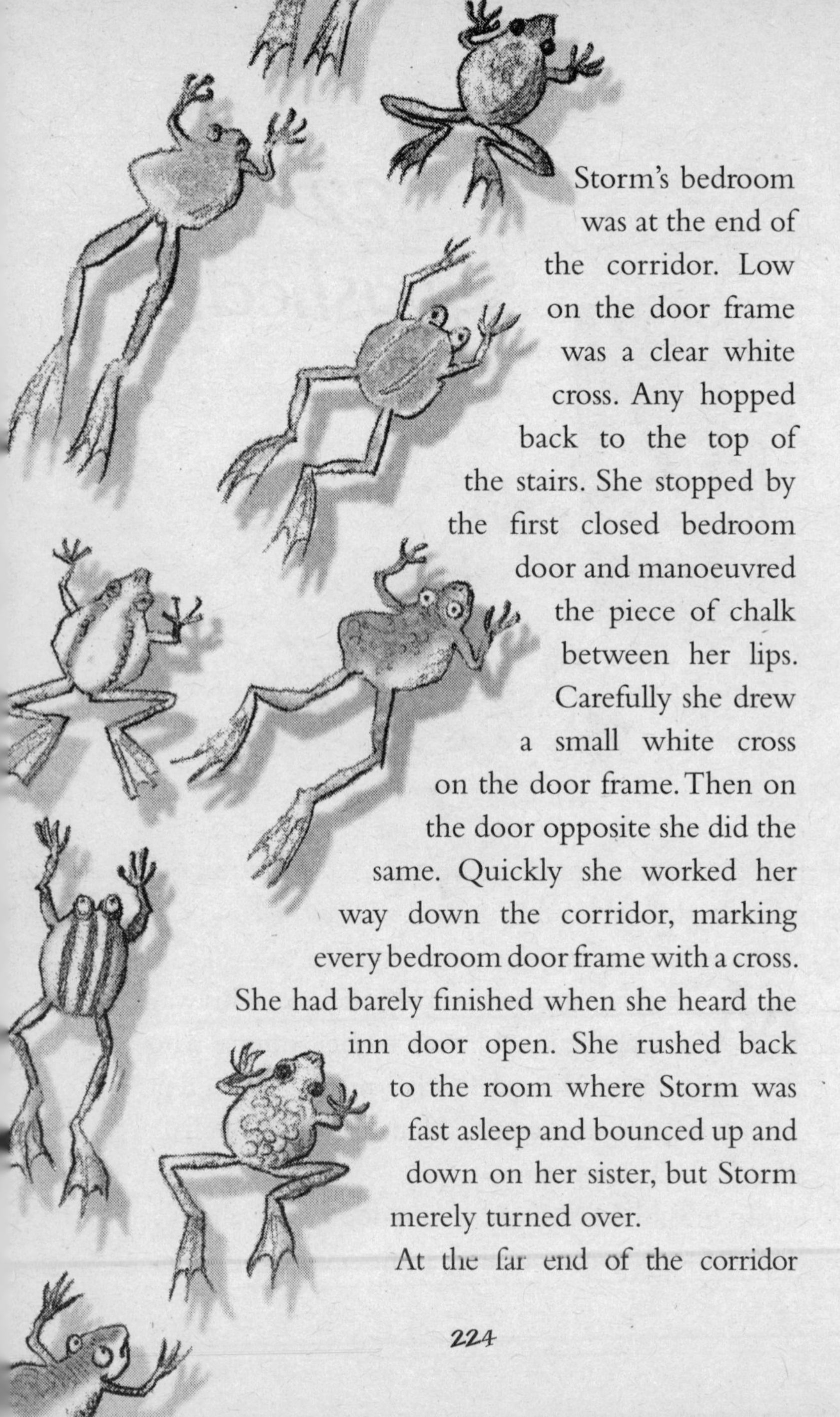

Storm's bedroom was at the end of the corridor. Low on the door frame was a clear white cross. Any hopped back to the top of the stairs. She stopped by the first closed bedroom door and manoeuvred the piece of chalk between her lips. Carefully she drew a small white cross on the door frame. Then on the door opposite she did the same. Quickly she worked her way down the corridor, marking every bedroom door frame with a cross. She had barely finished when she heard the inn door open. She rushed back to the room where Storm was fast asleep and bounced up and down on her sister, but Storm merely turned over.

At the far end of the corridor

came an almighty yell as Belladonna walked unannounced into the bedroom at the top of the stairs, which had an X clearly chalked on the door frame. Belladonna backed out of the room apologetically after discovering it was occupied by a party of Sumo wrestlers on their way to the world championships. Spying another chalk mark on the opposite door, Belladonna entered only to find herself retreating, rapidly pursued by two nuns. She surveyed the doors down the corridor through narrowed eyes. Every single one had a chalk mark on its frame. She gave a yell of exasperation and started pushing open all the bedroom doors, waking the furious occupants. Soon the inn was in uproar. It was also hopping with frogs, because on entering the room of one of the distinguished professors, Belladonna had knocked over his glass tank full of rare amphibians, and the frogs had all escaped. Belladonna was getting closer to Storm's sleeping quarters when Hermes finaly appeared at his door and pointed her to the right room.

Meanwhile, Any was croaking loudly in her sister's left ear. Storm wouldn't wake up, despite the commotion in the corridor. There was a little ledge over the bed which was piled high with books with titles such as *Tadpole Taming: Dealing with the Tantrum Years; A Moste Strange Weddinge of the Frogge and the Mowse; The Frog Prince – Fact or Fiction?* Any jumped up and pushed the tilting stack with her nose. The books cascaded down over Storm's sleeping head. A particularly heavy tome entitled *Don't Get Hopping Mad, Get Even* scored a direct hit on Storm's forehead.

Storm sat bolt upright. 'Are you trying to kill me?' she shouted angrily.

'No,' croaked Any, 'but Belladonna will be any second now, unless we get out of here.'

Storm leaped out of bed, pulled up the sash and was out of the window in a flash, climbing down the ivy on the side of the building.

'Hey, what about me!' yelled Any.

'Just jump,' said Storm, holding out her cupped hands.

'You do realize that's the equivalent of a human jumping off the high diving-board into a fish bowl?'

'You're a frog, aren't you? Jumping is what frogs do best. It's about all they do,' shouted Storm irritably. She heard a whinny at her shoulder.

Pepper had let himself out of the stable and was ready for a quick getaway. Any looked down anxiously. At that moment Belladonna and Hermes ran through the door of the bedroom pursued by several Sumo wrestlers, two nuns, and the professor. Hermes spied Any sitting on the sill and pulled down the sash. It dropped like a guillotine. Belladonna could see a little squashed leg still twitching under the window. She laughed: she may not have got the pipe as yet, but at least she had got rid of one of the troublesome sisters.

Hermes pushed up the sash to admire his handiwork. The professor rushed forward, picked up the dead squashed frog and gave a little howl. 'Sir,' he said furiously, 'you have destroyed my life's work. You have squashed the world's last known living no-neck robin-breasted frog. You have not just killed a frog, you have wiped out an entire species. You are a disgrace.' To the cheers of the other guests he gave Hermes a shove. Hermes toppled out of the window and landed in a wheelbarrow of steaming muck that the stable boy had just left beneath the window.

Belladonna slipped away in the mayhem.

Out in the forest the sure-footed Pepper galloped as fast as he could.

'Phew,' said Storm, 'that was a lucky escape.'

'I don't think luck had much to do with it,' said Any tersely.

Storm looked at her little sister. 'Thanks, Any, without you we'd be frog-spawn.' A look of astonishment passed over Storm's face. 'Hey, Any, I've just realized – I can understand you and communicate with you perfectly.'

'For someone quite clever, you are sometimes remarkably slow to catch on,' said Any with a sigh.

'I wonder why I can suddenly understand you?'

'Actually I don't think you do understand me at all, Storm,' said Any mournfully. 'I'm in a long dark tunnel of slimy green despair. But if you mean that you now understand the rudiments of Froggish, I expect it was the book falling on your head. Bangs on the head sometimes do funny things to the brain.'

'Well, it's very useful,' said Storm, 'and as even Netta can't do it, being able to speak Froggish makes me feel very clever.'

'Don't let your brains go to your head,' said Any. 'In any case,' she added tartly, 'your accent is absolutely unspeakable.'

'Is something wrong, Any?' asked Storm, hearing the tension in her sister's voice.

Squashed!

'I've got something terrible to tell you.'

'Aurora?' whispered Storm.

'No,' said Any. 'It's Kit, he's dead.'

Unable to take the awful news in, Storm closed her eyes. Her last conversation with Kit flashed through her mind. She felt horribly guilty.

Several hours later, Storm, Any and Pepper emerged from the edge of the forest and found themselves by a mill pond on the edge of a small town. A dilapidated signpost stood by the side of the road. To the central post was tacked a flyer proclaiming the imminent arrival of Mr Prometheus' Famed Fun-fair. One arm of the signpost pointed towards the town and declared: SOMEWHERE one mile. Another arm pointed back in the direction from which they had come and read: NOWHERE 24 miles. A third arm pointed to the left, declaring: ANY-WHERE 17,235 miles. The fourth arm of the signpost pointed to the right and sloped sharply downwards. It read: UNDERWHERE (and Underground station). Storm stood under the signpost, turning the pipe – wrapped in a strip of her skirt – over and over in her hand. She felt its warmth under the cloth and heard its persistent call for her to turn

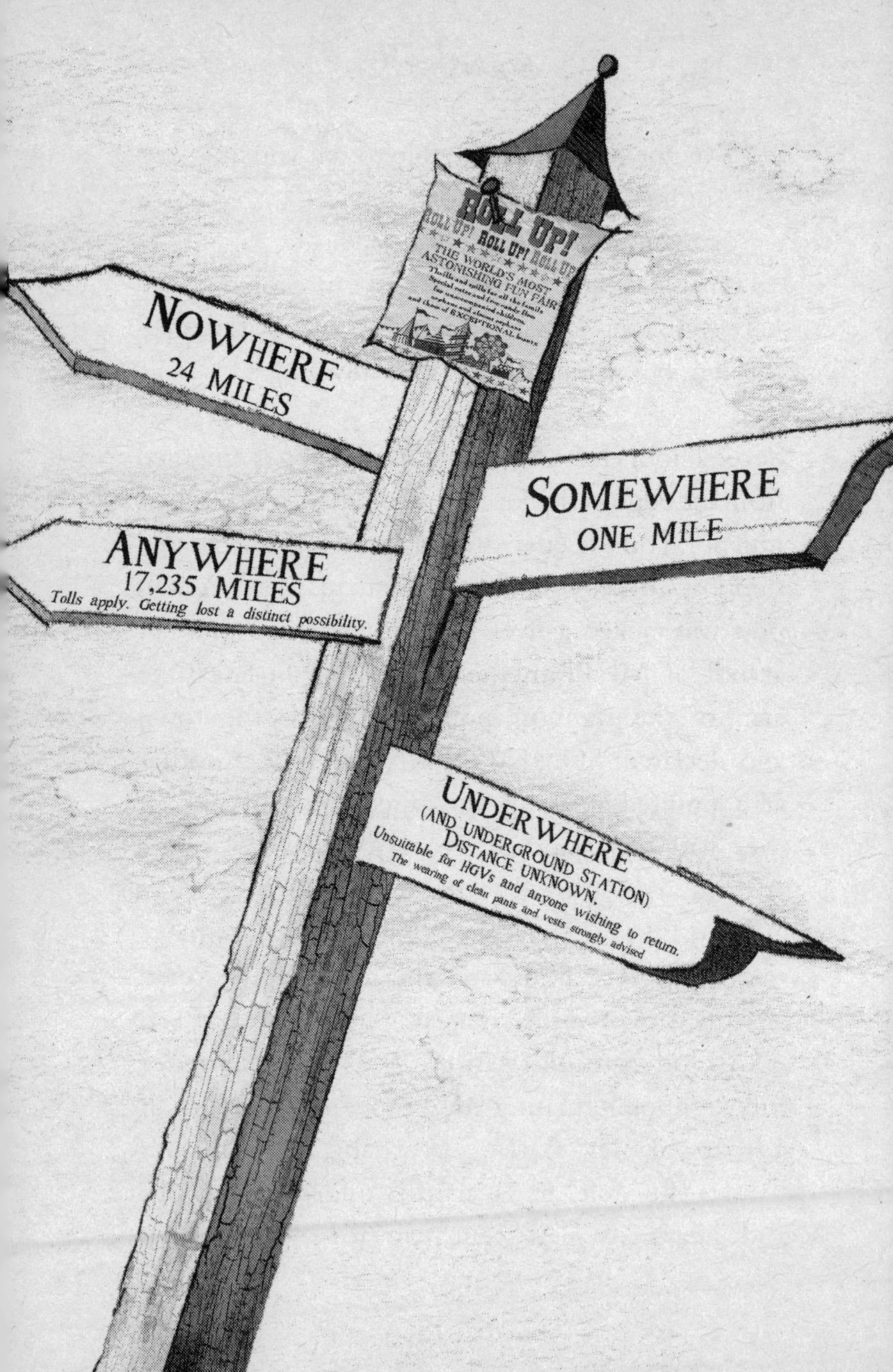
ROLL UP!
ROLL UP! ROLL UP! ROLL UP!
THE WORLD'S MOST
ASTONISHING FUN FAIR
Thrills and spills for all the family
NOWHERE
24 MILES
SOMEWHERE
ONE MILE
ANYWHERE
17,235 MILES
Tolls apply. Getting lost a distinct possibility.
UNDERWHERE
(AND UNDERGROUND STATION)
DISTANCE UNKNOWN.
Unsuitable for HGVs and anyone wishing to return.
The wearing of clean pants and vests strongly advised

round and go back. She closed her ears to it. She did not trust the pipe. She knew it would try and betray her to Belladonna. The pipe wanted to return to its owner, it didn't want to be taken to the Neverafters. Since they had left the inn, the pipe had not been quiet even for a second and its increased agitation made Storm suspect that the entrance to the Underworld was somewhere nearby. She sighed. 'Netta said she was sure we'd find Aurora in Somewhere. This must be it,' she announced, pointing to the town. 'I'm sure she's close, I feel her.'

The road to Somewhere looked dusty and had a dead-fly sadness that matched Storm's mood. She kept thinking of Kit and each time was overcome by a hot prickly feeling of shame. She felt responsible for his death. Any had explained that it was she who had insisted that Kit return to Eden End believing that Aurora would be safer if Belladonna thought that she had secured Aurora's heart.

'I thought we'd be able to fool Belladonna for longer,' explained Any tearfully.

'And I thought the worst of Kit and believed he had just abandoned Aurora to die in the forest,' said Storm bitterly. 'Any, I said the most terrible things to him. I misjudged him, and now he's dead and I'll never be able to put it right. Oh, I've made such a mess of everything.'

'You've been doing your best,' said Any soothingly.

'Yes, but my best is never good enough,' said Storm fiercely.

'It will be if you succeed in taking the pipe to the Underworld.'

'I'm afraid, Any. I don't want to die. I want to find Aurora as quickly as possible and go back to Eden End and stay there safe and warm forever. The three of us there alone, the three of us together.'

'That's wishful thinking,' said Any. 'As long as the pipe is in this world, Belladonna will always want it. If it's not her, it will be somebody else. We'll never be safe at Eden End, and you know it.'

'So you're saying I have no choice but to go into the Underworld?'

Any said nothing, she just looked sad.

'I don't want to die,' repeated Storm stiffly.

'We all die in the end,' said Any, and then she added in woebegone tones, 'Kit is already dead, and some of us will die sooner than others.'

Storm stared at her little sister. 'What exactly do you mean, Any?'

Any shrugged. 'I've discovered that the life

expectancy of my species of frog is around two years. I was already almost two when Belladonna enchanted me, so I probably don't have much time left. I could die of old age any minute.'

'Oh, Any,' Storm cried, scooping her sister up in her hand. 'I will find a prince to kiss you, I promise, and we will find Aurora and I will take the pipe back to where it belongs.'

'Well, I'm glad that's all settled and you've got everything under control,' said Any gloomily.

'Look!' said Storm, pointing to a large sign. 'We've arrived.'

The sign read:

23
The Very Grumpy Dragon

The closer they got to the centre of Somewhere, the stranger it seemed. The whole town was decked with black flags and bunting as if the buildings were all in mourning. The cobbled streets were deserted. Storm suddenly felt cold and very anxious as if something bad was about to happen.

'I wish my teeth would stop chattering,' she murmured.

'Perhaps they're trying to tell you something,' said Any.

'I don't think it's good news,' replied Storm, and at that moment from far away they heard the sound of people weeping and wailing. The sisters looked at each other and quickened their pace, following the terrible sound. What was going on?

Soon they found themselves leaving the town and taking a little track that wound up a hill towards a cave. Smoke blew across the hillside in dark plumes. A crowd of sobbing people was cordoned off a little way from the entrance.

'This way, this way,' shouted the security guards. 'Don't dawdle.' They threaded their way through the crowd. The hillside was covered in snow, but around the opening of the cave the snow had melted. The security guards nearer the front were keeping the crowd contained.

'Stay back! Stay back! We don't want anyone to get hurt.' Suddenly there was a huge roar and flames shot out of the cave. The crowd stopped crying to gasp and their cheeks turned rosy with the heat from the flames. As the flames died away to be replaced by curls of acrid smoke, Storm realized what was inside the cave: a dragon, and a particularly fearsome and angry dragon at that. With Any on her shouder she fought her way to the front of the crowd, where a kindly-looking man in ceremonial uniform was blowing his nose noisily.

'What's happening. Is it some kind of display?' asked Storm.

The Lord High Chancellor wiped away a tear. 'It's the annual sacrifice to the dragon.'

'So what gets sacrificed?' asked Storm.

The Lord High Chancellor stared at her. 'Two maidens,' he replied.

'But that's barbaric,' said Storm, appalled.

'You obviously don't come from these parts,' said the Chancellor. 'What went on before we came to an agreement with the dragon was far worse. The dragon just came into the town and ate whoever he wanted, whenever he wanted. No child was safe, not even our beloved prince who simply disappeared one day, presumed eaten. We had to find a solution. So we came up with an agreement – signed in blood. The dragon leaves our town alone if we satisfy his blood-lust with two maidens a year. Lots are cast on the night before the sacrifice. It's very democratic, nobody is exempt. In fact, this year the princess is one of the two maidens to be sacrificed.' The crowd gave another great wail and wept copiously.

'Oh,' said Storm, 'they must be so sorry that the princess is going to be eaten by the dragon.'

'On the contrary,' replied the Lord High Chancellor, 'they will be pleased to see the back of her, and none more so than myself. I cherish every moment that I don't spend with her.'

'Is she so unbearable?' asked Storm.

'I'm afraid so,' said the Lord High Chancellor. 'She is demanding, selfish, vain, rude and greedy. Everyone thinks so.'

'But if she's so unpopular, why are you all so upset?'

'Oh,' said the Chancellor, bursting into tears again and mopping at his cheeks with a large tartan handkerchief. 'We're crying because of the other maiden to be sacrificed. The palace cook. She only arrived in the town yesterday evening just before the lots were drawn but everyone in the town loves her already. She is a delightful girl, everything the princess is not. She has entirely rearranged the palace linen cupboard and she makes the most scrumptious chocolate madeleines.'

'Chocolate madeleines!' Storm shouted and Any croaked simultaneously.

'Yes,' said the Lord High Chancellor. 'Delicious little buttery cakes.'

'I know what madeleines are,' said Storm impatiently. 'What's the cook called?'

'Oh, look, here they come now,' said the Chancellor. Two small carriages were being pushed up the hill. In the first came the princess, her beautiful little face was as sharp as a splinter and everyone near her had to put their hands over their ears because she was screaming so loudly.

In the following carriage sat Aurora. Her face was pale and her eyes downcast and she distributed madeleines to the weeping crowds as the carriage made its way towards the cavern.

'Aurora! Aurora!' shouted Storm. But the weeping of the crowd was so loud and the numbers so dense that Aurora could neither see nor hear her sisters. She looked as cold as stone in the open carriage, entirely resigned to her fate.

'Aurora,' screamed Storm, but the whole crowd was now chanting Aurora's name and her call was lost in the hullabaloo. Aurora and the princess were helped out of their carriages, the princess struggling very hard. Surrounded by

security guards holding spears, Aurora and the princess were pushed towards the opening of the cave. There was another great roar and more fire shot out. The guards waited with Aurora and the princess and poured buckets of water on the grass to put out the small fires that had sprung up there.

'He's getting impatient,' said the Chancellor sadly, 'and to think he used to be such a sweet, gentle little dragon. He had the sunniest of dispositions, and then he lost his mate. She was winged accidentally during the javelin competition at the school sports day. She must have got frightened and disorientated and flown away. If only we could find her. Sadly, I fear that she is dead and that he is the only legendary four-tongued, three-footed, two-headed honey dragon left in the entire world.'

But he was talking to himself because Storm, with Any on her shoulder, was frantically pushing her way through the crowds towards Aurora. They reached the front of the crowd, just as the guards once more started to bundle Aurora and the princess into the cave. For a second the crowd fell silent.

'Aurora!' yelled Storm desperately. Aurora

swung round. She saw Storm and Any sitting on Storm's shoulder. A look of astonishment, then delight and then despair passed across her face. She opened her mouth to speak and as she did so, the security guard holding her gave her a push and Aurora disappeared into the mouth of the cave. Storm gave an anguished cry, ducked under the cordon and ran after her. The guards tried to stop her, but she pushed, kicked and shoved her way past, seizing one of the spears and a bucket of water as she went. Then she raised the spear above her head and with an almighty yell ran pell-mell into the cave. A terrible sight met her eyes. Aurora and the princess were pinned against the wall and a dragon was moving towards them ready to engulf them in flames. For a moment Storm was too frightened to move. Then the beast gave a growl like a rumble of thunder and opened both its mouths. A lick of flame shot out towards Aurora and the princess. Jolted into action, Storm threw the bucket of water into the flames, just as they ducked out of the way. The ground sizzled and steamed.

The dragon was now very angry and very hungry. It swung around and its tail lashed across

the floor narrowly missing Storm. It took a swipe at Aurora with its claws and caught her on the arm. Aurora stumbled and fell to the ground. Before it could strike again, Any bit the dragon's foot and Storm tried to plunge her spear into the dragon's back, but neither could penetrate the dragon's armour-like skin. The dragon raised itself up, ready for the kill, and as it did so, to the oohs and aahs of the crowd outside, Pepper the pony and Zeus the lion charged into the cave and ran straight into the dragon and knocked it over. The dragon was badly winded, but it was not finished yet.

Storm realized that the growling noise in the

dragon's throats heralded another explosion of fire. 'Help,' she shouted to the princess, and she ran outside to the buckets of water. The two of them picked up a heavy bucket each and ran back into the cave. The dragon was struggling to its feet. The roar in its throats grew louder and it seemed certain that the entire cave and everyone in it would be engulfed in flame. The dragon opened its mouths and as it did so Storm chucked the contents of her bucket down one throat and the princess chucked hers down the other. There was the hiss and sizzle of icy water hitting flame, and clouds of steam filled the air. Surprised and furious, the dragon tried to breathe fire again, but its lungs were drenched in water and only a tiny lick of flame came out, fizzled and died like a badly-struck match. The dragon snarled and the princess kicked him very hard in the shins. The dragon looked for a moment as if it might burst into tears, but instead it reared up ready to attack again, its terrible teeth and claws bared.

Storm, Pepper and Zeus ran forward but the dragon cast them aside with a deadly swipe. They recovered themselves, but the dragon was advancing upon them. The dragon took a step forward and everyone else took a step back.

The dragon pressed on again. Storm looked at her companions. They had fought valiantly but she knew that they were beaten. They would all be dragon meat. The dragon took another step towards them, and at that moment Netta, followed by a white mouse, burst into the cave. Everyone, including the dragon, froze.

In the little bubble of silence that followed, the mouse started to speak. It wasn't squeaking, but conversing in a strange guttural growly language that could only be dragonish. The dragon listened. Slowly it lowered itself to the ground to be closer to the mouse and an exchange of growls took place. Lost for words, the children looked at each other. Suddenly the dragon burst into tears. Netta gave it a little pat and it began purring like a very large, scaly cat.

Netta turned to the children. 'The mouse and I have located the dragon's mate – they're to be reunited.'

24 The Prince

The dragon, Aurora and the princess were sitting around a small wrought-iron table on the perfectly-striped lawn in front of the palace. The palace rose behind them with its tall white towers and turrets like an enchanted castle out of a fairytale. The princess and the dragon were playing tiddlywinks using real gold counters while Aurora popped pieces of madeleine into the dragon's mouths. Every now and again the dragon purred contentedly. Aurora thought he was rather sweet, and she had never thought she'd say that about a dragon. Especially not one that had tried to eat her!

Storm thought of her dead father and how much pleasure he would take in this idyllic scene. He would have loved to have seen that the legendary four-tongued, three-footed, two-headed honey dragon really was one hundred metres long and did indeed have the sunniest disposition of any member of the lizard family. Zeus and Pepper were getting to know each other, gently nuzzling each other's manes. Aurora kept throwing her arms around Storm, taking great care not to squash Any, and half laughing, half crying, she would say wonderingly, 'You're not dead. Belladonna told me that she had killed you both. But you're not dead at all.'

'I think you keep stating the obvious,' said the princess, cross at not being the centre of attention. 'Who are

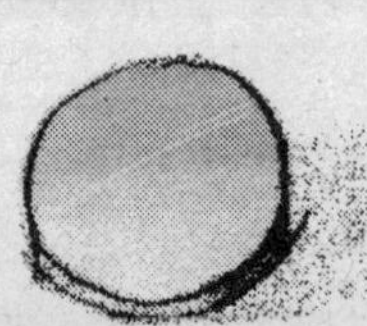

these people, anyway?'

'My sisters, Storm and Any.'

The princess eyed Any with curiosity and stretched out her plump little hand towards Storm. 'It's nice to meet me,' she said, 'the pleasure is all yours.'

Storm suppressed a giggle. 'Delighted,' she said, and then she added, 'You really are very pretty.'

'I know,' said the princess.

'And very good at tiddlywinks,' said Storm, watching the princess flip a counter into the bowl.

'I know,' said the princess, standing up and stepping on Storm's foot in the process.

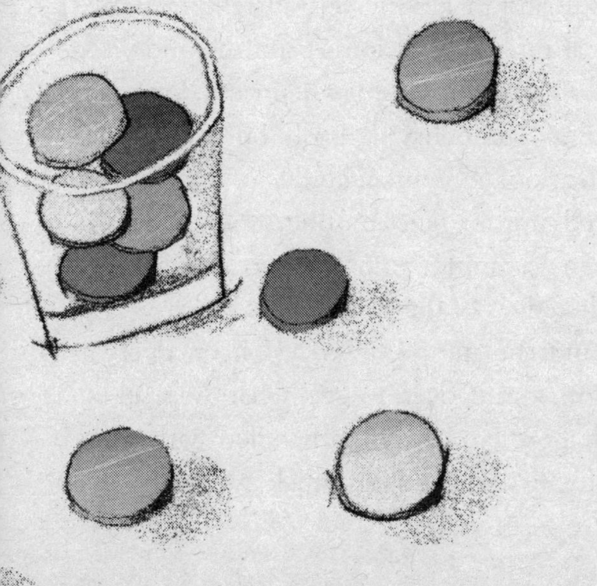

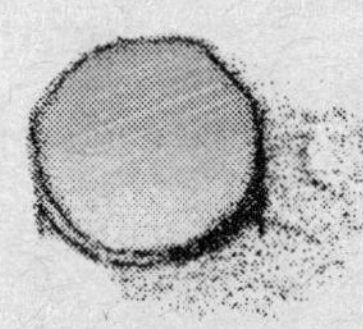

'Sorry,' blurted Storm, 'my fault.'

'I know,' said the princess.

'Actually,' said Storm. 'I think it was really your fault.'

For a moment the princess looked as if she would explode, she raised her foot to stamp it and then she smiled and sunshine broke out all over her pretty little face. 'You're right, it was my fault. Nobody ever says that to me.' She looked at Storm shyly. 'You're very brave. I can see why your sister loves you so much. My brother was brave and I loved him too, but the dragon ate him. He promised he'd teach me to be brave and take me on lots of adventures, but now I'm going to have to be queen, which is horribly dull and makes me very ill-tempered. You have to wear pink, which doesn't suit me, and wave and smile all the time even when you don't feel like it. I know I'm behaving badly, but I can't stop myself.' She looked reproachfully at the dragon, who started huffing and puffing agitatedly, little wisps of fire escaping from his two mouths and singeing the edges of the tiddlywinks board.

Netta and the mouse, who had been deep in conversation, came over to see what was upsetting the dragon. He had to be handled with some care due to his hot temper, which was still liable to flare at any moment with potentially disastrous consequences. Netta had said that it would probably take a few weeks for the dragon's naturally sunny disposition to reassert itself and he would be a great deal calmer when reunited with his mate, who the mouse and Netta had located in the mountains.

While the mouse and the dragon conversed animatedly, Netta gave Storm a long look. 'Haven't you got something you've got to do?' she asked gently.

Storm scowled and looked at the pipe lying wrapped in a strip of material on the bench beside her. 'I'm just enjoying having Aurora back, all to myself. I haven't forgotten about the pipe, Netta.'

'Good,' said Netta, 'because Belladonna certainly won't have forgotten about it.'

Any studied Storm's face with her bright little eyes. She knew how much Storm dreaded her trip into the Underworld and how dangerous it would be for her sister.

Storm was looking very closely at the mouse and the way it was gesticulating. 'There is something very human about that mouse,' she said.

'Of course there is!' said Netta calmly. 'Because it is human. The poor thing is suffering under an enchantment. Fortunately, mouse spells only ever last until the new moon. By the day after tomorrow he should be back to normal. I'm quite looking forward to meeting the man himself, because he is utterly charming and courageous as a mouse.'

'It's a pity it's not the same with frog spells,' said Storm sadly, looking at Any, who had hopped a few feet away. Netta nodded and dropped her voice to a low whisper.

'Unfortunately, that's a much more sophisticated spell and only a genuine prince can break it. I had hoped that things would work out as I had planned, but I fear my magic has been badly damaged by my injuries.' She touched her head where a scar was clearly visible. 'Time is running out to find a prince. In her current form, Any may only have a matter of days to live.' She didn't think Any had heard, but the little frog had and a tiny tear ran down her cheek.

The mouse had finished its conversation with the dragon and ran over to Netta squeaking excitedly. Netta listened, her head crooked on one side. A satisfied look passed over her face.

'Yes, you go and get the dragon's mate. The sooner they are reunited, the better,' she said to the mouse, which scurried off, taking the dragon and Pepper with him.

'It's just as I thought,' Netta explained to the children. 'The dragon says that although he is responsible for a great many deaths and is deeply sorry, he had nothing at all to do with the disappearance of Prince Christopher all those years ago. Indeed, he claims that while flying over the town on the night the prince vanished – looking, it is true, for a child-sized snack – he saw the boy being dragged away towards the mountains by a woman dressed in a nanny's uniform with the boy's pet lion cub in tow. He swooped down to get a better look, but the woman tried to hex him, so he flew away.' She turned to the princess. 'Do you know the name of your brother's nanny?'

'Belle,' whispered the princess sadly.

'Belladonna,' shouted everyone.

'Yes,' said Netta grimly, 'Belladonna.'

Aurora had turned very pale. 'Was your brother called Christopher?' she asked the princess.

'Yes.'

'And did you call him Kit for short?' whispered Aurora. The princess nodded.

'Kit! Kit's a prince!' cried Storm, and then she stopped and looked stricken, remembering that Kit was dead. She cast a look at Aurora's ashen face.

'You know him?' asked the princess, looking astonished.

'I'm sorry,' said Aurora, her voice cracking, 'but I'm afraid I've got the most terrible news. Your brother, Kit, is dead. Belladonna killed him in the forest.'

The princess broke into loud sobs. 'I had only just got used to him being alive and now he's dead again. This is most discombobulating.' Everyone gathered around the princess to comfort her, and Storm put her arm around Aurora and whispered, 'You knew! Oh, I'm so very, very sorry, Aurora, I'd do anything to bring him back. He loved you very much.'

Aurora gulped. 'We were going to be married, Storm. We were going to find a way to get rid of Belladonna and then we'd have all lived together – you, me, Any and Kit – at Eden End in our own happy ever after.'

Storm felt terrible. Her jealousy had destroyed her own beloved sister's happiness. If Storm hadn't deserted Kit in the woods, he might still be alive. How could she ever confess to Aurora what she had done?

25
Back From the Dead

At that moment there was a disturbance further down the lawn at the gates, where a number of people seemed to have gathered. A palace guard made his way up to the table.

'Beg your pardon, your highness,' he said, 'but we've got seven brothers and a corpse at the gate, and they are demanding to see you. The brothers that is, not the corpse. The corpse is very undemanding. They say they have important news for your majesty.'

'You'd better let them in,' said the princess, 'but make sure they wipe their feet. I don't want muddy boot marks all over my lawn.'

It was a strange procession that made its way up the lawn towards the table. The smallest brother walked slowly in front and behind him walked his brothers, three each side of a glass coffin, which they carried aloft on their shoulders. When they reached the princess and the sisters, they laid the coffin gently on the ground, and bowed down. Aurora gave a little gasp and covered her face with her hands.

'Your highness,' said the eldest brother, 'we found this young man dead in the forest covered in a makeshift shroud of leaves. We were following a silver hare and a white mouse, which you don't often see together, when we stumbled over the body. We recognized him at once as the young man who had passed by our cottage a few days previously, and we decided to take him home and bury him properly. It was when we were moving his body into the glass coffin that I noticed the dragon-shaped birthmark on the back of his neck and I remembered the missing prince who disappeared all those years ago. So we brought him here for you to see, your highness.'

'Kit, it's my brother, Kit,' cried the princess tearfully.

'Kit, it's my love, Kit,' cried Aurora, her voice cracking.

'My lost brother,' cried the princess.

'My lost love,' cried Aurora.

Storm put her arm around Aurora's shoulder and squeezed her hand.

'We will bury him in the palace graveyard,' said the princess.

Aurora walked forward and placed her hand on the glass coffin, staring down into Kit's face. His lips were pink, his cheeks rosy as if he had just settled down to sleep and was having the most peaceful, beautiful dream. She longed to touch his skin one last time, to give him one last kiss before he was swallowed up by the hard, dark ground forever.

The princess could see what was going through Aurora's mind. 'Open the coffin,' she commanded. 'We need to say a proper goodbye.' The brothers carefully lifted the coffin lid. The princess leaned over the coffin and kissed her dead brother softly on the forehead. She stepped back, tears rolling down her cheeks. Aurora took her place. She bent and placed a kiss on Kit's forehead. Her lips brushed his skin and it felt so warm to the touch. A sob escaped from her throat and her lips locked onto his lips and she lifted up his body to embrace him better. As she did so, the piece of poisoned apple dislodged from his throat and fell from his mouth and he opened his eyes and kissed Aurora back full on the lips.

'My Aurora,' he whispered.

'My Kit,' whispered Aurora back.

The princess gasped in amazement. Storm's mouth fell open. Zeus clapped his paws together in delight and a tear rolled down Netta's cheek.

'My only love,' whispered Kit, kissing Aurora again.

'I should jolly well hope so,' said Aurora. 'But this is no time for kissing me. You've got to kiss Any.'

Kit looked very confused. 'Aurora, I like your little sister very much, but I don't want to kiss her. I only want to kiss you.'

'I know you've been half dead, Kit,' said Aurora impatiently, 'but you're awfully slow on the uptake. You've got to kiss her because she's a frog and you are a one hundred per cent fully-verified genuine prince and it's the only way to break the enchantment.'

'A prince!' said Kit, looking even more confused. 'I'm not nearly charming enough to be a prince. Are you quite sure you haven't made a mistake?'

'Certain,' chorused Storm, Aurora and the princess together.

'Don't worry your handsome princely head about it, we'll explain later,' said Storm kindly. 'Just get on and kiss Any now before it's too late.'

Aurora was looking around as if she had lost something very important. 'Where is Any?' she asked in a puzzled voice. Everyone called Any's name.

Storm looked at the bench where she had been sitting. The pipe was gone. She felt in her pocket just in case. Nothing. She turned white.

'What's wrong?' asked Aurora, seeing Storm's face.

'I think I know where Any is,' whispered Storm. 'She's taking the pipe back to the Underworld. She knows she's going to die soon anyway, and she's taking it so that I don't have to go.' Her eyes filled with tears. 'She's sacrificing herself for me. Come on, we must go after her. We must catch her up.'

'There's no time to waste. We must take the road to Underwhere. Quick, we must all change our pants and vests before we set out,' urged Netta.

'I can take you in the palace charabanc,' said the

princess graciously. 'You can sit next to me, Kit, and tell me everything that's happened to you. I'll drive the charabanc round.'

'All right,' said Storm impatiently. 'But hurry, or we'll be too late. We'll meet you by the gates.'

The princess, Aurora and Netta ran towards the palace garage, a gold-plated building the size of a small mansion, but Storm put a hand on Kit's shoulder and stopped him. She turned bright pink and looked at her shoes as if they were the most interesting things she had ever seen. She was eaten up by guilt.

'Kit,' she mumbled. 'I did you a terrible wrong. I should never have said the things I did. They're not true. Aurora loves you very much and she always will.'

Kit gave a rueful little smile. 'Just as she will always love you, Storm,' he said gently.

'Don't be kind to me,' said Storm, angrily wiping away her tears. 'I was responsible for your death.'

'No you weren't,' said Kit. 'It was Belladonna, not you. Anyway, I'm alive, aren't I? So there's nothing to feel guilty about,' he added with a grin.

'I'm sorry,' whispered Storm.

'Nothing to be sorry about,' said Kit. He smiled at her. 'I'm not trying to take Aurora away from you, Storm. She's got enough love for both of us.'

There was the sound of a bleeping horn. Kit took Storm's hand and they ran to the charabanc.

26 Death In the Woods

'Stop!' yelled Storm. The palace charabanc screeched to a halt. The kindest description of the princess's driving was erratic. This was partly, but not entirely, because her crown was too big for her and kept falling down over her eyes. After one particularly terrifying hairpin bend she handed the crown to Kit, saying, 'Here, take this. It's yours, anyway. I'll be pleased to be rid of it.'

The back tyres of the charabanc were smoking from the princess's emergency stop, which had been executed with rather more interest in flair than safety. Storm leaped down from the car and ran around the front. She could see Any just peeping out from under the left-hand front tyre. For a terrible moment Storm thought that they had squashed her quite flat, but suddenly the little frog gave a huge leap and hopped off down the road. Storm set off in pursuit.

'Stop, Any! Stop! We've found a prince to kiss you.'

'I don't believe you. You're just trying to stop me taking the pipe into the Underworld,' croaked Any without slowing down.

'It's true, I promise,' called Storm.

'I bet you've got your fingers crossed behind your back,' croaked Any.

'I haven't,' said Storm.

'All right, show him to me,' said Any, stopping and hopping back.

Kit got out of the car. Any stared at him. 'That's not a prince, that's Kit. And aren't you supposed to be dead?'

Kit grinned. The emergency stop, which had caused him to bang his head on the windscreen, had both made his crown slip and given him a rudimentary grasp of froggish.

'I came back from the brink, and yes I really am a prince apparently. It's taking a bit of getting used to,' he said, straightening his crown.

Any looked him up and down. 'You must be joking.'

'He's not,' said Storm desperately. 'Just let Kit kiss you, then you'll see, the enchantment will be broken.'

'Oh, all right, let him kiss me,' said Any grumpily.

Kit kneeled on the ground with his face close to Any's.

'Go on, kiss her,' urged Aurora.

Kit leaned over and pecked Any on the forehead. Nothing happened.

'I knew it,' croaked Any furiously. 'It was just a ruse to get me to hand over the pipe.'

'I think you have to kiss her on the lips,' said Storm firmly.

Kit screwed up his face and kissed Any hard. There was a puff of green smoke and the real Any appeared in place of the frog. She gave a croak that turned into an enormous burp and looked very surprised. Her skin still had a greenish tinge.

Everyone clapped and Storm and Aurora ran to embrace her.

Kit wiped his mouth with his sleeve. 'Ugh, that was the slimiest kiss I've ever had.'

'It's not very charming of you to mention it,' said Any. She grinned at him. 'Our Kit! A prince! Whoever would have thought it? I suppose that means that Aurora will get to be a princess and live in the palace.'

The pipe began a poisonous seductive whispering in Storm's brain and she stared at Aurora and Kit. If Kit married Aurora they wouldn't be able to live at Eden End. They would have to live in the palace in Somewhere, because that was where Kit would be king. Storm suddenly felt a familiar itch that she recognized like an old, unwanted friend – jealousy.

She turned and started to walk on alone.

'Storm, where are you going?' called Any.

'To take the pipe to the Underworld,' called Storm brusquely.

'Not without us, you're not,' said Aurora firmly, running past her sister and blocking the way.

'Yes,' said Kit. 'We're all in this together and

we're all coming.'

'We wouldn't let you go on your own,' said Netta gently.

Storm considered their determined faces. 'All right,' she said in a tight little voice. 'Please yourselves.'

'It's best we go the rest of the way on foot,' advised Netta, who was worried that the princess's driving would kill them all before they got to the Underworld. 'Less conspicuous,' she added diplomatically. So they waved goodbye to the princess, who did a 33-point turn amidst much smoke and revving, and hurried onwards.

They walked parallel to the track, weaving their way through the trees and keeping a sharp eye out for Belladonna. They were sure she must be close now. Once or twice Storm thought she caught the sound of the merry-go-round being carried on the wind. She could see Netta walking ahead, hand in hand with Any. From behind they looked like a happy mother and daughter out for a stroll in the woods. Behind them came Aurora and Kit, their arms entwined around each other. Storm marched behind them alone, grumpily kicking at the stones. She felt furious with them all for being happy and furious with herself for feeling furious. The pipe was glowing red-hot in her pocket and seemed to be calling out insistently to her, telling her to abandon any attempt to take it to the Underworld. It was making it quite clear that it wanted to stay in this world. Storm had to fight its constant whispering and singing and her legs felt heavy as if she was walking through sludge.

Suddenly Netta halted and put her finger to her lips.

'What is it?' whispered Storm grumpily.

'I don't know,' said Netta, 'but I thought I heard something moving. Could you scout ahead for us, Storm?'

'Why me? Why's it always me who has to do the dangerous things?' whispered Storm fiercely.

Netta looked taken back by her vehemence.

'But you always want to do the dangerous things, Storm,' said Any, looking baffled. 'Normally we can't stop you leaping before you look.'

'It's all right, I'm very happy to go ahead,' said Netta softly.

'No,' said Storm tersely, filled with an uncomfortable mix of resentment and guilt, 'I'll go.' She pushed past them and walked forward quietly.

'What's got into her?' asked Any, almost on the verge of tears.

'The pipe,' said Netta. 'For Storm every step is a struggle because the pipe is trying to stop her from taking it to the Neverafters. The closer we get, the harder it is for her, because the pipe is fighting for its own survival. But I think there's more to it than that. I think she's realizing that things won't ever be quite the same if Aurora and Kit are going to be together. Sometimes the realization that change is here to stay is hard to bear,' said Netta sadly. She sighed. 'It'll pass. But we must be gentle with her.' She sat down on a fallen log next to Any.

Aurora and Kit moved a little further on into a glade so they could be alone. Kit took Aurora's hand in his. 'Can you ever forgive me, Aurora?'

'I already have, Kit.' She smiled at him. Her eyes were brighter than a hundred suns.

'Aurora, you once told me that if I ever had need of your heart I should come and take it. I know I've forfeited the right, but if the offer still stands then I would like it now, please.'

'My heart is yours and yours alone. I give it to you willingly,' said Aurora.

'And I give you mine,' said Kit. Their lips touched shyly and as they did so, Belladonna stepped out from behind a tree. Aurora screamed and Kit gave a cry of fear. Belladonna's face was etched with deep cracks like the parched earth in a desert, her eyes were polluted pools of the faintest blue and her body was twisted like the gnarled branch of a tree. She blanched when she saw Kit.

'You're dead,' she croaked.

'I've never felt better,' replied Kit with a grin, and he stepped in front of Aurora.

'I will have her heart. It is my right. I claim it as mine,' said Belladonna softly, with a wicked smile.

'You can't,' said Kit, very firmly barring her way with his body.

'You can't stop me,' said Belladonna, raising her knife.

'Yes I can,' said Kit unfalteringly. 'You're too late. You can't have her heart, because she's already given it away. Aurora's heart is no longer her own. It belongs to me.'

Belladonna's skin turned the colour of cold porridge, her eyes flashed black and she gave a scream of fury as she plunged the knife towards Kit. Aurora saw the glint of the blade and flung herself in front of Kit. The knife glittered for a moment in the air as Belladonna drove it blindly into Aurora's breast. A crimson ribbon of blood spurted from the wound in a great arc. Any, who had run into the glade followed by Netta, screamed. In a blink, Aurora's skin turned to parchment and she swayed like an unstable building. Blood flowered across her chest like a peony. Her knees crumpled and she would have toppled to the ground if Kit had not caught her in his arms and held her fast. For just a moment she gazed into his face – her eyes in his eyes lost.

'I love you, Kit,' she murmured. 'Take good care of my heart.' Her eyelids fluttered. 'Tell Storm . . . tell Storm . . . forever and for always . . .' She closed her eyes and with a tiny wistful sigh, she stopped breathing.

Kit gave a choke of despair but his broken cry was drowned out by a far more terrible sound from Belladonna. The witch was beginning to dissolve from the feet upwards as if she was standing in a vat of acid, and her cries were so horrible that the rabbits living in the forest dived into their warrens and didn't venture out again for two days.

'The rules! I've broken the rules,' she gasped. The

air around her crackled and hissed and she gave one last gruesome screech of distress and then she was gone, quite disappeared. All that was left of her was her lead heart and even that was so shrivelled and black it looked like a pickled walnut. For hundreds of years nothing would grow on the spot where it fell except the deadliest of mushrooms.

At once, the sound of a travelling fair was audible. The noise of rumbling caravans and tinkling merry-go-rounds grew louder and louder. The temperature suddenly plummeted. Netta put a warning finger to her lips. As the rides rolled by, the hustle and bustle of the fair could be clearly heard. The cries of 'Have a go, dearie,' and 'Everyone's a winner' rang through the trees, even though there were no customers to be seen. Shrieks and screams emanated from the ghost train, the merry-go-round turned and turned, and, most eerily, the swing boats soared backwards and forwards even though there was not a soul in them. The spooky sound of unseen children laughing and giggling hung in the air. At the very spot where Belladonna had disappeared, the leading caravans began to fizz and dissolve and eventually the entire fair – the big wheel, the ghost train and the hall of mirrors – disappeared into thin air, leaving only the faintest smell of candy-floss in its wake. The last thing they saw was a screeching Hermes scrambling after the fair, trying to prevent it being swallowed up until he himself was consumed by the earth.

As Hermes vanished before their eyes, Any ran to Kit, who was rocking back and forth cradling Aurora's limp body. She put her arms around him, and Netta – silent tears streaming down her face – encircled them all.

27
Messages From the Dead

'Aurora! Any! Aurora? Where are you?' Storm crashed blindly through the undergrowth back towards the clearing. She had scouted ahead and found nothing. She had been considering going a little further when she had been overcome by a whirling sense of panic, a feeling that the world had suddenly tilted and was spinning wildly out of control. She turned and ran back towards the others, her unease multiplying with every step. Through her panic she could hear the pipe calling to her.

She was puzzled. There was something different about the pipe, but she didn't know what. It was as if it was no longer fighting her so hard. Its song was sweeter and friendlier too, as if it was somehow welcoming her. As she ran towards the clearing she felt as if she was running blindly towards the edge of a treacherous cliff. She had almost reached the glade when Any appeared. She took one look at her little sister's wretched, forlorn face and knew immediately that something was terribly wrong.

'What is it? What's happened?' she asked urgently.

Tears welled in Any's eyes but when she opened her mouth the only word she could say was 'Aurora' over and over again.

'What is it?' insisted Storm. She searched Any's stricken face. 'Something's happened to Aurora, hasn't it?'

Any nodded mutely. 'She's . . . she's . . .' Any's voice broke with a sob. Storm anxiously scanned her face. Any opened her mouth again to speak.

'No, no, don't tell me. Don't tell me,' screeched Storm, putting her fingers in her ears as if she believed that until Any had imparted the worst, it couldn't be true. 'I don't want to know.' But she already knew. She could see the appalling truth written all over Any's desolate little face and she could feel Aurora's absence. It was as if part of herself had died.

She almost knocked Any down as she pushed past her. She reached the glade and took in the scene in a single glance, throwing herself at Aurora's body and hugging her. Aurora was still warm as if she was just in a deep sleep.

'Wake up, Aurora, wake up,' sobbed Storm, shaking Aurora quite roughly.

Netta laid her hand gently on Storm's shoulder. 'She can't, Storm. She's dead.'

'She can't be,' sobbed Storm. 'She always wakes up.'

'Not this time. This time she has gone,' said Netta.

'You must be able to do something,' sobbed Storm.

Netta shook her head sadly. 'I wish I could, but death is far more powerful than me or anything else on this earth.' She paused and looked at Storm's tear-stained face.

'But you could do something. You could go on and complete the quest. Return the pipe to the Neverafters in the Underworld. For Aurora's sake.'

'I don't want to go on. I want to go home,' Storm yelled, and her voice trailed away as she realized that without Aurora, Eden End would never really feel like home again.

'You'll have to make up your own mind,' said Netta, without a trace of judgement in her voice.

Storm stared at her. 'You're not supposed to say that,' she said crossly. 'You're supposed to persuade me to fulfil the quest.'

'Only you can decide whether to do that,' said Netta.

Storm felt the pipe glow so hot it was like being scalded.

'There's no point. Not without Aurora. Come on,' she said to Kit. 'Help me lift her. We'll take her back to Eden End, where she belongs.'

Kit looked gravely at Storm. 'She would have wanted you to go on.'

'How would you know?' shouted Storm furiously.

'Because I love her,' said Kit simply. 'Just as you love her. And Any and Netta love her too. You don't have a monoply on loving Aurora, Storm.'

Storm stared at Kit, her fists clenched. Her eyes burned dark in her white face. 'Well, if you love her so much, you can have her.' And she turned on her heel and walked away, back towards Somewhere. The pipe seemed to be cheering her on. But she could hear another voice, the voice of her mother urging her on to the Underworld.

Any ran after her. 'Storm! Storm! Please come back. I need you. We all need you to go on. Otherwise Aurora will have died for nothing.'

Storm kept on walking. 'No,' she said. 'Dr DeWilde's dead. Belladonna's dead. There's no pressing reason to take the pipe to the Neverafters.'

Any burst into tears. Behind them Netta was sitting very quietly, hunched up with her eyes tight shut as if concentrating on a sound from very far away. Suddenly she jerked upright. Her voice was strange, as though it was coming from a far-distant place.

'Storm! Come back. It is crucial that you go on.'

'No, Aurora is dead. It's over. I'm leaving. I can't go on,' called Storm over her shoulder.

'But you must,' cried Netta. 'I'm hearing Aurora. I'm getting a message. The Underworld has not yet fully claimed her. She's caught in a queue.

Something to do with rabbits. There is a chance – a very small chance – that if you go into the Underworld you may be able to bring her back.'

Storm swung around. 'I don't believe you. You're just trying to persuade me to complete the quest.'

'I'm not lying. I really am getting a message,' cried Netta, her voice tinged with desperation. 'I can hear her now. She's begging me to get you to help her. She says she's heard that the Underworld has no linen cupboards, so she doesn't think it will be her kind of place at all.'

'That's Aurora!' cried Any and Kit together. 'Storm, you must listen to Netta.'

'She's lying,' said Storm, her voice as cold as the grave.

'Hold on,' called Netta. 'There's something else coming through.' She shuddered as if her entire body was in spasm.

'She's telling me something else. I can't quite make it out . . . it's something odd, a phrase she keeps repeating over and over with your name, Storm. I can't quite make it out. Something like "Forever and for always".'

'What did you say?'

'It's coming through again.' Netta's brow was furrowed as if she was concentrating very hard.

'"The three of us alone. The three of us together. Forever and for always." There's somebody else there, a woman. She's saying something about chocolate truffles.'

Storm gave a huge sob, ran to Netta and threw her arms around her.

'It's true! It's Aurora! It really is Aurora. And it's Zella – our mother – too!' She stood up straight. 'Come on, Any, what are you waiting for? We've got to get going. We must rescue Aurora and bring her back from the Underworld.'

'But what if it's impossible?' asked Kit sadly.

'I specialize in the impossible,' said Storm. She gave an embarrassed smile and held out her hand to Kit. 'You'd better come with us. I know that Aurora will be longing to see you.'

Kit took her hand, held it in his own and squeezed it very tightly.

'If you're all going into the Underworld, I am too,' said Netta.

28
Into the Underworld

'Here? This is the entrance to the Underworld? I don't believe it!' said Storm.

'Well it is. Of course, it's not the only one,' said Netta. 'You find other entrances under ancient yew trees, filed under U in local lending libraries, and sometimes even in public lavatories. It's always those cubicles that have a sign on them saying *Out of*

Order. Once you've found one entrance, you tend to notice them all over the place.'

They were standing outside a small building with an ornate stone façade. Carved into the stone were the words: *Underground station*.

'Come on,' said Netta, 'We can't afford to waste any time. If we don't catch up with Aurora soon, it will be too late.' They walked through the ornate hall, past the barriers and the escalators that only moved in a downward direction, and up to a small window over the top of which was written Booking Office. A small wizened man with a face like an ancient baby sat behind the window.

'Four returns, please,' said Netta.

The old man looked at the little group curiously. 'Certainly not,' he said. 'It is quite out of the question. It would be more than my job is worth.'

Netta argued quietly with the man, who kept shaking his head, and Storm tapped her foot impatiently. A group of Sumo wrestlers walked into the entrance hall.

'Over here,' called the ticket man. 'Could you step aside?' he asked Netta.

The Sumo wrestlers stepped up to the window.

'Six of you? Is that right?' he asked, looking at

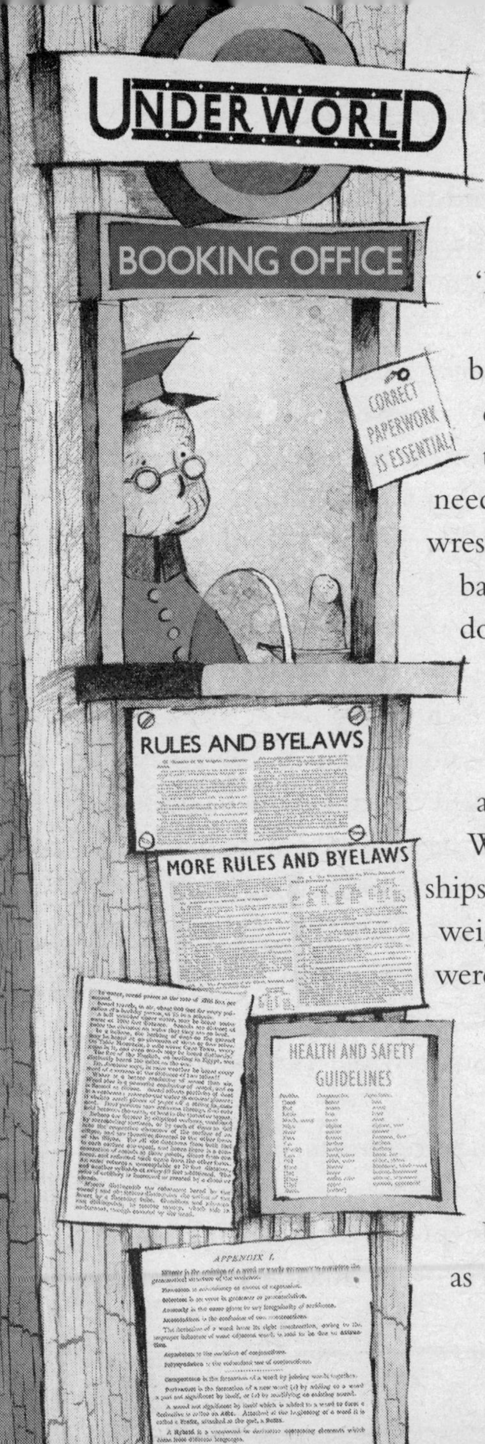

a form. One of the wrestlers nodded. 'Here are your tickets to get through the barrier. There's a train due any minute, but take your time, no need to hurry.' The Sumo wrestlers passed through the barriers and disappeared down the escalator.

The ticket man turned back to Netta. 'Floor fell in at the National Sumo Wrestling Championships. It couldn't take the weight. I'm surprised there weren't more fatalities.'

'Listen,' said Netta urgently. 'I know this is a most unusual request. But we really do need to get to the Underworld as quickly as possible. We're in a hurry. We're trying to catch somebody up.'

She had to stand aside again as two men came limping by with ropes and pickaxes slung over their shoulders.

'Let's just jump the barrier,' said Storm impatiently.

'Don't even think about it,' warned Netta. 'You might get over, but if you don't make it you risk ending up partly in and partly out of the Underworld. You'd be doomed to a half-life for eternity. It's like being in a waking coma.' She shivered. 'It's a terrible fate and not worth the risk.'

The ticket clerk handed over two tickets to the men with pickaxes and directed them to Platform One. 'Climbing accident on Everest,' he said as he watched them pass through the barrier. 'It's been a busy afternoon. I'm ready for my tea break. I'm looking forward to my madeleine.' He pointed to a large chocolate madeleine sitting on a shelf next to the kettle.

'Aurora!' cried Storm, Any and Kit together.

'Do you know her?' asked the old man. 'Lovely girl. You only just missed her. She was caught in a queue. We had to close the barriers for a while because of severe overcrowding on the platform. A sudden outbreak of myxomatosis felled several warrens of rabbits and they all arrived together. It took a while to get the situation under control. You'd think people would be pleased to have an extra half-hour to say goodbye to their past lives, but you wouldn't believe the complaining that went on. Everyone is in such a hurry these days. But not Aurora. She just handed out madeleines. Gave me one to have then and another for my tea break, and she put a shine on the glass on my booth. I can tell you, that girl is going to be eternally popular in the Underworld.'

'Aurora is my sister,' said Storm desperately. 'She shouldn't be going into the Underworld. She had her whole life ahead of her. She was going to be married and live happily ever after. Her death was a terrible mistake.'

'They all say that, the ones who come after the dead and try to get them back,' said the man, shaking his head.

Storm thrust her arm through the opening in the glass and held his hand. 'I can't live without her,' she whispered. 'Please.'

There was something in her eyes so desperate, so beyond hope, that the ticket clerk's heart softened a little. 'I wish I could help you, but I can't. And even if you could get into the Underworld to look for her, she probably wouldn't want to come back. Lots of people like the Underworld far more than they like this world once they get over the shock of finding themselves there. The facilities are unrivalled and the service is first class. And of course if she's already bathed in the River of Forgetfulness, she won't recognize you, anyway.'

'The River of Forgetfulness?' asked Storm, horrified.

'It makes you forget your past life. Numerous scientific studies have shown that those who bathe in the River of Forgetfulness settle down into the Underworld much more quickly. The staff down there recommend it for everyone.'

'I must find her before it's too late,' sobbed Storm.

A family of four – two parents, a boy and a girl – walked through the entrance and looked hesitantly around. The clerk leaned forward and beckoned them over.

'Here are your tickets,' he said cheerfully. He consulted his clipboard. 'That's funny, I was expecting five of you. Youngest daughter is missing.' He leafed through some documents. 'I'm afraid they all burst from over-indulging at the national pie, sausage and lardy cake fair,' he whispered to

Storm. 'Two adults, three children. Ah, here we are. Youngest daughter was issued with a return ticket, just in case, as there was some doubt over her status.' He looked further down the form. 'Right. Seems she was sick and won't be needing the ticket after all.' He gave a wave to the family. 'Right, on your way down to Platform One. Can't miss it. I'll cancel this spare ticket. Enjoy yourselves.'

'The ticket. Give it to me. Please,' begged Storm.

The old man's heart melted. 'All right,' he said to Storm, 'take the ticket. If anyone asks any questions about your status, it didn't come from me. Say you found it.'

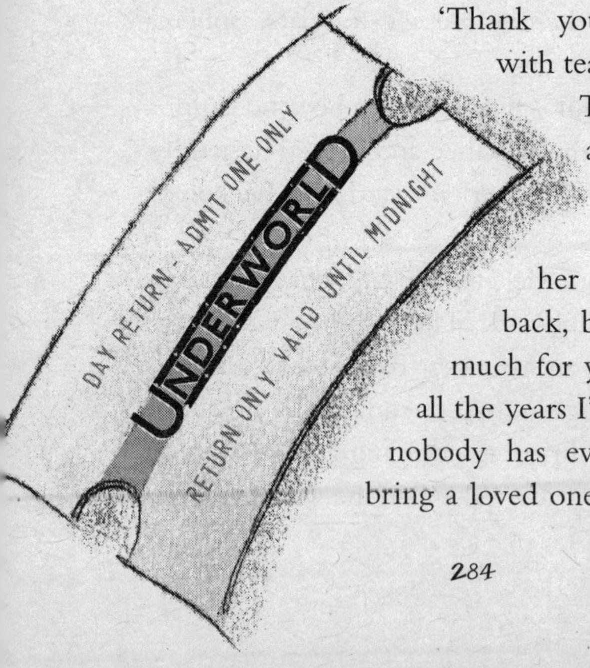

'Thank you,' said Storm, with tears in her eyes.

The man smiled and shook his head. 'I hope you can find her and bring her back, but I don't give much for your chances. In all the years I've worked here, nobody has ever managed to bring a loved one back, not even that chap Orpheus who had the same determined glint in his eye as you.'

'Whatever you do, make sure you're back here by midnight. The last train leaves from the other end at eleven forty-five p.m. It takes the last shift to their sleeping quarters, but it stops here on the way. Make sure you are on it. I pull the metal gates over the barriers and lock them at midnight sharp. If you're the wrong side of the gates at midnight, there's no coming back, you will have to stay in the Underworld for ever. Oh, and make sure you don't eat anything while you are there. If you do, the return part of the ticket becomes void. It's what happened to that Persephone, although if I remember, her mother kicked up such a fuss they came to some arrangement for her.' He smiled at Storm. 'I know you won't do anything silly because it will be hell for me. An administrative nightmare. I'll be filling out forms in triplicate for eternity.'

Storm turned back to the others. 'There's only one ticket, so I'm going,' she said firmly. There were protests from Kit and Any, but Storm was determined. She kissed them both and Netta held out her arms and gave Storm a hug. Storm felt as if she could have stayed in that embrace forever.

'You won't forget the pipe, will you?' said Netta.

'Not likely, not after all the trouble it's given me,' said Storm, and she felt it shift in her pocket as if it knew it was being talked about. Since Belladonna's death, Storm had been more aware of the pipe than ever. It was as if it was calling her all the time, almost serenading her.

'As soon as I've found Aurora, I'll take the pipe back to the Neverafters and then we'll be out of there.'

'Storm, you might not succeed in getting Aurora back, you do realize that?' asked Netta seriously.

'No, Netta,' said Storm. 'I'm not prepared to even entertain that possibility.'

'You will take care, won't you?'

'Of course. But I've faced Belladonna and Dr DeWilde and survived. So I'll take the worst the Underworld can throw at me, whatever that may be.'

Netta smiled uneasily. 'Storm, be on your guard. It's not just death that is your enemy, but the dead themselves. It is their world that you are entering. They will have the advantage.'

Storm ran to the barriers, touched her ticket against the reader, and set off down the escalator with a backwards wave.

29
The River of Forgetfulness

As Storm arrived on Platform One there was a sudden rush of wind through the tunnel and the next train arrived. The doors opened and Storm stepped into a carriage already occupied by several elderly people, a gerbil, a Labrador and two goldfish in a bowl of water. The train stopped at several more stations and a few people and a shire horse got on, but nobody got off. Then they pulled into a station and an automated voice announced, 'This is your final stop. All change please. All change.'

Everyone got out and headed towards the Way Out signs. Storm tried to weave her way through the crowd. People were queuing to get through the barriers. She could see a blonde head in the far distance.

'Aurora!' she called. Several people turned round. Storm pushed her way forward, murmuring apologies. She grabbed hold of the blonde girl's arm. It was not Aurora. A wave of disappointment swept over Storm. She reached the barrier. She touched her ticket against the reader and slipped through the open doors. She hurried on up a tunnel and came out into the sunshine, blinking.

She was on a well-manicured lawn with a clock tower at its centre. There were rattan tables and chairs scattered about, and cucumber sandwiches, scones, jam and cream and Black Forest cherry cake were being served by waitresses in black uniforms with white aprons. Nearby, people were playing croquet and bowls. Several uniformed young women with clipboards were directing the new arrivals and taking names. Storm hurried up to one of them.

'Aurora Eden. She's my sister. Has she come this way?'

The woman looked down a list of names. 'Aurora Rose Grace Eden. You've just missed her.'

'Where has she gone?' demanded Storm.

'She seemed a little distressed, so I sent her straight to bathe in the River of Forgetfulness. She'll be fine in a jiffy, probably already is,' said the woman kindly.

'Which way?'

'I need to know your name, I can't find another Eden on my list,' said the woman, looking puzzled.

'Which way to the River of Forgetfulness?' yelled Storm.

'All right, if you're in such a hurry to get there, we'll do the formalities later, although that's always tricky because you will have forgotten who you are, but as long as you keep hold of your ticket . . .' said the woman.

'Which way?' yelled Storm, frightening several rabbits.

'Past the tennis courts, left at the rock-climbing centre, through the woods past the archery, turn right at the dry ski-slope and you'll see the entrance to the River of Forgetfulness baths by the gazebo.'

Storm ran as fast as she could, tearing across the croquet lawn and leaping over the newly-arrived rabbits that were causing chaos on the bowling green. Her throat was on fire but she pushed herself harder as she ran past the dry ski-slope and saw the entrance to the River of Forgetfulness baths in front of her. A large sign over the entrance proclaimed:

Storm ran through the door. Signs pointed to male and female changing. She ran into the female changing room. A woman handed her a swimming costume, a robe and some goggles.

'Change in the cubicle. The River of Forgetfulness is to your left.' Storm rushed straight

towards the pool and the woman shouted after her, 'No outdoor shoes.' Storm didn't stop, but ran into a large chamber that looked much like a traditional swimming pool complete with several flumes down which laughing children were sliding. But it was clear that the pool had been built to incorporate a river that snaked through the middle of it entering at one end of the pool and exiting at the other. Several people drifted lazily on lilos, sipping cocktails, and in the shallow end toddlers wearing water wings were being taught to swim.

Storm looked desperately around. The place was crowded. She couldn't see Aurora anywhere. Then she caught sight of a slender figure at the far end of the pool. Aurora was standing on the first rung of the steps and was about to lower herself in. Her big toe had just grazed the water.

'Aurora!' yelled Storm. Aurora took no notice.

'Aurora,' roared Storm. Startled, Aurora looked up. For a moment it looked as if she would lose her balance. She started to fall backwards towards the pool. She reached out and clutched at the rail on the steps, righting herself just in time.

'Don't go in the water, Aurora,' yelled Storm, ignoring the No Running notice and dashing round to Aurora's side of the pool. She pulled Aurora away from the water and onto one of the loungers by the pool edge.

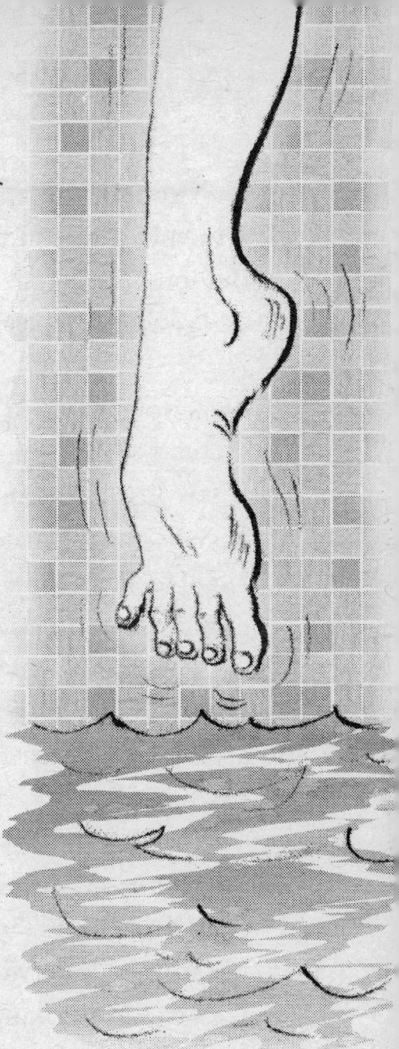

'Who are you?' asked Aurora dreamily.

'It's me, Storm, your sister,' said Storm, fiercely shaking Aurora.

Aurora frowned. She looked as if she was thinking very hard. 'I don't think I know you, but it's lovely to meet you,' she said with a sweet smile. 'Would you care to come for a swim? The water is lovely.'

'Aurora. Please. Please, Aurora,' begged Storm. 'Please remember me.' She looked down and saw Aurora's wet toe. She picked up a towel and rubbed the toe vigorously dry and all the time she was saying, 'It's me, Aurora, Storm. We're sisters. We've got a little sister called Any and we live together at Eden End. The three of us alone, the three of us together. Forever and for always.'

'Forever and for always,' murmured Aurora.

She stopped frowning. 'Of course,' she said as if remembering something. 'The three of us alone, the three of us together. Forever and for always.'

'Yes,' said Storm, laughing, 'Aurora, Storm and Any.'

Aurora frowned again. 'There's somebody else,' she said, looking puzzled.

'Yes,' said Storm. 'There is somebody else who is very important to you and you to him. There's Kit. He loves you with all his heart and you are going to be married.'

'Yes,' said Aurora, 'now I remember. Now I remember everything.' She laughed and flung her arms around Storm's neck. Suddenly she stopped laughing.

'I'm dead,' she said in shocked tones.

'Sssh,' said several people in outraged voices. 'Dead' and 'death' were the rudest words you could use in the Underworld.

'Strictly speaking, that's true,' said Storm, 'but I love you and I can't let you stay here. I'm taking you home. I promise.'

'Oh, Storm,' said Aurora sadly. 'I've always thought that love could conquer everything except chickenpox and really stubborn stains. But I'm not at all sure that it can conquer death.'

'Trust me, it can and it will,' said Storm firmly. 'But before we can leave we've got to take the pipe back to the Neverafters.'

30
Across the Ravine

Storm and Aurora stared at the narrow rope bridge which stretched over a deep ravine. It looked as if it had been there for centuries and was only clinging to either side of the ravine through habit. Some of the rope was worryingly frayed and it was apparent that a number of the rough wooden slats that formed the walkway were missing. It was getting dark. They needed to get a move on or there was no chance that they would make it back to the station by midnight. Aurora, thought Storm, looked dead on her feet. She realized the absurdity of the idea, and turned her attention back to the rope bridge. The pipe shifted in her pocket and urged her to give up.

When they had enquired the way to the Neverafters, the woman at the Information Desk had looked shocked, and said that it wasn't a suitable place for Storm and Aurora. She had tried to persuade them to join a yoga session or the poker for beginners class that was just starting in the entertainments hall.

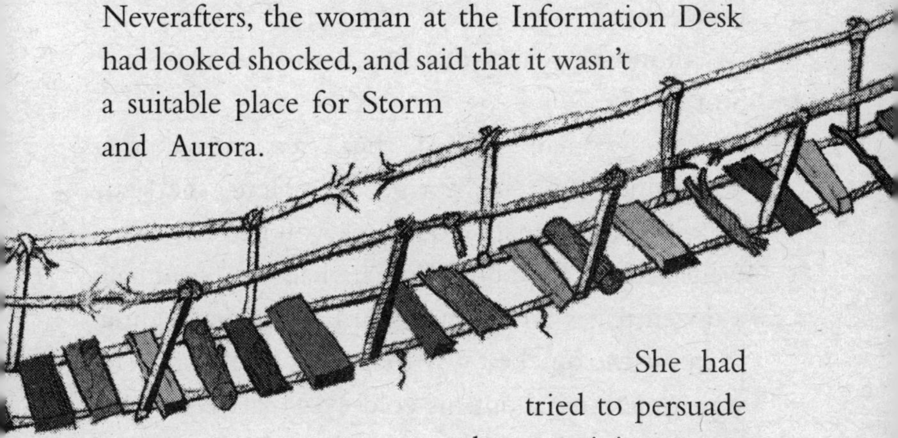

'You don't want to go to the Neverafters, not young things like you,' she said kindly.

'Why not?' asked Aurora, 'what's wrong with it?'

'It's just a bit wild and off the beaten track,' said the woman. 'It's very hard to get to, you'll never find it. Even with a map, it's almost impossible to locate. The only people who ever find the Neverafters are those who want to be forgotten: the outcasts, the misunderstood, the scapegoats and the truly heartless. They always seem to find the path; it's as if they are drawn there. It's not so much a place as a gap on the map where perhaps something was but is no longer.'

'Show me where that gap is on the map,' said Storm.

The woman sighed but recognized the determined glint in Storm's eye. 'Here,' she said, handing her the map. 'Good luck, you'll need it.' She went back to her book. But she had only read half a dozen pages when a man rushed up demanding to know the quickest way to the Neverafters. There was something about his cold eyes that seemed to bore into her and the long scar down his handsome face made her shiver. So she sent him the long way round on a route that would take him right through the middle of the wild goose chase that always took place on the second Wednesday of the month.

Now Storm and Aurora were standing in front of the rope bridge. They had found a path through the mountains, negotiated the swampy Badlands and managed to steer clear of a wild goose chase. But the rope bridge across the ravine was more daunting still. Looking down the narrow, deep ravine made Storm feel dizzy. The pipe in her pocket sang to her, insisting that they go back, not forward. Aurora kept looking fearfully behind her, she had a feeling they were being followed. There was an alternative path across the ravine via thousands of steeply cut steps that would take them down and then up the other side. But that path would be almost as perilous and would take much longer. They knew they didn't have the time.

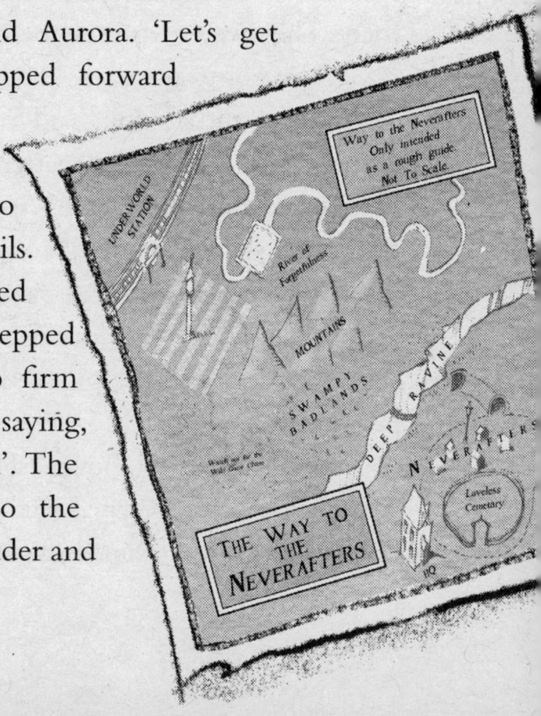

'Come on,' said Aurora. 'Let's get across.' Storm stepped forward onto the first couple of slats, holding tight to the rope handrails. The bridge swayed violently. Storm stepped back quickly onto firm land. The pipe was saying, 'Go back, go back'. The closer they got to the Neverafters, the louder and more insistent it became. She stepped forward again onto the bridge and immediately stepped back as a sudden violent gust of wind shook the bridge. Aurora scanned her sister's sweaty face. There was a look on it that she had never seen before. Storm was scared. It made Aurora feel scared too, because she had always believed that Storm was scared of nothing.

'You're frightened,' whispered Aurora.

'Of course I'm not,' said Storm indignantly, but her eyes told another story. Aurora scanned the zig-zag path up which they had climbed. Far below them she could see two dots moving up towards them. They were definitely being followed.

'We've got to go across,' said Aurora urgently.

'It's all right for you,' said Storm nastily. 'You're already dead. It doesn't matter if you fall off the bridge and into the ravine.' As soon as Storm said the words, she wished she hadn't spat them out. But she couldn't swallow them back again.

A look of hurt stole into Aurora's eyes. 'All right,' she said. 'Give me the pipe. You stay here and I'll take it.'

Storm stared at Aurora. The shock of what Aurora had said drowned out the clamour of the pipe in her head. Aurora had always deferred to

Storm in matters of courage. It was accepted in the family that Aurora was the pretty, practical one, Any the smart one and Storm the brave one. But maybe Aurora's time alone in the forest fending for herself had made her courageous too? If Aurora was going to go round being brave all the time, where did that leave Storm? Where was her place in the family? Just the middle one. The one squashed in between the eldest, Aurora, and the baby of the family, Any. A white-hot coal of rage burned in her stomach. She had come into the Underworld to save Aurora and protect their life together at Eden End by ridding herself of the pipe forever and now Aurora was criticizing her! She was furious.

'No, I'm not frightened,' said Storm. 'I'm going across. Now.' She shrugged. 'If you want to come, that's fine. I don't care if you do or don't.' She stepped onto the bridge. It swayed like a see-saw. She clung to the sides, her fingers clenched around the handrails, and took another step forward. Her stomach lurched, but she kept on going painfully slowly.

Storm had almost reached the middle of the bridge when she glanced back. Aurora was staring intently at her feet as if trying to persuade them to step forward. Storm gasped in horror. Bearing down fast upon Aurora was Dr DeWilde. Even at such a distance, she could sense his cold eyes boring into her and the malice that played around his lips and marked his handsome face with cruelty. She tried to warn Aurora, but only a squeak came out and her legs buckled and she sank to her knees. It had never crossed her mind that Dr DeWilde could be of any further danger to them, but of course they were now in his world, the land of the dead. Her heart hammered in her chest and she felt sick with fear, but she knew that she must act, and quickly, to save Aurora. She rose to her feet and began to edge her way back to her sister.

Aurora looked up and was puzzled to see Storm returning. She glanced behind her and immediately saw Dr DeWilde. Her legs stopped working but her brain went into overdrive. If Storm came back to help her she would simply be walking into Dr DeWilde's arms. Even if she continued across the ravine at her current rate, Dr DeWilde would be at the bridge before Storm could get to the other side. He would only have to cut the ropes at this end and the bridge would fall, sending Storm plummeting into the ravine below. He could then simply make his way down the steps to retrieve the pipe from Storm's body. Aurora knew she had to act.

The only thing to do was to catch up with Storm and persuade her sister to continue on but faster. If they hurried, they might just make it to the other side before Dr DeWilde got to the ravine. Maybe they could cut the rope and stop him using the bridge. He'd never catch them up if he had to cross the ravine using the steps. Aurora put one foot onto the bridge. It wobbled horribly. She tried to avoid looking down and took several tiny steps. With two of them on the bridge, it was swinging more violently than ever. Suddenly Aurora recalled what Storm had said. She was already dead. She had nothing to fear except fear itself. Instead of taking a small shuffling step, she took a large stride. The bridge pitched like a boat on a storm-tossed sea, but Aurora didn't care. Still holding the rope hand-rails, she broke into a run. The bridge juddered.

Storm, her face beaded with sweat and fright, saw Aurora coming towards her. A look of amazement crossed her face to see Aurora nimbly running across the swinging bridge as if she was running down the wide flat drive of Eden End. The amazement was replaced by fear as she saw the unmistakable, sinister figure of Dr DeWilde almost upon the bridge, knife ready in his hand to cut the cords. Aurora seized Storm's hand and pulled her onwards. They were within a few metres of firm land.

Dr DeWilde ran up to the other end of the bridge. He raised a knife and started sawing through the frayed ropes that held the bridge in place. He was in a foul mood; several goose feathers clung to his clothes. Storm and Aurora were just seconds away from reaching the end of the bridge. It began to swing more violently as Dr DeWilde sawed through the rope.

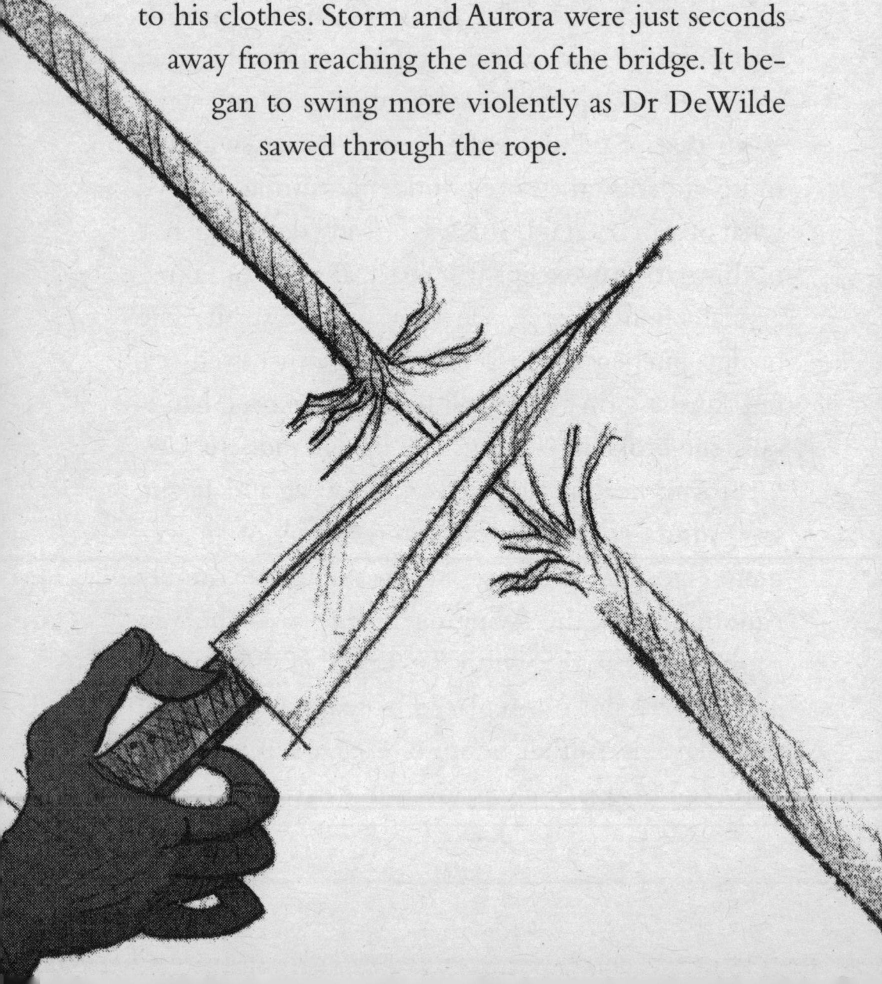

The bridge was now hanging only by several thick threads. It lurched with every step the children took. Several more cuts with the knife and it would collapse completely.

Dr DeWilde repositioned his knife and as he did so, a woman's honey and granary-toast voice softly called his name.

'Wolfie! Wolfie DeWilde. Or do you prefer Dr DeWilde?'

He swung round to face a beautiful woman whose violet eyes had a look in them as innocent as butter and whose captivating mouth curled with amusement. 'Zella Eden,' he said. 'I'd know that voice anywhere.' For a moment he almost looked frightened.

A fruity laugh filled the air, like diamonds in a drain. Then the delicious voice said silkily, 'Leave my children alone. If you hurt either Storm or Aurora, you'll regret it. I know you, Wolfie. I know how your twisted mind works, and if you hurt either of them I'll make sure you never get out of the Underworld.'

'Is that a threat?' demanded Dr DeWilde.

'No,' said the voice softly. 'It's a promise.'

'You can't frighten me, you're dead,' said Dr DeWilde.

Zella laughed again. 'So are you, and I already have. You should see your face. You look as white as a ghost.'

The tinkling laugh was more than Dr DeWilde could bear. 'Zella Eden,' he roared furiously, 'nothing, not even you, is going to stop me taking my revenge on Storm. I hold her responsible for my death, and she must pay the price.' He gave a sinister little smile. 'Your whole family will pay, the living and the dead.' His icy eyes glittered dangerously, and he leaned forward and hissed, 'Don't underestimate me, Zella. I will be ruthless and I will not rest until I have destroyed all you hold dear, and regained the pipe.'

'Well, you're going to have to get a move on,' said Zella, but there was an undertone of fear to the amusement in her voice. Dr DeWilde looked across the ravine. The children had reached the end of the rope bridge and were disappearing into the entrance of a tunnel at the other end.

'You've just been trying to delay me,' he shouted. He considered the bridge. He wasn't sure it would hold, but if he crossed the ravine via the steps, he would never catch up with the children. He had to get to Storm before she consigned the pipe to eternity. He stepped onto the rope bridge, which began swaying violently.

'Steady as you go,' said Zella sweetly. Dr DeWilde took another step. The bridge juddered. He made the mistake of looking down. The ravine fell away to nothingness and far, far below a river ran through the narrowest of gorges like a thin silver thread. Dr DeWilde's head began to spin. The bridge rocked wildly. Thinking only of the pipe and dropping to his hands and knees, he began the long, slow crawl across the bridge with Zella's laughter ringing in his ears.

31
Don't Look Back

Storm and Aurora edged along a dark tunnel keeping very close together. They could just make out the sides in the gloom. They kept casting fearful glances behind them, expecting Dr DeWilde to suddenly loom out of the shadows. Once Storm thought she heard a footfall behind them and her stomach lurched, her insides turned to water and she scuttled forward like a panicked spider. She knew that the bridge would not hamper Dr DeWilde for too long. He would let nothing stop him in his quest to regain the pipe and would hunt them down just as a cat stalks a mouse.

They came to a fork in the tunnel. They took the right-hand fork and had only gone fifty metres when they were faced with another choice. This time they took the left-hand fork. They walked on, and a few seconds later were faced with yet another choice. Storm studied the map intently, tracing the route that they were following with her finger. She knew that she needed to memorize the route carefully otherwise it would be difficult to find their way back through the tunnels again.

'Do you want some help?' asked Aurora, seeing her sister's face screwed up with concentration.

'I can do it by myself,' said Storm curtly. But every time they came to a fork in the tunnel, the pipe in her pocket seemed to sing a suggestion to her. It required all Storm's strength to ignore it. She was worried that their progress was too slow. At the rate they were going they would never make it back to the station by midnight. She hurried forward, took another sharp turn to the right, and in the distance she could see a small pinprick of light.

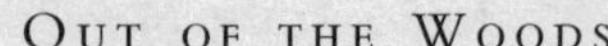

They came out under a lamp-post in a small cobbled street that was shrouded in murky fog. The street appeared to be deserted but the fog was as thick as cotton wool and it was hard to be certain that nobody lurked there.

'Which way?' whispered Aurora.

Storm studied the map. 'Not far,' she said. She took them through great clumps of fog down another narrow street which opened out into a small square. Beyond the square was an eerie park and at the end of the park was a graveyard around which mist swirled like cream in a cup of black coffee.

'That's where we need to go,' said Storm, pointing to a large crumbling mansion beyond the graveyard that rose up out of the fog like a fairground illusion, and was so old and derelict that it looked far too decrepit even to be haunted.

Aurora hesitated.

Storm reached out and took her sister's hand. 'I can't do this without you, Aurora,' she whispered gruffly.

Aurora grinned, she knew this was Storm's attempt at an apology. 'I couldn't do anything without you, Storm,' she replied.

'Together, forever and for always.'

'Forever and for always.'

They were so close to their goal. Storm looked back through the swirling mist, half expecting to see Dr DeWilde's leering smile. Nothing monstrous loomed out of the shadows. Tightly squeezing each other's hands, the girls walked through a little wooden gate into the graveyard. Tacked to the gate was a faded sign which read:

The graves were the saddest they'd ever seen, the stones tilted drunkenly against one another as if trying to comfort each other. The writing etched in the stones was faded and indecipherable as if someone was trying to obliterate memory itself. Weeds grew not just between the graves, but over and around them as if strangling the stones. It was a grim and desolate place made grimmer by the murky mist and boggy, treacherous ground.

'Watch out!' cried Storm, sinking up to her ankles in a boggy patch. Around them the earth gurgled and bubbled as if something or someone was constantly moving underneath, churning it up. The ground seemed to have a grudge against them.

'Perhaps it would be better to walk on the gravestones themselves,' suggested Storm.

'I think that would be a bit rude,' said Aurora. But after a few more unpleasantly boggy steps, she agreed.

Storm went first, springing nimbly from one stone to the next. Aurora was slower and soon fell behind. 'Hurry up!' called Storm, and she took a leap onto a particularly decrepit stone that looked as if it had lain forgotten in the cemetery for centuries. She paused a moment to wait for Aurora to catch up. As she did so she felt the gravestone below her crack and two hands reached out, grabbed her legs and began to pull her downwards into the earth. Storm screamed and Aurora lost her balance and stepped into a boggy patch of ground.

'I've got you now, Storm Eden,' cried the familiar voice of Belladonna as she rose up from the grave, a terrible rictus grin on her skull-like face. She leaned over Storm and began to push her into the soft, yielding ground.

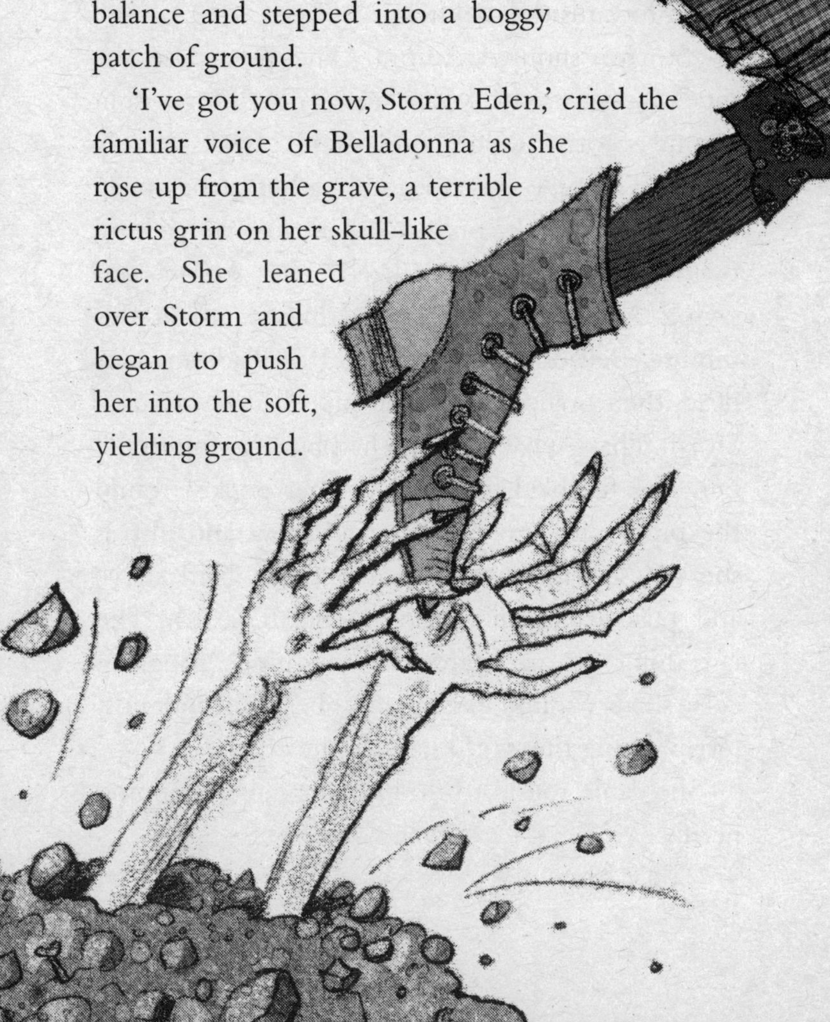

Storm was so shocked that for a moment she did nothing and then she began struggling with all her might. But Belladonna had the advantage and Storm felt her body being swallowed by the damp earth as she was pushed down towards the darkness.

'Storm!' shouted Aurora. 'The pipe. Use the pipe! It's yours. It's yours again now.' For a split second Storm didn't understand what Aurora meant. The pipe was no good to her; it belonged to Belladonna. It only worked for its rightful owner. But then she realized what Aurora was saying. Although it didn't feel like it just at this minute, Belladonna was dead! If Belladonna was dead, then ownership of the pipe had reverted to Storm. That's what the pipe had been trying to tell her! She fumbled frantically in her pocket, found the pipe, put it to her lips and blew, and just as she did so, Belladonna gave one last hard shove and pushed Storm's head under the earth. The last thing Storm heard was the pipe's song, an eerie shivery sound like the most beautiful and most terrible song the world has ever heard.

She came round to find Aurora gently slapping her face.

'What happened?'

'The pipe worked. The earth spat you out and swallowed Belladonna up.' Aurora shivered. 'It was horrible. I really don't think she'll be bothering us again.'

'The pipe?'

'You dropped it.' Aurora put it in Storm's hand. 'It belongs to you again now,' she said lightly.

Storm clasped the pipe tightly. She felt all powerful, as if she could control the universe. 'Maybe we'll just go home. We could take the pipe with us,' she said. 'Think how useful it would be. We'd never have to worry about money again, we could make everyone do as we pleased . . .'

A flicker of disappointment crossed Aurora's face. 'If that's what you really want, Storm,' she said in a strained voice. 'If you think that's the right thing to do.'

Storm struggled to resist the pipe's seductive song. It felt as if a battle was being waged in her head. Then out of the corner of her eye, she saw Dr DeWilde appear out of the mist at the graveyard gate.

'No,' she said, rising to her feet. 'I don't think it's the right thing to do.' She pointed to Dr DeWilde. 'He's the reason why. Him and Belladonna and all those other people in the world who would do anything they can to get hold of the pipe and who would use it for nothing but ill. Unless I get rid of the pipe forever we'll never be safe. Come on.'

They hurried onwards, and at the edge of the desolate cemetery Storm turned back. The fog swirled and eddied and she saw Dr DeWilde just stepping onto the first graves.

32
Pandora's Box

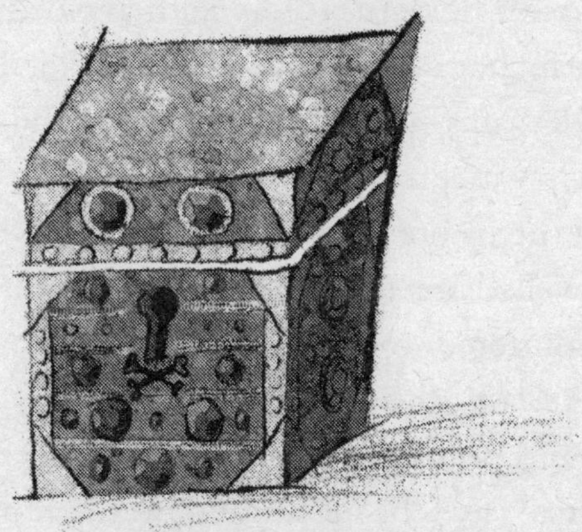

The girls stood at the front of the old crumbled mansion. A sign on the door read:

They walked into the hall. A tired voice called out: 'In here.' They pushed open another door and found themselves in a vast ballroom with a huge vaulted ceiling covered in painted clouds. The ballroom was piled with empty wine bottles. At one end, next to a grandfather clock, sat an old woman, her once beautiful face raddled with drink and despair. She sat huddled under a huge umbrella, which was protecting her from the rain that fell from the painted clouds above. She clutched a small bejewelled box in her gnarled hands and all the time she muttered to herself, 'Poor, poor Pandora.'

'At last! I've been hoping you would come,' she said softly, with a smile like tarnished gold sequins. 'I've been waiting for centuries to get the pipe back in my box, where it will be safe and

do no further harm in the world.' Pandora gave a bitter laugh. 'One less thing to be blamed for. One less thing to regret.' Her sigh filled the air, bringing with it the claggy odour of stale wine and disappointment. 'There have been many times when I thought it might come back to me, but I've always been wrong. Its corrupting power is too great. Your mother tried to return it but to no avail. Now at long last, Storm Eden, you have brought it back to me. Can I see it?'

Storm held it out. The pipe burned her hand and called out to her to turn around and walk out of the ballroom. For a moment Storm hesitated. She took a deep breath and tried to concentrate. The pipe sang to her insidiously. It was like trying to resist a really tormenting itch that wouldn't go away. She knew she couldn't live her whole life with that itch. It would deform and cripple her. She had to get rid of the pipe. The woman saw the determination in Storm's face.

'I have much to thank you for, my dear. For years I've been trying to collect back all the things that escaped from my box, but very few ever return to me once they are out in the world. Of all the things that escaped from my box, it is the pipe that I regret most. It has done untold harm. It has caused wars and famine. It has played a part in the deaths of millions and the enslavement of many more. It is a pestilence. I will be relieved when it is safely back inside.' She held out the box. 'If I open it just a chink, will you slip it in for me?' Storm hesitated. The pipe seemed to be screaming at her inside her head, telling her that she would be a fool to throw away all that power. Her entire body tingled with euphoria. She, Storm Eden, could rule the world. She would be invincible!

'Storm?' The old woman's eyes were bright with pleading and there was a crack of anxiety in her voice.

At that moment, the door of the ballroom was flung open and Dr DeWilde strode in. 'Storm Eden, don't listen to the old crone. If you put the pipe back into Pandora's box, it will be lost to the world forever. It would be a terrible waste. Think of the power you would have if you kept it.' His eyes glittered feverishly, the scar on his handsome face was livid.

'Ignore him,' said Aurora urgently. But Storm couldn't close her ears to the pipe's siren song. It had silted up her mind. She opened her mouth to say that maybe she would keep it after all, but as she did so, the room was filled with a rustling wind that made the window fastenings fidget, and a familiar voice said, 'Storm, my wild one. The strongest of them all.'

Storm and Aurora spun round. Zella was walking towards them. They stared; Aurora gave a great sigh and Storm choked back a sob. Zella clasped Aurora to her, and tears glistened in her eyes as she said tenderly, 'My, you are growing up beautifully. And you've been looking after my little Any. I thank you.' She squeezed Aurora's hand hard and then enfolded Storm tightly in her arms. 'The pipe was my special gift to you, Storm,' she whispered, 'my dying gift. I gave it to you because I knew that you would not betray my trust. I have heard the pipe's song myself, Storm. I know how hard it is to resist. But I gave it to you, because I knew that you could and would do what must be done. Nothing great is ever easy, but I know you have the strength.' Their eyes locked and Storm reached out a trembling hand and touched her mother's face.

'Come with us,' whispered Storm. 'Come with us back to the Otherworld. I need you so badly.'

Regret flickered across Zella's face. 'I can't, Storm, I've been here in the Underworld far too long.' She turned to Aurora and gently took her hand. 'I heard you were here, my darling. But unlike me, you don't belong here, Aurora. You have your whole life ahead of you. You must go back with Storm and marry Kit. And do please make sure that Reggie remembers to eat, he's so absent-minded.' She sighed, and another tear rolled down her cheek. 'I miss him so. I miss you all, my loves.'

'But Papa must be here somewhere. He's dead,' said Aurora.

Zella shook her head. 'I can assure you that he's not,' she said calmly.

Storm and Aurora looked at each other, stunned. 'So,' said Aurora slowly, 'where is he?' She grabbed Storm's arm. 'If Belladonna was lying about Papa's death, maybe she was also lying about marrying him.'

'Darling, of course she was,' laughed Zella. 'Your father would never remarry without telling me. He tells me everything, just like you do, Storm, when we have our chats by my grave.'

Storm broke into a great big grin as the grandfather clock struck the tenth hour.

'But you must hurry,' said Zella, who had been keeping a watchful eye on Dr DeWilde. He was circling the little family group like a bird of prey ready to swoop for the kill. 'Unless you get to the gates by midnight neither of you will be able to return.'

She turned to Storm. The pipe immediately increased the volume of its song as if trying to drown out Zella's words. 'You are wasting precious time here, Storm. Put the pipe in the box. If you can't do it for yourself, do it for me.'

Storm felt as if she was being pulled apart. The noise in her head from the pipe was like the most beautiful melody she had ever heard; but Zella's voice and presence were seductive too. She thought of Eden End and how she felt when she lay on Zella's grave, hugging the silver birch sapling. Suddenly her mind cleared and the insistent singing of the pipe was drowned out by her love for her mother and her mother's love for her.

'I will,' said Storm. 'But you must promise to come with us.'

Zella looked at Pandora. 'Is it possible?'

'Unprecedented, improbable, but maybe just possible with enough hope. I will give you what help I can.'

'I promise that I will try to come with you,' Zella told Storm, with a sad smile. 'But we may fail in the attempt.'

'Don't listen to your mother, Storm. Listen to me and listen to the pipe,' said Dr DeWilde. 'Think of the wealth and the power. You could rule the world.'

But Storm closed her ears to him and the pipe's insistent whispering. She didn't want to rule the world; she wanted to be safe at home at Eden End surrounded by her family. She turned to Pandora and reached out her hand towards the box. Pandora opened it the tiniest chink and the entire room was filled with green and gold light and a roaring noise like a terrible wind. Storm uncurled her fingers and as she did so, Dr DeWilde shouted 'No!' and leaped towards her. The pipe clung for a moment in mid-air, twinkling and winking like sunlight on razor blades. Dr DeWilde's hand grazed the pipe as it fell into the endless depths of the box. There was a noise like a loud explosion and he was thrown back as if hit by a huge electric shock.

Pandora looked down at him. 'That was very silly of him. He'll live, but it will take him at least twenty minutes to recover.'

Dr DeWilde groaned and shuddered on the floor as if he was experiencing a terrible nightmare.

'He's coming face to face with his past,' explained Pandora.

'It's his past I feel sorry for,' said Storm, hugging Zella tightly.

'You'd better be on your way,' said Pandora, handing Aurora and Zella two tickets for the train. 'You're cutting it fine, and once Dr DeWilde recovers, I rather imagine he'll try to catch you up.' She leaned forward to Storm. 'My advice to you is don't look back. You'll only trip over your own feet. Keep your eyes on the road ahead. On the final ascent to the Otherworld you must go first, Storm. If you turn back and see your sister's or mother's face, you will forfeit them.' She smiled at Storm and beckoned her forward. Then she opened the box just the tiniest chink and reached in. Once again the room was flooded with a light stained green and gold. She pulled back her hand quickly as if something inside had tried to bite it, and snapped the box shut as several things inside seemed to be fighting to get out.

'Put out your hand,' she said to Storm, and she dropped something in it. It was a tiny, perfect pearl.

'This is my thank-you to you,' said Pandora.

'What is it?' asked Storm, looking at the glowing pearl in her hand.

'It is a pearl of hope.' Pandora looked very sad. 'I'm afraid I can't spare you a nugget. I have very little hope left at the bottom of my box. But take this pearl out into the Otherworld for me and carry it with you wherever you go. Now be off. And remember: Don't look back.'

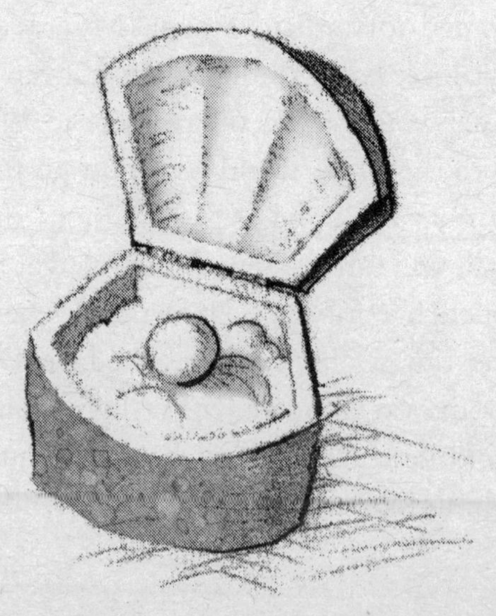

33
forever and for Always

The clock in the square showed the time as just a little after five. The journey back had been difficult. They would have got utterly lost in the tunnels if Aurora had not had the foresight to lay down a trail of madeleines on the journey there. They had decided not to risk the bridge with its dangerously frayed ropes.

Instead they set off down the steep steps of the ravine and up the other side as fast as they could. In the Badlands the wild goose chase was still going on and they had had some near misses. But there had been no sign of Dr DeWilde and now the journey's end was almost in sight.

The last few Underworld workers were hurrying through the barriers towards the train. When the last couple disappeared down the tunnel to the platform, the attendant got out a large key and locked the barriers shut. Storm, Aurora and Zella arrived just as he was turning out the lights. He looked up and saw them.

'Too late, too late,' he said, waving them away with his arm.

'But we must go through!' cried Storm. 'It's a matter of life and death. Please.'

There was something about the catch in her voice and her shining face so full of hope that reminded him of himself when he had been a boy. It was like suddenly rediscovering something he had lost or misplaced a very long time ago.

'Come on, then,' he smiled, and was surprised to hear his voice saying, 'Rules are there to be broken.' And he opened the small gate to the side of the barriers, normally reserved for shift workers with heavy luggage, and let them through. 'You'll have to hurry. You're cutting it fine to get the last train.'

As they raced down the tunnel, they heard the train screeching into the station and the doors open. They charged onto the platform just as the doors began to close again. Storm flung herself into the gap. The doors slid open and Aurora and Zella fell into the carriage behind her.

'Made it,' gasped Storm. 'Safe. Nobody can catch us now. All we have to do is make sure we get out of the Underworld before midnight.' The carriage was deserted except for one man who was reading a newspaper, his face obscured behind it. The train pulled out of the station, and Storm, Aurora and Zella collapsed into the seats.

The man folded his newspaper, stood up and sauntered towards them. 'How lovely to see you all,' said Dr DeWilde with an evil grin. 'I was so desperately worried that you might miss the last train.' He turned to Storm and said quietly, 'I find the Underworld very dull, Storm. And it's all your fault that I'm here. You are entirely responsible for my death in the Ginger House fire, so the least you can do is make it up to me. I want the return part of your ticket to get me out of here. You can rot here for eternity with your sister and mother. I'm sure you will have a lovely time with that double-crossing witch Belladonna. Perhaps you could all play board games together.'

'Keep away from us,' said Zella, stepping in front of the children.

Dr DeWilde advanced towards them, his knife glinting in his hand. 'I'm going to kill you, Storm Eden,' he said pleasantly, 'and I'm going to enjoy every minute of it.'

He was almost upon them when the train screeched into the next station. The doors opened and as the knife descended towards Storm she ducked and the three of them leaped out, ran down the platform and dashed into the next carriage. Dr DeWilde had stooped to retrieve the knife and was not quick enough to follow them.

Storm, Aurora and Zella made their way to the end of the carriage to get as far away from Dr DeWilde as possible. He snarled at them through the glass partition that separated the carriages, like a caged wolf in a zoo. The train drew into another station. Storm, Aurora and Zella were out of the doors as soon as they opened, and running down the platform. Dr DeWilde was after them. 'Doors closing' came the announcement. Just in time, they nipped into the next carriage, leaving Dr DeWilde on the platform.

'We've done it! We've lost him,' crowed Storm triumphantly. 'He can't catch us up now. There isn't another train.'

'Don't be too confident,' said Zella. 'We're not out of the woods yet. He's a very determined man. He'll stop at nothing to prevent you leaving the Underworld.' She turned to Storm. 'Ours is the next stop. Now remember. Once we're off the train, you must go ahead, Storm. Whatever happens, whatever you hear behind you, you mustn't look back. If you do, Aurora and I will be lost to you forever. Whatever you hear happening behind you, keep your eyes straight ahead and just keep going upwards. Once you get beyond the barriers,

OVERWORLD
2359

Storm, you must wait for Aurora and me to pass you. Only then can you walk through too so we can be together again forever and for always.'

The train drew into the station and the three of them ran off the train in single file, Storm followed by Aurora and then Zella. The platform clock said one minute to midnight.

'Hurry,' called Storm, running faster. She could hear the drum of Aurora and Zella's feet behind her. She dashed onto the long escalator that led up to the booking hall. The escalator only went in a downward direction and it was hard work running against it. She could hear Aurora gasping for breath behind her. Storm pounded upwards, willing her sister and mother to hurry. All the time she fingered the tiny pearl of hope. Nearing the top of the escalator, she heard the booking hall clock begin to strike the hour.

Bong! The ticket hall clerk turned a key in the escalator to stop it moving, and began to pull the metal grille across the front of the ticket barriers. It was heavy and kept getting stuck. *Bong.*

'Hurry up,' yelled Storm as the escalator jerked to a halt, almost throwing her backwards. The going immediately got a little easier. Behind her she could hear the clatter of feet. She was not certain, but she thought she could hear more than two pairs. She desperately wanted to look behind her. It took all her strength to resist. *Bong* went the clock.

'Keep your eyes ahead,' gasped Aurora as if reading Storm's mind. *Bong*. Storm reached the top of the escalator. She passed through the barriers and stood by the small gap in the grille. *Bong*. She could see the anxious faces of Netta, Kit and Any. Suddenly they broke into smiles and cheers and she guessed they could see Aurora coming up behind her. She stood by the grille, still just inside the Underworld. Aurora put her ticket in the barrier. It opened. She dashed past Storm and fell into the arms of Kit, Any and Netta. *Bong*.

'Quick, Storm,' cried Netta. 'Come through. What are you waiting for?' *Bong*.

Storm hesitated. Where was Zella? Feet pounded behind her. Suddenly the smiles on the faces in front of her turned to horror. Any screamed. Aurora covered her face. Then she heard Zella's voice from further down the escalator calling, 'Storm! Storm! Turn round. You must turn round. Quickly, my darling! Listen to me! He's got my ticket. You must look back.'

Storm hesitated.

'Turn round,' shouted everyone in the

booking hall. She whipped around. Dr DeWilde was upon her, a look of triumph on his face. His knife was poised to plunge into her back. Instinctively, she put out both her hands and shoved him with all her strength and in that push was all the hurt, and jealousy and loneliness she had felt since that day when they had set off to the fair in such high spirits.

With a great cry, Dr DeWilde fell backwards, twisting and tumbling down the escalator past Zella, who stepped nimbly out of the way. *Bong.* Storm ran back down the escalator towards her mother. She picked up the ticket that Dr DeWilde had dropped and held it out to Zella.

Zella looked up into her daughter's face, her eyes glistened. Storm felt a sob rising in her throat. Zella smiled at her sorrowfully and shook her head. 'It's no good, Storm, I can't come with you. You've seen my face.'

'You saved me, you sacrificed yourself to me,' whispered Storm. 'If you hadn't called out for me to turn round, Dr DeWilde would have killed me, but you might have still made it out.' She stretched out her hand to Zella. 'Please, come with me. I need you.'

Zella was becoming more difficult to see as if she was slowly fading away. *Bong.*

'I can't,' said Zella sorrowfully. 'But I will always be with you. As long as you remember me, I will remember you. Forever and for always,' and she reached up to Storm and planted a whispering kiss on her head. She was fading fast. 'Now go, my bravest one,' she said, 'go before it's too late.'

Reluctantly, her heart breaking, Storm turned. Her mother's ticket fluttered out of her hand as she ran up the escalator. *Bong.*

'Storm,' called Zella after her. 'Chocolate truffles. Bring them as often as you can. I do like them so.'

Storm didn't turn, but she smiled and raised her arm.

'Oh,' called Zella, her voice becoming ever fainter. 'Tell your father that he should remarry. I want him to be happy. You too, Storm. Forever and for always.'

'Forever and for always,' Storm whispered as she climbed the final few steps. 'Forever and for always.' And she fell through the grille into her sisters' arms. *Bong*. She turned round and looked back. There was just the faintest glow like a fast-fading golden smile in the spot where Zella had been standing. The ticket office clerk pulled the grille across. *Bong*. The clock struck the final chime of the hour. He locked the grille and put the key in his pocket.

'Time to go home,' he said.

'Yes,' said Storm with a hiccup, 'it's time to go home.' Wave after wave of pain swept over her, a great deluge of unbearable loss. It was as if she had lost her mother twice over, and the second time was far worse. The others sensed this and said nothing, but they hugged her and held both her hands and squeezed them tightly. Together they left the station.

A few minutes after they had departed,

Dr DeWilde crawled to the very top of the escalator. In his hand he clutched the ticket. He stood desperately shaking the metal grille and angrily demanding to be let out. He howled – a truly desolate sound – until the lights were quite suddenly extinguished, and then there was only silence.

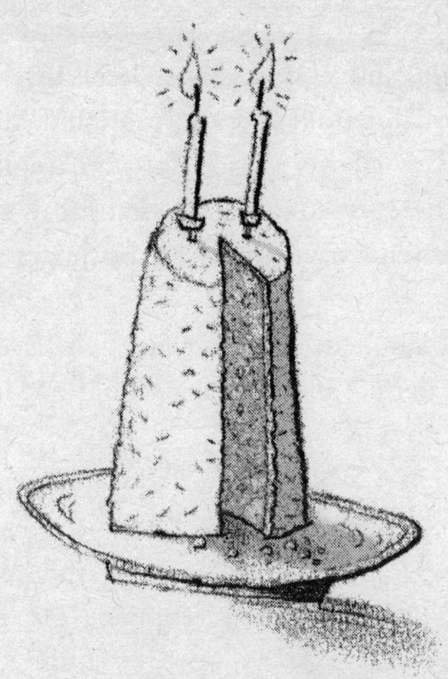

Epilogue

'Happy birthday to you, happy birthday to you.'

Everyone clapped and cheered as Any blew out the candles on the giant madeleine that Aurora had fashioned into a birthday cake. 'I wish it was my birthday every day,' she said, tearing the wrapping paper off a present from Netta – a collection of

Grimm tales and a book about Greek mythology.

'But you'd get old so soon,' protested Aurora.

'Birthdays are very good for you,' replied Any firmly. 'There is considerable statistical evidence that those who have the most birthdays live the longest.'

Aurora laughed. Then her face fell. 'Everything would be perfect if only Papa would get in touch to let us know he is safe.'

Netta and the children were all sitting in the kitchen stuffed full from a supper of broccoli soup and the madeleine cake. Any was snuggled on Netta's lap. Aurora's trunk was sitting packed in the corner. Tomorrow she was going on a three-week visit to Somewhere to join Kit who was doing a crash course in kingship and dragon husbandry. Netta was going to stay at Eden End and look after Any and Storm until they joined Aurora the following week.

'It will be such fun having you with me. I'll be able to show you how I've rearranged the palace linen cupboard. They've got a truly dreadful system, it will take me weeks to get it straight,' said Aurora.

Storm smiled, but it was a smile with very little hint of happiness in it. Nothing was ever going to be the same again at Eden End.

'Have you opened your card from the princess yet?' asked Aurora.

'Yes,' said Any. 'She says that the reunion of the dragons has been a complete success and they have such sunny dispositions that they spread happiness throughout the town. And they are firm friends with Pepper and Zeus. Oh, and she's taking a rally driving course and once Kit has been crowned king she's planning to drive across the world all by herself.'

'Gosh,' said Aurora, 'we'll all be keeping well away from the roads, then.'

As the others laughed there was a knock at the door.

'I wonder who that can be?' said Storm, surprised. She pulled open the door. A sliver of

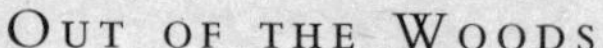

new moon hung in the sky. There didn't seem to be anyone there. There was a squeak from by her feet. She looked down and saw that it was the little mouse which had escaped from Belladonna's hair and which had been such a help to them. The mouse was struggling to drag a teapot many times its own size, and on closer inspection Storm realized that it was no ordinary teapot but the Cherished Family Teapot.

'Let me help you,' said Storm, and as she bent towards the little creature, the first beam from the new moon touched the mouse's back and its fur began to fizz, then disappear and then most disconcertingly the mouse began to grow. It squeaked, and the squeak turned to a whoop and then a laugh, and in a blink sitting just outside the door was not a mouse, but Captain Eden, who was laughing heartily and clutching the Cherished Family Teapot.

Everyone's jaws hit the ground. 'Papa!' screeched the children.

Captain Eden held out the teapot to Aurora, and said, 'I redeemed it at the pawn shop on my way back.' He looked at their astonished faces and grinned. 'What we all need is a nice cup of tea.'

After several cups of tea and a great many hugs and explanations, Any asked shyly, 'Papa, now that you've found the four-tongued, three-footed, two-headed honey dragon, will you stay at home more?'

Captain Eden swung her into his arms. 'I will, Any,' he grinned. 'My fortune is made. With the money I got for finding the dragon's mate, I'll even be able to afford to fix up this place a bit. I'm going to spend much more time with you all and I hope that you, Aurora, will invite me to visit you and

Kit in Somewhere. Such an interesting place.'

Storm suddenly noticed that silvery faraway look that her father got in his eye when he was planning a new expedition, so she wasn't in the slightest bit surprised when he added, 'Actually, while I was there I picked up some rumours that maybe the dodo isn't extinct, after all. When I've rebuilt the west wing I think I might check the rumours out.' He looked at the remains of the birthday cake. 'Can I have some?'

Aurora passed him a large slice. Any put her hand out for the last piece of cake. 'Oi, Anything Eden,' said Aurora, 'that's my piece. You'll burst, you've already had four slices.'

'Well, I want to have my cake and eat yours too,' said Any, 'otherwise there's no point being the birthday girl.'

'You can have it later,' said Aurora. Any counted to ten and reached for the cake.

'It is later,' she said.

'Later, later,' said Aurora.

Any gave a deep sigh. Aurora showed every indication of becoming a grown-up, the first sign of which was telling you that you could only do things later that you badly wanted to do at this very minute. She picked up her book of Greek myths and began to read the story of Orpheus and Eurydice.

Storm glanced over at her father and Netta, who were talking together quietly by the fire. There was something in the way that they looked at each other that made her wonder if Aurora and Kit's marriage might not be the only one on the cards.

Aurora picked up her knitting and looked with satisfaction at the quiet scene in the kitchen. 'There will be days and days like this,' she said contentedly to nobody in particular.

Unnoticed, Storm slipped out of the kitchen door and ran through the park to the graveyard. She kneeled in front of her mother's grave and hugged the silver birch tree.

'I love you. I miss you,' she whispered. The wind rustled through the leaves on the tree.

'Everything is changing,' she whispered, 'and I don't like it. I wish I could freeze everything as it is at this moment.' The wind sighed. 'I feel as if I've already left so much behind me and I seem to lose people along the way. You. Now Aurora. Even Any's growing up. She'll never turn two again. Soon she won't be a baby at all. It's as if the best is already behind me.'

She heard the crunch of feet on crisp snow and

looked up to see her father standing there. She suddenly felt shyer than a church mouse in a cattery. He came and sat down next to her. They sat in silence for a moment and then he said, 'I love it here.'

Storm smiled. 'Zella said that you came here too.'

'Whenever I can. It's so peaceful.' He smiled. 'I always admire the care you take of Zella's grave. Shall I tell you a secret? Sometimes I bring her chocolate truffles as well.'

Storm grinned at him. Silence enveloped them again like a warm cloak. 'I miss your mother very, very much, Storm. But I think you miss her even more.'

'Are you going to marry Netta?' asked Storm fiercely.

Her father looked at her, surprised. 'I don't know, Storm. I don't know if she will have me. But I won't ask yet, anyway. Not for a long time.' Then he added, 'Would it upset you very much if we did get married?'

Storm was about to blurt the word 'yes', but then she stopped and thought about it. She thought of Netta's enveloping arms and her smell like caramel pineapple and night-scented stocks that was so like Zella and she thought of Zella's message to Reggie, which she knew that she must deliver to her father. 'Maybe not,' she mumbled. 'But I don't like change. Everything's changing and I just want it to stay the same.'

'Things can change for the better, not just for the worse.' There was another long silence. Then Captain Eden said, 'I hope I've changed, Storm. I was never a good father and then when your mother died, grief made me even more neglectful of you three girls. I'm sorry. I'd like to get to know you all better.'

'But Aurora won't be here, she'll be in Somewhere with Kit being a queen and taking charge of the kingdom's linen cupboards.'

'Yes, but not for some time; they are not getting married immediately and even when they do there will be holidays and visits. We'll all be together a great deal of the time.'

'But it won't be the same!' cried Storm passionately.

'No, it won't,' admitted Captain Eden. 'But different can be good. You never know if you are going to like different until you try it. Listen,' he said, taking her hand. 'I've got something I very much want to ask you. I'm planning to stay here for several months and spend time with you. But eventually I will need to go on another expedition, and when I do, I wondered whether you might like to come with me? I could do with a companion, somebody who will look out for me and make sure I don't get turned into a mouse again.'

'Me? Go with you on an expedition? Just the two of us?'

'Why not? We'd be a good team. You are brave and resourceful and fit as a fiddle. You've proved that, Storm.'

'What about Any?'

'Any's too young. Besides she doesn't have your lion heart, Storm. She can stay with Aurora. They are not really adventurers, your sisters. Not like you.'

Storm said nothing, but a tingle of pleasure like a tiny electric shock ran through her. The air suddenly seemed to have more oxygen in it; the world brighter colours. Her father, who she had always thought didn't have much time for her, thought she had a lion heart. She wanted to purr out loud.

'What about Eden End?'

'It will still be here when we get back.'

He stood up. 'You don't need to give me an answer

now. Just think about it. It might be another kind of different, a different that you find that you enjoy very much and which you also have a talent for,' he said.

Storm watched him walk back to the house. It was beginning to snow again. The flakes danced in the air. Storm sat alone and watched the sky turn indigo and the stars begin to peep through. She turned the pearl of hope over and over again in her pocket and listened to the wind swish and whoosh through the trees and call out her name. Then when it was quite dark, Storm hugged the silver birch tree that bent its branches over as if to caress her. The sky swarmed with stars. Somewhere in the dark she thought she heard her mother's voice whisper, 'Look forward. Keep your eyes on the road ahead. Don't look back.'

Storm smiled, stood up and walked briskly into her future. She could see Aurora and Any waiting anxiously for her by the kitchen door. She ran towards them, smiling.

'Are you all right, Storm?' they asked in unison.

'Yes,' she grinned. 'I'm going to be just fine.' She encircled them both with her arms. 'Even if we have to be apart sometimes, we'll always be there for each other, won't we?'

Aurora and Any nodded vigorously and they encircled Storm with their arms too.

'The three of us alone, the three of us together. Forever and for always.'

The End

forever
AURORA
STORM
&
ANY
and always

'There were several very
toothsome words on this page
but they were gobbled up
by a wolf.'

Granny Ridinghood's Double Chocolate Brownies with Hot Fudge Sauce

For the Double Chocolate Brownies:

115g (4oz) butter
115g (4oz) plain chocolate
300g (10oz) caster sugar
3 drops vanilla essence
2 large eggs
140g (5oz) plain flour
2 tbsp cocoa powder
100g (3.5oz) milk chocolate chips

For the Hot Fudge Sauce:

230g (8oz) plain chocolate
Small knob of butter
300ml (half pint) double cream
1 large tbsp golden syrup

Preheat the oven to gas mark 4/180°C/350°F. Grease and line an 18cm or 7" square cake tin. Melt butter with broken-up plain chocolate in a bowl over simmering hot water.
When melted stir well and remove from heat to cool a little. Stir in sugar and vanilla essence. Beat together eggs and then gradually add to mixture stirring all the time. Sift flour and cocoa powder together and then stir into the mixture. Stir in chocolate chips and pour mixture into the tin. Cook for 35 minutes. It should be crusty around the edges but firm and still moist in the centre. The trick is not to overbake.

For the Hot Fudge Sauce:
Melt chocolate and butter in a bowl over simmering water. When melted take off the heat, stir and add cream. Put back on heat and, stirring continuously, heat through thoroughly but do not allow to boil. When hot stir in golden syrup.
Remove from heat, beat well and serve over still warm brownies.

'Aurora baked all the words on this page into a cake, and very tasty it was too.'

GRIMM
TALES

'If I was ever going to read a book, it would be this one.'

Endorsement from

The Princess

LYN GARDNER works as a theater critic for the *Guardian*. She goes to the theater five or six nights a week, which should leave no time for writing books at all. She and her two daughters have one venerable goldfish (there were two, but one came to a tragic end) and a horse—who is the most demanding, temperamental, and expensive member of the family.

MINI GREY was born in a Mini in an icy car park in South Wales. She has written and illustrated a number of critically acclaimed and award-winning picture books, including *Ginger Bear, Traction Man Is Here!,* and *The Adventures of the Dish and the Spoon.* Mini lives in Oxford with her partner, Tony, two-year-old son, Herbie, and cat, Bonzetta.